I0775471

Who Am I?

The Jane Brooks Story

Who Am I?

The Jane Brooks Story

ALAN SAKELL

For Matthew,

My brother, my friend, my lifesaver.
I would not be here on this earth if it was not for you.
I will never forget that.

Love Always,
Alan

Dear Reader,

When I wrote this book, I did so with you in mind.

I want you to feel like you are a part of the Jane Brooks story.

As you read the words, I want you to be the narrator.

You are the one telling Jane's story to the world.

To make it more interesting, I am not telling you which character you are in the story.

That is for you to figure out.

I will give you one hint for now: you are not Blue.

Are you up for the challenge?

Sincerely,
Alan Sakell

Intuition

> ➢ a natural ability or power that makes it possible to know something without any proof or evidence.
> ➢ a feeling that guides a person to act a certain way without fully understanding why.
> ➢ often referred to as a gut feeling.

Have you ever contemplated the affects your intuition has on you? If not, do not fret. I have contemplated it enough times for both of us. I am doing that right now as I, once again, find myself with my butt pressed into the toilet seat, my elbows dug into my knees, and my head in my hands. Yes, this is one of the affects your intuition will have on you. It usually starts with me arguing back and forth with myself, a devil on one shoulder and an angel on the other. The closer the devil comes to winning the argument, the more my hands start to sweat. As the angel starts sliding further and further off his shoulder, the more my stomach starts to turn. When the devil is just about to throw his arms up in the air as the champion once again, I find myself making a mad dash to the bathroom. The result of letting the devil continue his winning streak is yet another regret to add to the already very long list.

Prologue

Jane Brooks was never anything special to look at. Her awkward high school years had lasted a lot longer than those miserable, sometimes unbearable four years. The three most popular girls in her school gave a new meaning to the word *bullying*. Granted most of what they said about Jane or called her right to her face was not far from the truth, but that did not make it any easier for her to hear. Jane may have been on the heavy side, and was definitely not one of the prettier girls, but she was neither deaf nor blind. Jane saw what they saw every day in her own mirror. Her almost-constant acne breakouts did not help the situation at all. Never mind the freckles that covered almost every inch of her body and her incredibly frizzy red hair. Jane did have one thing going for her: she was much smarter than any of them.

By the time Jane had graduated from high school and had received a degree in hospitality management from an online college, her life had started to turn a corner. She no longer had an acne problem. and she had lost all her extra weight. There was nothing Jane could do about her freckles or her crazy red hair except embrace them as part of what made her the woman she is today. Thanks to Jane's overactive brain, she had made the dean's list constantly. She was at the top of her class every single year. When it came time to find her dream job, working in one of the nicest hotels in Miami, she blew the competition away. She may not have the looks. She may not have a man in her life. But she does have the brains and the job she always wanted. Nobody's life is perfect. It is what you make of it.

There is one other thing that Jane has a lot of in her life: regrets. The funny thing about regrets is that they can either be from things you have done or things you have not done. For Jane, it is almost a tie though lately, the number of regrets from things she has done is starting to edge its way past the amount of regrets from things she has not done. This is not a good thing for anyone. It is like a snowball that starts to roll down a mountain in Colorado. The bigger it gets, the more dangerous it can be. At the present time, Jane's snowball is the size of Frosty's head. All that is missing is a corncob pipe, a button for his nose, and some coal for his eyes.

Jane's problem is that she has not been listening to her intuition lately. She has been letting the devil win, which, without fail, leads to yet another bad decision. Thus, another regret. She knows before the thought has even fully entered her mind that the answer should be no, yet before she knows it, she has blocked out the angel completely. For a woman as smart as Jane, it is hard for her to fathom why she continues this same pattern. Her only way to justify it to herself is by repeating over and over again: the devil made me do it, the devil made me do it, the devil made me do it.

Chapter 1

It is almost lunchtime on yet another boring Monday. Jane has been at work since 9:00 a.m., and she will not be free until 7:00 p.m. Ten-hour shifts can be rough, especially when you are dealing with the public most of the time, but Jane loves her job. She loves working at a place where she deals with so many different people every day from all over the world. Living and working in Miami can be a challenge for some people, especially those that do not speak Spanish. Luckily, Jane is fluent in English and Spanish. There are a few other languages which she knows just enough of to get by with. The hotel she works at tries it hardest to instill the philosophy that the customer is always right. Jane's philosophy is the customer is usually wrong, but just nod, smile, and agree.

Jane's newest addiction has become dating apps on her cell phone. She spends more time on them every day than she does anything else. They have pretty much taken over her entire life. She has been on every single one she could find for straight women. Living in Miami, which is known as a transient city, can definitely have its advantages. There are new faces for Jane to see every time she logs on, which is why she spends so much time every day swiping right or swiping left. You never know whose face will show up on your screen next. The excitement of the chase is too much for Jane to resist.

Today Jane, decides to take a walk during her lunch break and heads to her favorite Greek restaurant. Another major plus of living in Miami is there are so many different kinds of restaurants to choose from. She makes it to the restaurant in ten minutes. She orders her favorite lunch special, the lamb gyro platter, and sits at the only seat left in the place. This place is packed every day of the week during lunchtime. The food is delicious and cheap, so being stuck at a table in the corner by herself is no big deal. Besides, she plans on spending as much of her lunch break on her app as possible even while eating every last bite of her gyro. The last thing she needs is some nosy kid trying to see what it is she is doing on her cell phone the whole time. There are so many people in Miami that, by being just a ten-minute walk away from the hotel, all the faces are new once again.

Although Jane has been on all the different apps, her favorite one is definitely Mingle. It is one of the newer ones on the market. She can do almost anything she wants to do when she is on Mingle, from chatting, sending pics, sending videos, or scheduling parties. She can even chat with the men through a video stream, allowing them to see each other while they chat. The video stream is the only option that Jane refuses to use. The excuse she always uses is that the camera in her phone is broken, so the video does not work. If they knew the truth, would they still have swiped right?

When Jane first started playing around on the apps, she found that none of the guys she was swiping right for were doing the same with her. The only possible matches she was making were older, usually fat bald men. It was always the same thing on all the apps. It seemed that the men Jane found herself attracted to did not find a woman with frizzy red hair and more freckles than you could ever possibly count worth a swipe to the right.

After about a month of the same thing happening and never matching with anyone that she found herself even remotely interested in, Jane decided to try something different. Last Friday night, while she was sitting at home with her beautiful Russian Blue cat, which she ironically named Blue, she decided she needed some excitement in her life. She took out her laptop and did something that she absolutely hates doing: she opened Facebook. Here's the thing about Facebook, which you may or may not already know. If you are one of the less popular people out there, Facebook can be downright depressing.

When Jane opened Facebook and signed into her account, she noticed instantly that she had no new messages and no new friend requests. This was exactly what she was expecting even though she had not signed on in over a month. When she looked at her list of friends, she was once again reminded that only two of the eleven friends she had connected with on Facebook are not family members. They are not really friends either, as a matter of fact. They are two of the people that work under her supervision at the hotel. Jane is pretty sure they only accepted her friend requests because they either felt bad for her or they were scared she would fire them if they did not accept the request.

Blue started pacing back and forth as he often does when she is not paying enough attention to him. He is a very needy cat. He loves when Jane rubs his head, especially the little spot right between his eyes. He is a bit high maintenance for a cat. Jane blames it on him being raised in Miami. If there is ever anything in his litterbox besides the gravel or his own urine, he will jump right back out. He will instead use the pot holding Jane's almost-dead ficus tree. She is pretty sure it is dying, thanks to Blue using it as his dumping ground. Jane got up, checked to make sure his litterbox was as he likes it, and grabbed a couple of his favorite treats. She went back to her desk and picked Blue up off her laptop, which he was now lounging across. She placed him gently into his own little bed right on the side of hers and gave him the treats. She reached over and gave him a good rubdown, making sure to spend most of it right between his eyes, which made him purr so loud she started to laugh out loud. That should keep him happy for a little while.

With Blue taken care of, Jane turned her focus back to the matter at hand. As she sat there, just about to type in the first of three names, her palms began to sweat. The devil was taking round one. Was she really going to do this? To stoop this low just for a little attention? The way Jane saw it, she had no other option. With her palms sweating, she started thinking back to those three girls that made her life a living hell for four whole years at high school. As her stomach started to tie in knots, damn, that devil is strong, she typed in the first of the three names; Stacey Maddox, and hit Search. In high school, her name was Stacey Sanchez, but she married a very rich doctor a few years after graduating from high school. Jane only knows about this because she has been doing Facebook stalking on the three of them for years. Stacey lives in a very nice house on Miami Beach with her husband and two sons. She is still one of the most beautiful people Jane has ever laid eyes on. From her long blond hair, beautiful hazel eyes, gorgeous smile, all the way to her new addition of very large breasts. Stacey Maddox is the woman most women wish they were, including Jane.

As the devil claimed victory once again, Jane found herself running to the bathroom with her laptop in hand. As she had anticipated, Blue came running in right after her. Sometimes, he behaves more like a baby than he does a cat. Every minute Jane is home, and he is awake, Blue must be in the same room she is in, or he will start making the most horrifying noises she has ever heard. With Blue curled up on the bathroom mat and Jane letting nature run its course, she started working her way through Stacey's Facebook page. How is it even possible that she can look perfect in every single photo she posts, even the ones from when she was very pregnant with both of her boys? Some things in life are just not fair. Jane found the three most recent photos Stacey had posted of just herself. She right clicked on all three of them and downloaded them to her laptop.

Jane finished in the bathroom the same time she finished with the photos. She went back to her desk with Blue two steps behind her. This time, he just sat there at her feet, looking up at her with the saddest eyes possible and making the cutest little crying noise. She slid back in her chair and let him climb into her lap. After turning around in circles a few times, he finally curled into a ball right in the middle of her lap. This is his favorite place in the world to be. He was fast asleep in the matter of minutes, which gave Jane the peace and quiet she needed to finish part one of her plan.

The next name she typed into the search bar was Melissa Miller. Melissa is a brunette version of Stacey. She is as stunning to look at in person as she is in photos. Unlike Stacey, Melissa kept her breasts the way God made them, which is still several sizes larger than Jane's. Melissa has not been as lucky in the romance department as Stacey has. At the ripe old age of twenty-eight she has already been twice married and twice divorced. She changed her last name back to Miller after each divorce to keep her father happy. With the amount of money he has to leave her as his only child, she does whatever Daddy wants her to. Jane skimmed through Melissa's most recent photos as she did with Stacey's. The majority of Melissa's photos are of her in a bikini at the beach or at her father's poolside. Jane copied one of the bikini photos onto her laptop and then found two other ones that were recent but show Melissa actually wearing more than a bikini. This was a tougher task than it should have been.

Two down, one more to go. The last of the three names was Monica Roberts. Monica is very different than Stacey and Melissa, but she was just as cruel to Jane. Monica, who has the most American-sounding last name out of the three of them, is the only one that was not born in the United States. She came to Miami from Cuba. Because she has that Cuban blood in her, she looks like she has the perfect tan all year long without spending even one minute in the sun. She has jet-black hair, huge brown eyes, and the most perfect smile, thanks to a few years of wearing braces right before entering high school. She has long, toned Tina Turner legs and a waist the size of a preteen girl. The other difference between Monica and the other two mean girls is that she is a lesbian. This makes no difference to Jane whatsoever. Jane scrolled her way through Monica's photos. There was a lot more flannel and a lot less bikini to look at while selecting the three photos she wanted for her plan. Once Jane found the three photos she liked the most, she downloaded them onto her laptop too.

With phase one complete, Jane logged out of Facebook and shut her laptop down. Blue came back to life and let out a very long yawn. He stretched his body out so much he nearly rolled out of her lap. They both made their way to the bathroom, Jane to brush her teeth and Blue to watch her in between yawning. When she was done in the bathroom, she changed out of her clothes and threw on a loose

T-shirt and a pair of sweatpants. She picked up Blue and gave him a little rub between his eyes and a good night kiss on his nose before putting him back in his bed. Jane then shut off the lights and climbed into her bed. Before she had even managed to get comfortable, Blue was there at her feet. By the time she had started to fall asleep, Blue had once again inched his way from the foot of the bed all the way to the other pillow right near Jane's. Another exciting Friday night in the life of Jane Brooks.

Chapter 2

The next day was the first Saturday Jane did not have to work in months. She actually allowed herself to sleep in late. Of course, sleeping in late to Jane meant sleeping past 7:00 a.m. When she opened her eyes, she saw two very different things at the same time. Out of her left eye, she saw the sun making itself known through the slats in her window blind, which never happens at her usual wakeup-time. Out of her right eye, she saw Blue with his head propped up on her pillow, just staring at her. This cat really needs to get a life. Talk about two peas in a pod.

Jane gave Blue his usual good-morning rub to which he purred in appreciation. Then she got out of bed and turned on the coffee machine. While she waited for the coffee machine to work its magic, Jane cleaned out Blue's litterbox to prevent another ficus tree visit. Once the coffee was ready, she put a cinnamon bagel into the toaster and grabbed the low-fat cream cheese from the refrigerator. While Jane waited for the toaster to pop, she filled Blue's water bowl and food dish. When it comes to feeding Blue his breakfast, it is all about the timing.

If Jane feeds him before her breakfast is ready, he will gobble his down as fast as he can, sometimes actually making himself choke. Then he will make his way over to Jane's side as she eats her breakfast. He will not take his eyes off her for even a second. Do you know how awkward it makes you feel when someone or something watches you eat your food? On the other hand, if Jane feeds him after her breakfast is ready, he will not even touch his until he has watched her eat hers first. The only way for Jane to eat her breakfast in peace is to feed Blue his breakfast at the same time she starts eating hers. I told you he is a high-maintenance cat.

Once they were both done with their breakfasts and Jane had taken her morning shower, with Blue curled up on the mat just outside the shower, she threw on a clean pair of underwear and the same T-shirt and sweatpants she wore to bed the night before. She had no plans of leaving the house, so why not be comfortable? She grabbed what was left of her morning coffee and sat down at her desk. To Jane's surprise, Blue was not at her side. Before she had even turned around, she knew exactly where he was. Getting up later than usual had thrown Jane's morning routine out of whack. She had not made her bed, like she usually does after her morning shower. She looked over at the bed, and sure enough, there was Blue curled up in a ball right on top of her pillow. Okay, so he is not only high maintenance, but he is also just a little bit spoiled.

With Blue out of her hair for a while, Jane got right down to business. She turned her laptop on, and while she waited for it to start up, she freshened up her cup of coffee with what was left in the coffeepot. When the laptop was awake and ready for her, Jane opened her folder with the photos she had downloaded from Facebook the night before. There were nine of them in all, three of each woman. Jane opened each photo and did a little editing to get them ready. Most of them were perfect just the way they were. A little crop here and a little crop there was about all she actually had to do. Once she was satisfied the photos were ready, she transferred them from her laptop to her cell phone. While she waited for the photos to transfer, she noticed that ever familiar feeling of her hands starting to sweat.

"Here we go again. I know, I know. I should not be doing this. But who is it really going to hurt? Is it so wrong for a woman to want to feel wanted, to be paid attention to?" Once the last photo had downloaded onto her cell phone, Jane shut the laptop down and joined Blue in her comfortable bed. He was sound asleep, and Jane would prefer him to stay that way, so she very slowly slid the pillow he was sleeping on over to the other side of the bed. She gave him a little loving rub between his eyes, which, luckily, did not even make him flinch.

Jane opened the Mingle app she had been using for the last month and deleted her current profile. Nobody would miss it anyway. She then started creating three new profiles, one for each of her high school bullies. Before Jane was even done with the first profile, the devil let her know he was again kicking the crap out of the angel by tying her stomach in very tight knots. She knew she really should not be doing this.

Jane is a beautiful, very busty blond in her first new profile. Her name is…What is her name? Jane had not thought this part through enough. She does not want to use Stacey's real name, nor does she want to use her real name. Damn this devil. He was starting to gloat again. Jane got out of bed as quickly and quietly as she could as to not rouse Blue and ran to the bathroom. She made it just in time once again. She felt like she was doing a cleansing for a colonoscopy, but it did not deter her. Jane finally settled on Lacy for her blond persona. She entered some fake details about Lacy, which she is pretty sure most people do anyway, and then she downloaded one of the photos she took from Stacey's Facebook page. Jane had downloaded three different photos because most people on these apps are always asking to see more photos, and she does not want to have to go back onto Facebook anytime soon to get more photos to send.

Once Jane was sure it was safe to leave the bathroom, she slid back onto her side of the bed and created a profile for Melissa, her brunette persona who is now known as Lisa. When she was done creating Lisa's fake details and downloading the photo with the least amount of skin showing, Jane moved on to bully number three. Monica became Mona, Jane's jet-black-haired, tanned Cuban persona. It was tough to decide which one of Monica's three photos to use on the app. Although she is wearing flannel in all the photos and has no makeup on at all, she is still beauty queen material. Jane ended up choosing the one with the best smile and downloaded it to her third new profile. Phase two was done for now.

Jane was going to create these same three profiles on all the apps she had used before, but if she did that it may become difficult to remember which lies she had told to which man, depending on what question he might ask her. The last thing she needs is to be talking to the same man on two different apps and telling him different lies to the same questions. Jane needs to be smart and ease herself into the world of the popular people.

For the rest of her first weekend off in months, Jane never left her house. She was constantly glued to her cell phone. She barely paid any attention to Blue, which he was not happy about, and he made it known by visiting the ficus tree more than one time. She became completely obsessed with her three new personas. She logged on as Lacy first and swiped right for every man she imagined Stacey would go for. As Jane waited to see which men Lacy would match with, she logged out as Lacy and switched over to her Lisa profile. Jane then swiped right for all the men she thought Melissa would be interested in. Next, Jane did the same thing for Mona's profile though, truth be told, Monica would not be swiping right for any of these men. They are all the wrong sex.

Once Jane finished swiping right for all three of her personas, she started switching from one profile to another, checking for matches. She was not surprised to see how many men all three of them were matching with. She was also not surprised how many of the same men were matching with all three of them. When Jane was doing her swiping right for Lacy, Lisa, and Mona, she tried to not pick the same man more than once, but after looking at so many different photos, she was pretty certain she had selected a few of the same for all three of the profiles. Some of the men were so handsome Jane did not want to miss out on chatting with them. Besides, just because Lacy swiped right for a man does not mean he would swipe right for her. Maybe he is only into brunettes and would match with Lisa instead. Having the same man match with two or three of her personas could make this tricky for Jane, but it could also make it a lot more interesting. Let the games begin.

Chapter 3

With her lunch break almost over, Jane shuts down the Mingle app, throws the trash from her lunch in the trash can, and heads back to the hotel. The walk is short, yet she still sees things that no one should have to see when walking the streets in the United States. There are homeless people on almost every corner, and the scent of urine lingers from them as Jane walks by without ever daring to make eye contact. These are the times when she realizes there is more to life than beauty.

Jane makes it back to the hotel with one minute to spare. There is nothing she wants more than to jump right back on Mingle, but considering she is in a supervisory role, she fights the urge and puts her cell phone in her office. The last thing she needs is to have one of her staff members catch her surfing a dating app while on duty. Never mind if her supervisor made a surprise visit and caught her. She would be out of a job before she could even finish swiping right.

The next six hours drag by. Mondays are the slowest day for the hotel. Most guests check in on Fridays and out on Sundays, which is why Jane does not mind working on the weekends. She gets to meet a lot more people and the days fly by. For quite a while, Jane had convinced herself that she would meet the man of her dreams while he was checking in or checking out of the hotel. They would have a whirlwind romance and get married in the gardens of the hotel where they met. Sadly, after working at the hotel for almost five years now,

Jane has only been asked out on a date twice by a hotel guest, and both times she was cancelled on. No wonder she is so desperate for a man's attention even if it will never be more than a few fake photos and a bunch of lies.

Jane knows that even though she may be chatting with lots of men on Mingle, it will never be possible for her to meet any of them in person. They would show up expecting to meet a beautiful blond or brunette or a tanned Cuban beauty queen, and instead they would meet a freckled, frizzy-haired redhead. How long do you think it would take for them to run away as fast as they could? Jane has received more attention over the last few days since she started her three new profiles than she has received her entire life. She finally knows what it feels like to be one of the popular girls even though, deep down, she knows it is not her that is popular; it is her three other personas. For now, she could not be any happier.

Finally, 7:00 p.m. comes at last. Jane says good night to the rest of the staff, grabs her keys and cell phone from the office, and heads out the door. It is a beautiful night out. The sun is finishing its descent and the stars are just starting to sparkle. The air is cool with just the slightest breeze. It is nights like this that Jane wishes she did have a special man in her life to go walking along the beach with hand in hand. Instead, she hurries home knowing that Blue will be waiting at the door for her the second she puts her key in the lock. He has been home alone for just about eleven hours with no one to rub him or play with him or, more importantly, to give him treats.

Just as Jane expected, Blue is right there to greet her as soon as she opens the door. She closes the door, drops her keys on the table, and bends down to greet Blue. She gives him what he wants most: a nice gentle rub between his eyes and a kiss on his nose. Blue may be a needy cat, but he is also very easy to please. Jane does a scan of the ficus tree pot and is relieved she will not have to be cleaning up after Blue again. She then gives his litterbox a quick cleaning while he supervises her work.

Jane has been on a salad-only diet for dinner for as long as she can remember. It was the only way she could lose the weight she wanted to lose, and it worked, so she has kept it going. She takes everything she plans on having in tonight's salad out of the refrigerator and starts cutting it up. Blue has jumped up on the kitchen counter so he can get a better view. Typically, Jane does not allow him to be on the counter, but she knows he was home alone all day, so she lets it slide. Once she has everything sliced and diced, she throws it all together in a bowl and adds some salad dressing. With her dinner complete, she grabs Blue's water bowl and food dish from his placemat that Jane bought especially for him. She cleans them out in the sink and dries them off. Blue has not taken his eyes off Jane since she walked in the door. This is the part he has been waiting for the whole time.

Jane fills Blue's water bowl with bottled water and places it back on the placemat. She then opens a can of salmon cat food, which is Blue's favorite, and empties it onto his food dish. She takes a fork and breaks it up into bite-size pieces for him and then places it right next to his water bowl. Now that both of their dinners are ready, Jane sits down at one of the stools she has on the outside of the kitchen island. Blue jumps down off the kitchen counter, and they both start eating at the same time.

With the dishes washed, both hers and Blue's, Jane grabs her cell phone and cozies up on the sofa for some Mingle time. Blue, of course, follows her and claims his spot dead center of the sofa. Tonight, for some reason, Jane feels hesitant as she is about to select which persona to log on as first. The devil has been behaving lately, but Jane always knows when he is about to make an appearance. She can suddenly start to feel the clamminess in her palms that happens right before they start to sweat. Strangely, Jane almost decides to close Mingle for the night, but the pull is just too strong for her to fight. As she decides to start with Mona's profile, Jane's palms go from clammy to full-on sweating. What is it with this devil tonight? He has not been bothering Jane any of the other times she has logged on in the past couple of days. What is so different about tonight?

With Mona's profile loaded on Jane's Mingle app, she starts swiping her way through all the possible men to match with. So many possibilities that will never have a chance to come to fruition. Being popular is not as easy as Jane thought it would be. It is a lot of work keeping up with all the messages she has been receiving. She tries to keep her responses as short as possible without sounding uninterested. Jane has also been trying her hardest to give each persona a different voice than her own. This has been toughest when she is responding to messages sent to Mona due to Monica being from Cuba. Some of the wording Monica would use in her responses may vary from the wording Stacey or Melissa would use in their responses. It has also been very exhausting keeping up with all the lies she has been telling all these men.

The interesting thing about the Mingle app is that it is more useful to women than it is to men. When a woman logs on, she gets to see all the men's profiles that are in her area, and she gets to swipe right if she wants to potentially match with the man or swipe left if she is not interested. When a man logs on, he only gets to see the women that have already swiped right for him. It is up to him if he wants to confirm the match or reject it. That is the main reason Jane selected Mingle as the app she would use for her three personas. If every man on the app could see all three of her profiles and they all swiped right for all three of them, she would never be able to keep up. Life is really tough for the popular people.

Blue starts stirring; nap time is over. He looks over at Jane, and he is not happy that she has not noticed he is awake. He jumps off the sofa and relieves himself in the ficus tree pot. If that does not get Jane's attention, nothing will. Unfortunately for Blue, Jane's full attention is on the man in the photo on her cell phone screen. She knows she has seen this man's face somewhere before, but for the life of her, she cannot place him. She reads the few details he has posted in his profile in hopes of getting some helpful hints. He has his name listed as Tim. He lives on Miami Beach. He is thirty-one years old. He is five feet, ten inches tall and weighs one hundred and eighty pounds. He has his occupation listed as *helps others*, whatever that means. He enjoys sailing, running, and spending time with those that are close to him.

As Jane reads Tim's profile, she cannot help but wonder if any of it is actually true. After all, there is not one single word in any of her three profiles that is true. The more time Jane spends deciding which way to swipe, the more intense the knots in her stomach become. To hell with you, devil! Three things happen simultaneously: Jane swipes right on Tim's profile, Jane runs as fast as she can to the bathroom, and Blue follows right behind her. Why in the world would this stupid little devil have any interest in Jane's decision about which way to swipe for Tim?

Once Jane is done in the bathroom, she climbs into bed with Blue right behind her. Jane has had enough excitement on Mingle for tonight. With Blue curled up at her feet, let's see how long that lasts, she shuts Mingle down. She has no idea why, but she has a very strong feeling that she just did something that she absolutely should not have done. As Jane pulls the covers up to her chin, the sudden movement startles Blue. He slowly makes his way up the bed and plops down on the pillow right near Jane's head. Jane lets out a little laugh, then leans over and gives him his good night rub right between his eyes and kiss on his nose. There has not been one single night since she brought Blue home that he has actually stayed at the foot of the bed. Never mind in his own bed. He always starts there but never stays for very long.

As Jane lays in her nice comfy bed waiting to fall asleep, she starts hearing dings coming from her cell phone, letting her know she has new matches and new messages coming in on Mingle. All the horny men on the app at this time of night looking to make an instant match. It takes all the willpower Jane has to switch her cell phone to silent mode without even opening Mingle. She can hear Blue already snoring away, and she lets his cute little snores drift her away into a nice deep sleep. All is good in the Brooks house tonight.

Chapter 4

The next few days, Jane manages to avoid opening Mingle at all. She can see from the notification alerts that she has lots of new messages on all three of the profiles, but she still has an uneasy feeling about the devil's reaction to when she swiped right on Tim's photo. She is not completely convinced that is what infuriated the devil, but something was different about him that night. Typically, when the devil is going to make an appearance, it always starts with Jane having the same argument back and forth: Should I do it? I shouldn't do it! Should I do it? Over and over again. This last time, he skipped right over that part and went right to making her palms clammy.

To keep her mind busy, Jane has instead been trying as hard as she can to remember where she has seen Tim's face before. She is pretty certain that when she saw him that night, it was the first time she has seen him on Mingle. If not there, then where? Working in the hotel as much as she does, it is possible that Jane had seen him as he was checking in or checking out, but that does not seem right to her. It was in a photo, not in real life. Of that, she is almost positive.

After another long shift at the hotel, Jane is very happy to be back home with Blue even if he seems to be irritated with her for some reason. If only he could speak instead of just meowing. He was not even at the door to greet her when she walked in the house. Life is funny sometimes. Jane finds Blue's constant need for her attention annoying at times, but the one time he is not there at the door as she opens it, she misses seeing him there waiting for her. Any attention is better than no attention when you live the life Jane lives.

After a little investigating, Jane is pretty sure she knows what Blue's issue is tonight. Before she left for work this morning, she somehow forgot to clean out his litterbox, which he had used sometime during the night. Due to his extreme stubbornness, he would not dare to step into the litterbox before Jane cleaned it out for him. Instead, he once again caused havoc on her ficus tree. By the looks of it, Jane can tell that Blue also decided to eat some of the lower leaves off their branches. She can see bits and pieces of them in Blue's vomit, which is waiting for her to clean up on her Persian rug.

After Jane has cleaned out the ficus tree's pot and cleaned up the vomit off the rug, she picks up Blue and sits down on the sofa with him in her lap. She knows she should punish him in some way, but isn't vomiting up the remains of leaves from a ficus tree enough punishment already? So instead, Jane spends some quality time making him feel loved. She rubs him between his eyes and then all down his back and even through the length of his tail. He purrs through all of it, his way of saying, "I love you too, Jane." Just like that, all is forgiven.

Then it suddenly hits her. Have you ever heard the old saying "All you have to do to remember something is to not think about it"? It makes absolutely no sense whatsoever, but while Jane was giving Blue his rubdown, she was so focused on him that she had stopped thinking about where she had seen Tim's face before. Jane picks Blue up in her arms, no sense upsetting him again, and walks over to her desk. She sits down in her chair and lets Blue do his little circle routine before crawling into a ball right in the center of her lap. She turns her laptop on, and once it is ready, she opens Facebook and logs into her account. Her hands start to sweat, letting her know she is on the right track. She goes directly to Stacey's page and clicks on the link for her photos. As they load, she feels her stomach clench up good and tight. Getting closer every click. She starts scrolling through the photos, and sure enough, there is Tim. He has one of his arms around Stacey and the other arm around their oldest son. Their youngest son is sitting up on his broad shoulders.

Jane knows from the Facebook stalking she has done over the years that his name is not Tim. It is actually Steve Maddox. Married and father of two boys. Jane had seen this photo when she was scanning Stacey's photos, looking for the three she wanted to use on Mingle. Holy Shit! Is this what the devil was all up in arms about? Jane logs out of Facebook and shuts down her laptop. She picks Blue up off her lap, which wakes him up. He does not seem to mind because he knows he is about to land right on top of the pillow on his side of the bed. Cats, like children, do not become spoiled by their own doing.

As Blue curls up nice and tight in a ball, Jane sits up in bed with her back against the headboard. She is not quite ready to call it a night yet. She starts replaying everything she has read or seen on Stacey's Facebook page regarding Steve. To Jane's recollection, there was never anything negative posted on the page about Steve. She is one hundred percent certain that there is not one single photo anywhere on Stacey's page that does not show all of them with the biggest smiles possible. One big happy family. Or is it all for show?

Jane is tempted more than ever to open the Mingle app and see if Mona is now matched with Tim, but before she does that, she needs to come up with a new plan. As soon as Jane swiped right on Tim's photo, he was sent a notification that he has a new potential match. The next time he opens the app, he will see the notification waiting for him to do his swiping. He will be seeing a photo of Monica, one of Stacey's best friends from her high school days. Jane does know that since the day Monica came out to Stacey, their friendship has turned to crap. Stacey took it very personally that Monica had kept her lesbian secret from her for almost ten years. If Jane has any luck at all, Steve will not recognize Mona from any of the old photos Stacey had posted of herself with Monica.

As Jane slides down under the sheets, she cannot stop thinking about all the what-ifs once Steve sees the photo of Mona as one of his potential matches. If he does not recognize her, will he swipe right? Is Mona even his type? If he does recognize her as one of

Stacey's high school friends, will he swipe left to keep Mona from seeing him on the app again? Would he even go so far as to delete his profile? If all the details he posted and his name are lies on Mingle, could the photo be a fake too, just like they are in all three of the profiles Jane created for herself? If she does not ever agree to meet him in person someday, how will she know if it really is Steve or not?

Chapter 5

Even though it is Jane's day off, she is still wide-awake before the sun has had a chance to fully rise. Her sudden movements startle Blue out of his canary-chasing dream. They both take care of their morning business before sitting down to breakfast together. As Jane makes her way through a bowl of Froot Loops, she gives into the urge and opens her Mingle app. Before the devil can even start his dirty work, she logs on as Mona. Her curiosity about whether she is now matched with Tim has overpowered anything this little devil can dish out. Jane does not even bother looking at all the new men she can swipe with. She goes right to her messages to see if there is one from Tim.

Sure enough, there is one. Jane opens the message, and as she reads the three words he wrote, she starts to shake uncontrollably, *You look familiar.* Jane instantly logs out of Mingle and throws her phone down on. The noise of the phone crashing down has caught Blue's attention. He casually strolls over to Jane's chair and just sits there staring up at her. He knows he is not allowed on the kitchen island no matter what. That is about the only house rule that Blue actually follows most of the time.

Jane is so bewildered by Tim's message that she does not even notice Blue is at her feet, which is not working for him. He stretches up her leg and rests his chin on her knee. Jane bends over, picks him up, and plops him in her lap. As Blue makes himself comfortable, Jane cannot help but think how much more depressing her life would be without him in it. Getting Blue was the best decision Jane has ever made, even if he continues killing her ficus tree.

Having Blue in her lap has actually calmed Jane down a bit. She contemplates what she should do next now that Tim has accepted her match and sent her that message. Jane has no idea if it is really Steve behind the Tim profile. Just because he said Mona looked familiar doesn't necessarily mean it has to be Steve. It could just as easily be some guy named Joe who stole Steve's photo the same way Jane stole Monica's photos. "What a tangled web we weave, when first we practice to deceive." Jane's snowball has started rolling down that Colorado mountain again. Look out below.

Here he comes again. With sweaty palms, Jane has all the confirmation she needs to know that what she is about to do is the absolute wrong decision. She picks up her cell phone and opens her Mingle app. She logs back on as Mona and opens the message from Tim. Instead of hitting Delete or Block, like the angel wants her to do, she hits Reply. Two can play this game. Jane types, "Have we met before? I don't think I know anyone named Tim" and hits Send. The next move, or shall we say, the next lie is his. Jane has not decided if she wants it to really be Steve or not. What if it is really him? What does she do then?

It has only been a week since Jane created her three new profiles. Though she has been enjoying all the attention she has been getting, the guilt she has been feeling for lying to so many men, is starting to outweigh the excitement of it all. Maybe that devil was on to something after all. Blue has become bored of just sitting in Jane's lap. He jumps down and starts playing with the new toy she bought him a cute little gray mouse filled with catnip. Jane makes a very rash decision and deletes the profiles she created for Lacy and Lisa without even checking the new messages and the possible matches they both had waiting for her. She considers deleting the one for Mona too, but she cannot get herself to do it. Deleting two out of three at one time is drastic enough. Besides, her curiosity is piqued to the max about this Tim man.

Jane does not want to be vindictive, but if perfect Stacey's husband is on Mingle, trying to match with other women, it would bring a fair amount of joy into her sad, lonely depressing life. Can it really be him? Can it be Steve using the name Tim? Finding a way to see who the man is behind this Tim profile has just become Jane's new obsession. No matter what it takes, she will find out if it is Steve or if it is another poser just like her.

Jane needs to do some grocery shopping for the coming week. When you eat salads for dinner every night, you go through a lot of vegetables, which unfortunately do not stay fresh for long. There is a Whole Foods market in walking distance from Jane's condo, which she absolutely loves, just like everybody else that lives in this part of Miami. The prices are a lot higher than the other local grocery stores, but they have a great produce department, which is Jane's main priority. She grabs her keys and her purse from the table by the door. Blue drops his mouse at her feet, sits down, and just stares up at her. He knows she cannot say no to him when he tilts his head to one side and gives her the saddest-looking face he can muster up. Jane caves into him again. She grabs his leash and attaches it to his collar, then they are out the door.

The walk takes a little longer than normal because Blue keeps stopping to smell pretty much anything and everything along the way. Jane likes taking Blue for walks when she has the time. He loves being outside, but Jane will never let him outside without his leash on. Once they are in the store, Jane grabs a carriage and puts Blue in the front basket. They have done this many times before. When Jane first started taking him to the store with her, he would keep trying to jump out of the carriage, almost strangling himself with his leash. After a few bad mishaps, he gave up on doing his own shopping. Now he just lays down in the basket with his head hanging over the side. He likes it when people rub his head as they walk by.

Jane works her way through the aisles and grabs everything on the list she made, including kitty litter and enough food for Blue to last a month. He is a very finicky eater. When Jane finds his favorites, she buys as many as they have of them on the shelf. Her last stop is the produce department, which is where she is headed now. Without the ability to understand Blue's meowing, Jane does not know if he likes this section of the store or if he hates it. Every time Jane turns the carriage into the produce section, Blue sits up in the basket and his nose starts twitching out of control. The vegetables are very fresh at Whole Foods, so the stronger-smelling ones fill the air as you walk by them. There are certain vegetables that, for some reason, make Blue start meowing until he is far enough away from their scent. One of them being onions, which Blue has already picked up on. Here comes the meowing. Jane rubs his head to quiet him down and walks past the onions as quickly as she can. Once and only once Jane made the mistake of going into the seafood department with Blue in the basket. He made noises she did not even know he could make. Jane learned that lesson very quickly.

Jane stops to pick out some fresh vine tomatoes, which she loves in her salads, especially when they are a bit firm when she picks them up. In the midst of selecting her tomatoes, she hears a woman's voice say, "Is it really you?" Though she hears it, she assumes it is not meant for her. Jane has never bumped into anyone she knows here. She continues searching for just the right tomatoes. Then the same voice comes again, but closer to her this time. "Is that you, Jane?" Unless there is another Jane in the very near vicinity it must be her the woman is speaking to. Blue is sitting at full attention now and looking right past Jane.

Jane drops one more tomato into her little plastic bag. She ties the top of the bag in a knot, drops it in her carriage, and turns around. Jane nearly passes out right there in the aisle of the produce department in Whole Foods. Standing in front of her is none other than Stacey Maddox. As Jane looks past Stacey, she sees Steve and their two boys picking out some bananas. This is more than Jane can handle right now. She has got to get out of here as quick as she can. She does the only thing she can think of: she lies. "Sorry, my name is not Jane" she says and pushes her carriage as fast as she can away from Stacey and, more importantly, away from Steve.

Jane finds the shortest checkout line as far away from them as she can and does not even look back in their direction. Once she is through the checkout line, Jane grabs the two bags in one hand and Blue in the other. What in the world are they doing in Jane's Whole Foods? They live on Miami Beach, and Jane knows there are at least two other Whole Foods on the beach. Why come all the way to this one?

Chapter 6

Back in the safety of her own home, Jane puts her groceries away and gives Blue some of his treats for sort of behaving during their shopping trip. Blue prefers to walk when they go out, but Jane did not want him slowing her down this time, so she carried him the whole way home. He had his two paws up on her shoulder and his head resting on them, as if he was keeping watch behind them. Once Blue has chowed down his treats, he surprises Jane and climbs into his own bed for a nap. He must be extra tired from their outing.

Jane cannot stop thinking about seeing Stacey in person after all these years. She is shocked that Stacey even recognized her, never mind actually remembered her name. They have not seen each other since graduation when Jane was almost one hundred pounds heavier than she is now. Granted, her frizzy red hair is just as frizzy as it was back then and none of her freckles have faded away over the years. No such luck there. Stacey, on the other hand, is even prettier than she was back then if that is even possible. Jane was hoping that Stacey was touching up her photos before posting them, but again, no such luck.

Seeing Steve with his two boys like that has given Jane very mixed feelings. One part of her is angry with him for being on Mingle looking for other women while he has Stacey and his boys at home. Even if things are not perfect with Stacey, he still has to think about his boys. Another part of Jane, the crazy part, is very busy daydreaming about her taking Stacey's place as Steve's wife and as the mother of Steve's boys. What is she, insane? That would never happen, not even if Stacey suddenly disappeared or accidentally passed away. Jane comes back to earth and again realizes that she still has no idea if it is really Steve behind the Tim profile. She is even more determined now to figure that out, but how?

Jane opens her balcony door, which wakes Blue from his nap. They both make their way outside and sit down on the chairs she has set up on the balcony. Jane likes sitting out here when the weather is not too hot or too cold, just like it is right now. She finds it relaxing to be outside and not have to be around anyone for a change. Blue likes it when there is a little bit of a breeze blowing in his face. Sometimes he will sit up in his chair and try to catch the breeze in his mouth. Jane loves it when he does that. It makes her laugh every time. Jane finds herself wondering how Blue would handle having to share her attention with Steve and the boys.

There is no breeze today, so Blue curls himself into a ball and picks up his nap where he left off. Life is just as tough for Blue as it is for the popular people. Jane sits back in her chair and lets the sunshine down on her. With her fair skin, she burns very quickly, so she only dares to sit out here in the late afternoon when the sun is not as strong. She closes her eyes and tries to stop her mind from working overtime. She needs to come up with a way to see this Tim man in person without him even knowing it is happening.

After about ten minutes, Jane can feel her skin starting to get hot from the sun. The last thing she wants is to start burning. All that does is bring out her freckles even more. She moves her chair into the shaded part of the balcony and is surprised Blue does not wake up from the noise. He must be having another canary-chasing dream. Sometimes when Blue is having a really intense dream, he will swat his front paws back and forth. He must be chasing a mouse or some other small creature that he can never seem to catch. Right now, the ball he is wrapped in is so tight Jane cannot even see his head. She relaxes back into her chair and just breathes in the fresh air.

A plan enters Jane's mind. It would take a lot of planning, a lot of scheming, and a hell of a lot more lying, but it could work. Is it really worth the time and effort it will take just to find out if it really is Steve? What is Jane hoping to accomplish by doing any of this? Even if it really is Steve, it is Monica he thinks he is matching with, not Jane. What is her real motivation here? Is her life really that dull and boring that she has nothing better to do than possibly break up Stacey's marriage? I think we both know the answer to that question.

Jane goes inside and grabs her cell phone, then she rejoins Blue on the balcony. He must be in a deep sleep because he did not move at all when she got up again. That outing must have really done him in. She opens her Mingle app and logs on as Mona. Again, she completely ignores all the new faces to swipe through and goes directly to her new messages. Her palms are full of sweat and her stomach is in knots as she clicks on the new message from Tim. This time he wrote, "I don't think we have met, but I have seen you somewhere before. Perhaps we should change that". Perhaps we should change that? Is he asking to meet Mona in person this soon? They have only sent one message to each other. Does he move this fast with all the women he matches with on Mingle? Before the devil has the chance to knock the angel completely off Jane's shoulder, she shuts down Mingle. No time for a bathroom run now. She has a plan to figure out.

The new message from Tim, though alarming, fits perfectly into Jane's plan she thought of earlier. If Jane does agree to meet up with Tim, he will be looking for a woman that looks like Monica, not a woman that looks like her. The tricky part is, what if it is not Steve that is behind the Tim profile and the real man using Steve's photo shows up instead? How will she know it is him when he arrives? If they are both using fake photos, neither of them will be able to spot the other. What in the world has she got herself into this time?

Blue finally decides to join the land of the living again and heads in to use his litterbox. Jane takes this opportunity to head back in herself. The sun is going down, and her stomach is starting to growl. Blue must be ready to eat by now too. She makes herself a delicious-looking salad with some fresh butter lettuce, a third of a cucumber, and one of the fresh vine tomatoes she just picked up at Whole Foods. She dices up a half of a grilled chicken breast she had left over from yesterday, mixes it into the salad, and then tops it off with some French dressing. Blue gets one of his favorite cans of salmon dinners. They both eat in silence side by side. Jane has some thinking to do, and she always does that better on a full stomach.

With a happy stomach and her thinking cap on, Jane settles in on the sofa. The sun has gone down, and without it, her living room gets pretty dark, but she does not turn any lights on. She finds it easier to focus and concentrate when she is in the dark. There are less things to distract her except for Blue, of course, who is now lying across the sofa with his head hanging over her leg. I wonder what he is waiting for. Jane knows this routine by heart. It has played out a million times. She gently rubs Blue between his eyes. He purrs continuously until he has had enough. He then moves to his spot on the sofa, curls himself up nice and tight, and goes back to sleep completely satisfied. If only Jane's life was so easy. What she wouldn't do to switch places with Blue even for just one day.

Jane is so calm and relaxed sitting in the dark like this with Blue already asleep next to her that she starts nodding off herself. As her head starts to bob forward and then back, it suddenly comes to her. She sits up straighter to keep herself awake as she carefully thinks through everything she will need to do for her plan to be a success. It is going to be a bit risky or maybe even a lot risky, but it will work.

Chapter 7

Jane has another long ten-hour shift ahead of her as she arrives at the hotel. It is a Friday, so she knows it will be busy her entire shift, which is exactly what she needs to make the day fly by and to stop her from obsessing about this Tim man, whoever he really is. Jane has not logged on to her Mingle app since she read her newest message from Tim. She knows she must play this smart for it to work. She has her plan figured out. She just needs to be brave enough to go through with it. This is taking Jane way out of her comfort zone. She has always played it safe and avoided taking any major risks in her life. That is all about to change. The devil is going to be in heaven.

While Jane stands behind the front desk with her two staff members as they hurriedly check in guest after guest, she cannot help but wonder if she is the only one in the lobby living a life of lies. Jane has always prided herself on being a good, kind, honest person. When you do not have much going for you, it is important to focus on any positive traits you can. With all the lies Jane has been telling over the last week, she can scratch honest off her list. Thank God she will always have Blue to go home to.

After the morning rush of guests checking in is over and Jane has given both of her staff members their lunch breaks, she heads to her office to eat the lunch she brought from home. It is tough for Jane to take an hour lunch break and leave the hotel during her weekend shifts. There can be mobs of people arriving at the same time, usually on shuttle buses from the Miami International Airport. That would be too much for just her two staff members to handle without any of the guest getting upset about their wait times.

Jane's lunch today consists of two leftover slices of Hawaiian pizza, a Granny Smith apple, and a can of Diet Coke. Luckily, there is a microwave and a toaster oven in the staff room for Jane to warm up her slices of pizza. Some people love cold pizza, but Jane is not one of them. Once she has heated up her pizza in the toaster oven and does a quick check of the front desk, she settles into the chair at her desk to stuff her face. With her office door closed, Jane does what she had promised herself she would never do; she opens her Mingle app. She has a few new messages, but none from Tim. Time to put her plan into action. She opens the last message from Tim and hits Reply. Damn, this devil is loving this. Her palms are dripping sweat, and her stomach feels like one of those Auntie Anne's cinnamon pretzels she loved growing up, all twisted up in a knot. She types in, "Care to share a few more photos?" and hits Send. She logs back out and closes Mingle and her cell phone.

It has only been a half hour, but Jane is done eating her lunch and is already back at the front desk. One of the shuttle buses from the airport is making its rounds and just dropped off enough guests to fill the lobby again. Her mind is all over the place after sending her message to Tim. She is having a hard time focusing on work. She looks out at all the guests waiting to check in and finds herself wondering if the real Tim is among them. Jane is trying to convince herself that there is no way Steve would be cheating on Stacey. It just does not make sense. It must be someone else, but who? She refocuses back on getting all the guests checked in before they start getting rowdy. Her staff members do not seem to notice how distracted she is, which is a huge relief. Jane is always trying to set a good example for everyone that she supervises by always being friendly and smiling even when she really does not want to.

By the time her shift is over, she is dead on her feet. It was an extremely busy day at the hotel today, which means Sunday is also going to be ridiculously crazy. That is when most of the guests that checked in today, along with most of the guests that check in tomorrow, will all be checking out. Jane was so busy the rest of her shift she did not have any time to check if Tim has responded and hopefully sent along some more photos.

As soon as Jane gets home, she picks Blue up. She gives him a nice big hug, rubs him between his eyes, and kisses his nose. The love they have for each other is unconditional. She then cleans Blue's litterbox and gives him a couple of treats while she gets his dinner ready. Jane decided on her way home from the hotel that she is going to spoil Blue tonight. She fills his water bowl with some warm milk, which she has not done for him in quite a while. She then fills Blue's food dish with StarKist all-white tuna. Blue goes crazy for StarKist tuna fish, but she only gives it to him once a month. After eating it, he will not touch his actual cat food until he is literally starving.

While Blue eats his dinner, Jane takes a quick shower. Her stomach has not been feeling right since she ate her lunch, so she is skipping dinner tonight. She is pretty sure there was nothing wrong with the food she ate for lunch. It is most likely a lingering effect of the devil's visit earlier. After she is done with her shower and Blue has finished licking every last drop of tuna oil off his chops, they both crawl into bed. Blue does not even bother starting at the foot of the bed tonight. He goes right for the pillow he spends every night on. Jane stands her pillow up against the headboard, grabs her cell phone, and logs on to Mingle. She has tons of profiles to swipe through, but once again, she goes right for her new messages. She sees a new message from Tim. Her heart starts to race before she even opens it. When she opens the new message, the first thing she sees is what he wrote, "Hope you like them. Send me some of yours in return". Then she sees the two photos he sent her. The first photo is of Steve in a tank top, drinking a beer at what looks like a cookout. The second photo is of Steve with no shirt on, sitting in a lounge chair at the beach.

Jane jumps back out of bed and walks over to her desk. She turns her laptop on and tries to steady her nerves as it starts up. Blue looks over from his pillow, but he does not move an inch. When her laptop is ready, she opens Facebook and does a search for Steve Maddox. She cannot believe she didn't think to do this sooner. Once she finds him, she clicks on his profile. Luckily, it is not set to private. She starts scrolling through his photos. One by one, she finds all three of the photos she has seen of him on Mingle. This tells her that it either really is Steve or someone went onto Steve's profile page and copied his photos to use on Mingle. Who would do such a thing?

She shuts down her laptop and crawls back in bed. Blue lifts his head as he waits for his good night rub and kiss on his nose. Jane does not make him wait long. The scent of tuna is still very pungent. Her next move is a risky one. She is pretty sure it may even be illegal, but it is the only way for her plan to work. She opens her Mingle app again and logs back on as Mona. She opens the most recent message from Tim and hits Reply. Before she can even type one single letter, she is jumping out of bed again and racing to the bathroom. The devil is very pleased with himself once again. With the way this devil is acting, Jane may be able to stop eating so many salads. While sitting on the toilet, she picks up where she left off, and she types, "Great photos! I bet all the ladies on here like them. Here are some of mine. Hope you like". She then sends Tim the other two photos she had downloaded from Monica's Facebook page. She knows he will be drooling when he sees them. Any straight man would. The plan is going exactly as she expected it to go so far. She shuts down Mingle, silences her cell phone, shuts off the lights and crawls under the covers.

Chapter 8

Jane is back at the hotel bright and early the next morning. Considering the hotel is already eighty percent full, she is not expecting any major rushes of guests today like there was yesterday. The weatherman is forecasting rain the whole weekend, which is normal for this time of year in Miami. Jane's day got off to a bumpy start. She left her house this morning without an umbrella and got caught in a downpour. Her naturally frizzy red hair now looks like a Little Orphan Annie wig gone wrong.

While it is quiet at the front desk Jane plans on staying in her office to work on her staff's schedule for the following week. First, she makes a cup of coffee and then gets to it. She has done the schedule so many times she could probably do it in her sleep. As she starts filling in the blank time slots, Jane hears her phone ping and instantly knows she just received a new message on her Mingle app. She checked Mingle this morning before leaving her house, but Tim had not responded yet. Jane looks out the window in her office, which faces the front desk and the lobby. She can see one of her staff members is checking in an older couple, and the other one is busy straightening up the brochure display. She quickly grabs her cell phone and opens the Mingle app. She logs on as Mona and checks her new messages. The newest one that just came in is from Tim. She opens the message and reads it, "Glad you liked my photos. Yours are smoking hot! So now what?" She shuts down Mingle without even logging out first. No man has ever referred to her as hot before. She can feel herself blushing even though she knows it is not her that Tim is talking about. So now what is right?

Jane knows she is playing a dangerous game no matter who is on the other side of this Tim profile. She has him hooked. All she needs to do is reel him in. She finds herself doing a little quiet chuckle. Reel him in just like a catfish. This could go wrong in so many ways. Jane has watched the *Catfish* show on MTV many times. It never ends well. She goes back to working on the staff's schedule. She needs some time to work out her next move.

The rest of her shift goes by quickly and smoothly. The hotel is now at ninety percent capacity, which is better than she was expecting on a rainy weekend. A majority of the guests had booked rooms in advance, which makes checking them in much easier. The guests will not be able to enjoy the beautiful gardens Jane hopes to get married in some day or the impeccable pool area. Fortunately, there are still plenty of indoor attractions close by to keep them busy during their stay.

Luckily, the rain has stopped long enough for Jane to make it home as dry as she was when she left the hotel. She does have a license and a car, but with the hotel only a little over a mile from her condo, she tries to walk back and forth to work every day. A little exercise never killed anyone, or so they say. As she opens her door, Blue starts meowing very loudly. On days like today when she has to work the early shift, she tries her best to not wake Blue up. She leaves his breakfast for him and sneaks out the door as quietly as she can. That was the case this morning, and Blue is not happy about it. He has not been rubbed, kissed, or fussed over for far too long, and he makes sure Jane knows it. She scoops him up in her arms as soon as she closes the door. She kisses his nose and rubs him between his eyes. In response, he gently rubs his head against her cheek. She then gives him a couple of his favorite treats. All is better in the life of Blue.

To Jane's surprise the ficus tree's pot has no new mess for her to clean. That means she needs to clean Blue's litterbox before they eat dinner. One of Jane's favorite inventions is the kitty litter you can flush down the toilet. She does clean the litterbox completely on her days off from work, but on workdays she just scoops and flushes. With the litterbox out of the way, she makes dinner for both of them before finally getting to relax. She is feeling a little guilty about having the day off from work tomorrow knowing how busy it is going to be for her staff. Whenever she works Friday and Saturday in a row, she always takes the Sunday off. Knowing she did schedule an extra staff member during check out time makes her feel a little better.

Before she is even done cleaning up from their dinners, Blue is already fast asleep in the center of the sofa. Jane's life is so boring and predictable that even Blue knows her next move before she makes it. She finds the remote for the television and flicks through the channels, which is something she has not done in a while. Jane has no interest in watching reality shows, and these days, that is all there seems to be on almost every channel. Why would she want to watch all these rich and famous housewives, or the fake wannabes make complete fools of themselves with all the fake drama just to be on television? She is, however, a sucker for a good *Dateline* or Forty-Eight Hours mystery. Now that is good television.

After a quick scan and finding nothing that interests her, Jane shuts the television off and starts thinking about what her next response to Tim should be. She does not want to come on too strong and possibly scare Tim away even though he is coming on pretty strong himself. She has to remember that while she is on Mingle, she is a woman that looks like Monica, not a woman that looks like Jane. Having a man that looks like Tim, or rather like Steve, asking her "So now what?" after only sharing a few photos is a lot different than asking Monica the same thing. A woman that looks like Monica having a real profile on one of these apps must be insane as Jane was starting to find out, especially when she had all three different personas going at the same time. Jane has not bothered swiping right or left for any new possible matches since she started messaging with Tim.

At the same time, she does not want to come off as uninterested and have Tim lose interest in her. What would Monica say if she was in the same situation? That is what Jane needs to figure out. She also still needs to figure out what she is going to do once she knows for sure if it is or is not Steve that is messaging her. What will he do if it really is him and he finds out he has been messaging and sending photos to Jane instead of to Monica, A.K.A. Mona? She cannot let that happen no matter what.

She brushes her teeth and takes a quick shower before calling it a night. Blue does not even bother following her into the bathroom. He goes straight from the sofa to the pillow, which, it seems, he has claimed as his own. Jane is pretty sure he sleeps on it all day while she is at work too. Spoiled rotten is what he is. By the time she climbs into her side of the bed, Blue is already snoring away. She bends over and kisses him lightly on the top of his head. Sweet dreams, Blue.

Chapter 9

Jane is awoken by Blue when he climbs onto her chest. She opens her eyes one at a time and sees Blue sitting there, just looking down at her. This is something new for them. She is always awake before Blue. She looks over at her alarm clock on her bedside table and cannot believe what she is seeing. No wonder Blue is up and ready for his breakfast. It is almost 9:00 a.m. Jane has not slept this late in years. She must have really needed some good sleep. She gives Blue a nice gentle rub between his eyes before he jumps off her and walks over to the kitchen. He starts pacing back and forth in front of his placemat with its empty food dish and water bowl and lets out a very loud meow. Message received.

Jane gets out of bed, does what she needs to do in the bathroom, then proceeds to make breakfast for both of them. After breakfast, she empties Blue's litterbox and gives it a very thorough cleaning before refilling it with new kitty litter. Blue's way of saying thank you is by climbing into it as soon as she puts it back on the floor and taking a leak. At least he didn't water her ficus tree instead. She then brushes her teeth and takes a shower. Blue waits patiently for her on the bathroom mat. Jane is pretty sure if Blue was not so afraid of water, he would actually join her in the shower. She did try washing him once in the bathtub shortly after she got him. Needless to say, that did not go over well. She had very long, very deep scratches up and down her arms that actually drew blood. She never made that mistake again.

Jane has decided she needs to put the ball back in Tim's court. She opens her Mingle app and replies to his most recent message of "So now what?" She does not want to sound needy or desperate because she knows Monica is neither of those. She simply types "That depends on what you have in mind" and hits Send. As soon as she sends the new message, she logs off Mingle and shuts down her cell phone.

Blue is very hyper today. It must be a side-effect of sleeping so long. He usually takes a nap shortly after breakfast, but instead, he has been playing with his catnip-filled mouse all morning. He picks it up in his mouth and throws it around the condo. Then he swats it back and forth with his paws just like a cat would do with a live mouse before moving in for the kill. Jane takes a look outside and sees the sun is actually making an appearance in between rain showers. She throws on a pair of jogging pants (Jane has not worn shorts since her high school trip), a T-shirt, sneakers, and a baseball cap. Before she can even grab Blue's leash, he is sitting by the door, waiting for her. She really is that predictable.

There is a nice little pet park that was added to the neighborhood last year. It is probably only intended for dogs, but Jane takes Blue there occasionally. Blue is not intimidated by the dogs even though they could tear him to shreds in less than a minute. Jane keeps him very close to her while they are there. They make it to the park in about five minutes. There are only a couple of other people there at this time of the day. Most people are either sleeping in or going to church. Jane walks Blue around the outside perimeter of the park away from a large dog. You can never be too safe.

After they do a lap around the entire park, Jane finds a bench away from anyone else and sits down. She is regretting not bringing a bottle of water with her. Blue jumps up on the bench and lays down with his head in her lap. Is he ever satisfied? She takes the subtle hint and rubs him between his eyes as requested. As they both relax on the bench, Jane notices two women entering the park with a very little chihuahua. For some reason Blue is infatuated with chihuahuas.

Every time he sees a chihuahua he tries to jump on it which they do not appreciate very much.

As the women get closer to where Jane and Blue are sitting, the chihuahua spots them and starts yapping away, which catches Blue's attention. Blue is up in an instant and jumps off the bench. Jane pulls on his leash to keep him from getting any closer. She had not realized that the women had taken the leash off the chihuahua until he is right there next to her feet. Blue is twice as tall as the chihuahua though it does not seem to notice or care. They take turns jumping on each other and rolling around on the ground. Jane does not take her eyes off them.

Now the women are close enough for Jane to see their faces, and she freezes. One of the women comes over and apologizes to Jane for her dog attacking Blue. If they were fighting instead of playing, Blue would win hands, or rather paws, down. As the apologizing woman tries to separate her chihuahua from Blue, the second woman approaches. Jane has still not moved or said a single word since she realized who the chihuahua belongs to. Once they are only a few feet apart, Jane starts freaking out on the inside. On the outside, she is as still as one of the statues they have throughout the park.

Then it happens. The second woman, otherwise known as Monica, otherwise known as Mona, says, "Aren't you Jane Brooks? I think we went to school together". Jane knows she has to act fast as she sits there looking up at the woman she is pretending to be on Mingle. First, Stacey in Whole Foods and now Monica in the pet park. Is no place safe to go anymore? Jane finds the nerve to speak in as much of a disguised voice as she can and lies once again. "Sorry, my name is not Jane, and I did not go to school around here." Monica does not look like she is buying the lie or the fake accent. Jane gets up from the bench, picks up Blue in her arms, which he is not happy about, and starts walking away before Monica can ask her any more questions. Another bullet temporarily dodged.

When they are about halfway home from the pet park, Jane puts Blue on the sidewalk and lets him walk the rest of the way home. He has been fidgeting in her arms the entire time she has been carrying him. He is not happy she stopped his playtime with Monica's chihuahua. Jane knew Monica lived in the same neighborhood she lived in, but this is the first time she has ever seen her. Jane cannot help but wonder how Monica would react if she ever found out that Jane is using her photos on an app, trying to meet men. *Flattered* is not the first word that comes to mind.

They make it home quicker than she had expected considering she let Blue walk half of the way. He was either too tired from their walk, or too upset with Jane to stop and smell the roses or anything else for that matter. Jane goes right to the refrigerator and grabs herself a bottle of water. Blue laps up the rest of his water before Jane pours half of her bottle into his now empty bowl. Before she can make it to the sofa, Blue has already claimed his spot. He circles around in the center of the sofa before landing in the same exact position he always does, curled in a ball with his head facing Jane. It seems she is not the only predictable one in the Brooks house.

Jane is not a big believer in coincidences, but what are the chances she would bump into Stacey and Monica within days of each other after not seeing either of them for years? Is it just another sign that she is doing something she really should not be doing? Blue starts snoring within five minutes of settling down. The life of a cat is a tough one to live. Jane, on the other hand, is really getting herself worked up over wondering what Tim's response will be to her newest message. Never mind the ramifications if Monica, Melissa, or Stacey find out what she has been up to on Mingle. She knows nothing good can come from any of this, yet she cannot get herself to stop. She has never had this much excitement in her life before. The thought of stopping her plan before she, at least, finds out if Tim really is Steve seems ridiculous to her.

Jane snaps out of her deep thoughts when she hears her cell phone ping. A new message on Mingle has been delivered. It is 2:00 p.m. on a Sunday afternoon. As she grabs her cell phone, she realizes her palms have started getting clammy. Should the devil really be making house calls on the Lord's day? Jane has not even opened Mingle yet, but she knows the message is from Tim and so does this little red guy with a very sharp pitchfork. She logs on to Mingle. When she sees it is a new message from Tim, the sweat starts seeping through the pores of her palms. As she reads the message Tim sent, the pitchfork starts jabbing about in her stomach. Where is the so-called angel when you need her? This time, Tim's message reads, "A fun time is what I have in mind. How about you?" So much for the angel coming to her rescue. Jane makes a mad dash to the bathroom. Blue lifts his head just enough to sneak a peek, then covers his head with his paws. Damn this devil to hell!

A fun time. Jane has not had a *fun time* ever. She is still a virgin at twenty-eight years old. The chances of that changing anytime soon are zero to none. Jane was raised in a very Catholic home, so she had intended to save herself for the man she would marry. That is turning out to be much easier to do than she had thought. She wants to take some time to think about her response before sending something she might regret sooner rather than later. She logs off Mingle, finishes in the bathroom, and joins Blue back on the sofa. Jane needs to think like a woman that looks like Monica. Would Monica agree to a fun time with a stranger after only sharing three photos and a few messages back and forth? A woman that looks like Jane most definitely would if the man looked like Steve. Is Tim really Steve? That is the question she needs an answer to.

Chapter 10

Another rainy Monday morning means another very long ten-hour shift at the hotel. It was raining too hard for Jane to walk to work this morning, so she drove in. The parking in Miami can be horrendous at times, but luckily, Jane has an assigned parking spot in the small hotel garage. One of her two staff members that was scheduled to work the morning shift with her called in sick. There is only Jane and one other staff member on duty. It will not be busy, so Jane does not even try to find a replacement. The only negative aspect of being short one staff member on a rainy Monday is that she will not be able to leave for her lunch break. Unfortunately, she did not know this before she left her house, so she did not pack herself a lunch. Jane has a collection of menus from most of the restaurants close by for just this reason.

The day is really dragging by with so few guests to check in and socialize with. Jane does not have an issue being social with the guests at the hotel. It is once she walks out the hotel door that she becomes socially inept. When she is at work, she feels needed and wanted. Sadly, that also changes once she walks out that door, well except for Blue. Jane and her staff member both order lunch from an Asian place down the street which delivers it to them in less than ten minutes. Jane lets the staff member eat first while she watches the front desk and then they switch off. Not one single guest checked in or out during either of their lunch breaks.

Jane has spent most of her shift thinking about how to respond to Tim. She has not logged on to Mingle since she read his last message. She knows she has new messages to read, but she wants to be prepared before opening the app. A few of the other men that she has matched with have also been sending her messages, but she has left them all unread. She has more than she can handle with just Tim. Never mind involving anyone else. Jane cannot comprehend how any one man or woman can juggle dating more than one person at a time.

Jane makes it home in under five minutes, thanks to having her car with her today. Blue comes running toward her as she opens the door. If only he were a man instead of a cat. Blue stretches up her leg as she takes her raincoat off. At least he missed her today. She bends down and picks Blue up into her arms. She gives him his favorite rub and a sweet little hello kiss on his nose. She carries Blue into the bedroom and puts him down on the bed as she changes out of her work uniform into something much more comfortable. Blue just sits there, waiting for her to finish.

After she has switched her work uniform for sweats and a T-shirt, she scoops out Blue's afternoon mess from his litterbox before sitting down at her desk. She starts up her laptop and opens the dreaded Facebook. She wants to do a little investigating. First, she opens Monica's page. She is not exactly sure what she is looking for, but she will know once she finds it or if she finds it. She starts with the photos Monica has posted. She sees there are some new ones since she last looked. There are a few photos of Monica with the woman Jane saw her with at the pet park, and there are a few of the chihuahua they had with them that day. Nothing exciting to see there. She keeps scrolling through the photos. She sees the three photos that she now has posted on Mingle and keeps scrolling and scrolling. If she was half as beautiful as Monica is, she would probably have this many photos posted for everyone to see too. Stop! She knew she would know it when she saw it, and she just did. Luckily, Monica has not deleted any of the photos she has posted in years.

The photo on her laptop screen from Monica's Facebook page was taken at their ten-year high school reunion which was just over a year ago. Jane was a definite no-show. She had no desire to be reminded of those awful years of her life. It is, however, very clear to see from the photo she is looking at right now that her three bullies were all in attendance. In the photo, Melissa is all the way to the right. She has her left arm around Stacey's waist. Stacey has her right arm around Melissa's waist and her left arm around Steve's waist. Steve has his right arm around Stacey's waist and his left arm around Monica's waist. Monica is all the way to the left. She has her right arm around Steve's waist. All four of them have the biggest smiles on their faces. Steve did go to the same high school, but he was a few years ahead of their class. Looks like Stacey brought him along as her guest.

If Steve was at the reunion a little over a year ago and had his arm around Monica's waist, why would he be sending a message saying, "I don't think we have met." If any man met Monica in person, there is absolutely no way, he would not remember it so soon after, which means Tim is either not Steve or if he is Steve; he is testing Monica to see if she remembers him as Stacey's husband. More than ever, Jane is determined to see this Tim man in person.

Jane's next Facebook mission is Steve's profile page. She searches for Steve Maddox and finds him right away. This would be so much easier if Jane could just add him as a friend, but that is not an option. Jane has been ignoring the sweat that is once again building up in her palms but, ignoring the twisting of the knot in her stomach is not as easy a task. This evil little imp is definitely not a fan of Tim. Jane does not wait for him to claim defeat. She knows he is going to knock out the angel again. She takes her laptop and heads for the bathroom. Blue comes running out of the bedroom and starts following her. As she takes her seat on the throne, Blue changes direction and heads back into the bedroom. No doubt he is going to curl up on his pillow and continue his afternoon nap.

Jane wants to check two specific things on Steve's profile page. First, she goes to his photos and starts scrolling through them. Unlike Monica, Steve has not added any new photos recently. Jane is not surprised by this. For some reason, men, well, straight men, that is, do not typically post half as many photos of themselves as women or gay men. She keeps scrolling until she finds it, the same photo Monica has posted on her page from the class reunion.

The second thing she wants to check is Steve's friends list. If it is not Steve behind the Tim profile, it must be someone who knows him in one way or another. It would not make any sense for a stranger to just happen to find Steve's profile and use three of his photos for Mingle. She works her way down the list, looking for anyone she might recognize, considering in the first message Tim sent her he said she looked familiar. Jane does not see any familiar faces until she sees Monica. Now isn't that interesting? Jane had not even thought to check Monica's friends list for Steve. With her investigation complete for now, she logs out of Facebook. Once she finishes in the bathroom, she heads back to her desk. After everything she now knows, what are the chances that Tim is really Steve? Monica and Steve are Facebook friends. They both have the same photo from the class reunion where they have an arm around each other on their Facebook pages and yet Tim says, "I don't think we have met".

Considering the devil has already tortured Jane, she decides it is the perfect time to respond to Tim's message. She grabs her cell phone and opens her Mingle app. She again completely ignores all the new profiles she has available to swipe through and goes straight to her messages. She skims her new messages just in case Tim has sent her another one before going to her old messages. She clicks on the latest one from Tim and hits Reply. Jane types, "A good time sounds fun, but how do I know you are who you say you are?" After hitting Send, she logs out of Mingle and shuts it down. If this was a game of chess, Jane would be two steps away from putting Tim in checkmate.

Chapter 11

Blue sleeps the rest of the afternoon away while Jane catches up on some house cleaning and laundry. Not the most exciting way to spend an afternoon, but she has put it off for as long as she could. All her work uniforms were in the laundry basket, waiting to be washed. Jane hates ironing clothes. She always takes her clothes out of the dryer before it has a chance to stop. This prevents her clothes from sitting there in a pile and wrinkling. As she hangs all her clothes on hangers, Blue wakes up and supervises. He has not moved off his pillow all afternoon.

With the laundry done and put away, Jane goes to the kitchen to make dinner for them both. Blue gets a can of turkey with giblets in gravy while she has yet another salad with a grilled chicken breast. After they are both done eating, Jane spends some time playing with Blue. She throws his catnip-stuffed mouse from room to room. He finds it and brings it back to her, then drops it at her feet. At least it is a toy and not a real mouse. After about a half hour of playing cat and mouse, Blue has had enough and takes his place on the sofa. Jane grabs her cell phone and joins him. She is anxious to see what Tim replies with this time. Will he come clean about not being the man in the photos, or will he keep up the charade? The same charade that she is playing with him.

Blue must be having one of his mouse-chasing dreams again because he is swatting his front paws back and forth even though he is fast asleep. His playtime with Jane must have carried itself over into his dreamland. Jane loves watching him while he does his swatting in his sleep. People are known to sleepwalk, so why can't a cat sleepswat? She uses her cell phone to make a short video of Blue in action. She then opens her Facebook app and logs in to her account. Jane is not big on posting anything on any of the social media outlets, but this video is just too cute to not post even though she has less than fifteen friends that will get to see it. After she uploads the video to her Facebook page, she notices she has some new notifications waiting for her which never happens. She clicks on the notification icon, and when she sees what they are, she goes into a complete panic.

Why in the world would both Stacey and Monica be sending a friend request to Jane? One thing becomes very obvious; Stacey and Monica both know she was lying to them when she said her name is not Jane. If they have looked at her Facebook page, they would not have seen very much about her personal life, but they would have seen her profile photo, which is very recent. No denying the person they both bumped into is, indeed, Jane Brooks, the victim of their high school bullying. Do they really expect her to accept their friend requests after everything they put her through for four years? She ignores the friend requests and logs out of Facebook.

Jane is tired after getting up so early for her morning shift. She brushes her teeth and climbs into bed. It is no surprise at all that Blue is right behind her. Blue went from starting out in his bed and working his way to the foot of the bed and then to the pillow to now just going right to his pillow. Jane does not even bother moving him. He will end up on the pillow sooner or later. Blue is out like a light and snoring away in minutes while Jane tosses and turns for what seems like hours. It is impossible for her to fall asleep when her mind is racing like it is tonight. She can't stop thinking about Tim's messages or about the friend requests from Stacey and Monica. None of it makes sense.

Ping! Just as she was starting to doze off, she hears her cell phone, letting her know she has a new message on Mingle. She knows there is absolutely no chance she will be able to fall asleep now unless she checks her new message. She does not even know if it is from Tim, but her curiosity will keep her awake the whole night. She reaches over to her bedside table and grabs her cell phone. Her palms instantly start to sweat, and her stomach starts to turn. Now she knows the message is from Tim before she even opens the app. The devil takes round one and round two. Will he ever let *me* win? She opens Mingle and sees she has a couple of new messages. She goes right to the one from Tim that just came in and opens it. As she reads what he wrote, the knot tightens more and more. "I could ask you the same question. I guess we will have to meet in person to find out if either of us are who we say we are." Jane makes a mad dash to the bathroom with her cell phone still in her hand. What does this devil know that Jane does not know? She logs out of Mingle and sets her cell phone to silent mode. When she finishes in the bathroom, she climbs back in bed. Jane knows sleep will not find her anytime soon.

*****

When her alarm goes off the next morning, she cannot believe it is already time to get up. She feels like she has not slept at all. She is pretty sure she saw almost every hour pass by on her alarm clock. Blue slowly comes to life on the side of her, yawning and stretching himself awake. At least one of them got a good night's sleep. Blue jumps right over Jane and off the bed. He strolls over to his litterbox for his morning leak. Jane knows she needs to get up and start their morning routine before she falls back to sleep, which Blue would not be happy about.

When she finally manages to get herself out of bed, she makes breakfast for herself and Blue. Then she takes a quick shower and gets ready for work. She has no extra time to make her lunch. It looks like she will be buying her lunch again today. Hopefully, none of her staff members will call out sick again today so she will be able to leave the hotel for her lunch break. Jane gives Blue a quick rub between his eyes and a kiss goodbye on his nose before she rushes out the door.

By the time Jane takes her lunch break, she has already had three cups of coffee, trying to wake herself up. She has been yawning for most of the day. Today, she decides to go to Pollo Tropical for lunch where she orders her favorite lunch special, the Tropichop, with no black beans. Everyone in Miami loves black beans and rice, but just the sight of black beans almost makes Jane gag. The service is quick as always and almost friendly for a change. Good help is definitely hard to find. That is especially true in chain restaurants where they usually pay minimum wage.

Jane picks a table as far away from any other customers as she can. She knows she will be opening Mingle, and she does not want any prying eyes all up in her business. She adds some of their signature curry mustard sauce over the top of her Tropichop and digs in. Once she is done eating, she opens her Mingle app and logs on as Mona. As she is logging in, a thought enters her mind. What would have happened if she had swiped right for Tim while she was logged in as Lacey? If whoever is behind the Tim profile knows Steve, then chances are he knows Stacey too. Jane contemplates logging back out and deleting the Mona profile too. She knows there is a good chance she is playing with fire, especially where the devil is concerned. She is so close to finding out the truth about Tim that she just can't get herself to delete the profile, at least not just yet.

She ignores all the telltale signs that she is once again about to do the wrong thing and opens the last message Tim sent her. It is time she steps up her game and goes for the checkmate. She hits the Reply button and types, "Perhaps you are right. Should we get a drink, or should we get a room?" Even as she types the message, she cannot believe she is doing it. But let's not forget it is Monica that is replying, not Jane. She shuts down Mingle, takes her tray with the remains from her lunch on it, and dumps it in the trash barrel on her way out the door. She could not get out of there quick enough. The damn devil had claimed victory again, and she had no intention of using the ladies' room in Pollo Tropical.

Jane's plan is going exactly how she hoped it would go so far. The next part is the one that she has been worrying about. She knows that she cannot actually meet Tim face-to-face. But if her plan goes the way she wants it to, she will be able to see once and for all if it is Steve or if it is someone else using Steve's photos. His next response will either put him in check or make Jane change her plan. She is nervous, excited, and anxious all at the same time. This is a game she will not be playing again no matter what the outcome is.

Chapter 12

Jane spends the rest of her shift at the hotel, working on the staff's schedule for the following week. She has the day off from work tomorrow, and the hotel is almost completely booked for the rest of the week. She most likely will not have any extra time to work on the schedule any of those days unless she works late to do it. She finishes the schedule with a few minutes to spare, then she heads home. She is looking forward to a relaxing night with Blue. Jane will definitely not be setting her alarm tonight. She has a lot of sleep to catch up on after last night's fiasco.

Before Jane can even manage to get the key in the door, she can hear Blue meowing for attention. As she opens the door, he is right there waiting to be picked up. Most cats are very antisocial. They like to be left alone and do their own thing. Russian Blues are typically very loyal to their owner and require lots of attention and affection, which is exactly Blue's personality. Being single and living alone, Jane is glad Blue is the way he is. She picks him up into her arms, kisses his nose, and rubs him between his eyes. She then holds Blue against her chest with his head on her shoulder in a gentle loving hug to which he starts purring very loudly. 'Tis love.

Jane decides to live on the edge tonight and orders herself a shrimp pesto pizza from Pizza Rustica. This is her favorite pizza. She limits the times she allows herself to get it out of fear of gaining any of her extra weight back. Jane knows Blue will smell the shrimp and try to get it like he does every time, so she makes sure he gets his favorite can of salmon for dinner. Hopefully, when Blue smells the shrimp, he will think it is his salmon. Very doubtful but worth a try. She makes sure to open his can right before the pizza is delivered.

Jane eats half of the pizza and saves the other half for lunch tomorrow. Blue did not fall for her attempt at seafood trickery. She ended up cleaning the pesto off one of the shrimps and gave it to him. Blue is still savoring the taste as he curls into a nice tight ball in the center of the sofa, awaiting Jane's arrival. Out of boredom, she turns the television on and does a channel scan. The only thing that interests her is a rerun of an episode of *Catfish*, which she has already seen, but she leaves it on anyway. In this episode, a lesbian is pretending to be a man that is in an online relationship with one of her straight best friends. Talk about messing with someone's head. Nev and Max convinces the lesbian she needs to come clean and come out to her best friend. Needless to say, there will not be a happily ever after.

Jane is so exhausted she starts to doze off on the sofa before the episode even ends. She shuts the television off, brushes her teeth, and goes to bed. Blue comes running into the room after using his litterbox and jumps right up on the bed. He makes a pitstop right near Jane's face for his good night kiss on his nose, then he settles in on his pillow. Jane grabs her cell phone and sets it to silent mode. The last thing she needs is a repeat of last night.

*****

After a long nine hours of sleep, Jane, and Blue crawl out of bed at the same time. She heads to the bathroom, and Blue heads to his litterbox. They are in unison this morning. Today's breakfast turns into a circus act. Jane decides to make herself an omelet with some ham, cheese, and fresh mushrooms mixed in. She dices up the ham and mushrooms and adds them to the eggs she whipped together with a little bit of milk in a bowl. Once she has everything ready to go, she puts a little butter into her frying pan to prevent the omelet mixture from sticking when she folds it in half. While she waits for the butter to melt, Blue decides to jump up on the kitchen counter to see what is going on. Jane is too busy moving the butter around in the frying pan to pay Blue much attention until he puts his paw on the rim of the bowl as he sticks his face in for a closer inspection and tips the bowl over. The omelet mixture spills all across the kitchen counter and down onto the floor.

After cleaning up the mess Blue made all over the kitchen, Jane settles for a bowl of Life Cinnamon cereal and a banana. Blue gets dry cat food, which he is not a fan of, and tap water instead of bottled water. Once the breakfast dishes are washed and Blue's litterbox is cleaned out, Jane and Blue move out to the balcony for some fresh air before it gets too hot out. Blue claims his usual chair and takes a catnap with the sun shining down on him. As Jane is standing there looking over the balcony, she realizes that she never turned her ringer back on. Her cell phone is still on silent mode. She heads back inside and grabs her cell phone off the bedside table, then heads back out on the balcony. She switches her ringer back on and opens her Mingle app. She has several new messages. One of which is from Tim. She sits down in her chair as her stomach starts to cramp and opens the new message from Tim. It is exactly what she was hoping for: "I am down to get a room. Where and when?" The message came in a little after midnight. Good thing her cell phone was on silent.

With very sweaty palms and intense knots in her stomach, she hits Reply and types, "This Friday night at the Marriot in Downtown Miami. Does that work for you?" She hits Send and logs out. Holy shit! She is really doing this, well, sort of really doing this. She will cancel last minute right after she sees who shows up at the hotel. Jane would never have the nerve to be so forward with a strange man, but Monica just might. That is, if she was not a lesbian.

Jane heads back inside to take a shower as Blue continues his nap. As she waits for the water to hit the right temperature, she realizes she is shaking, and it is not from being cold. Sending messages like she just did to Tim and telling lie after lie is not something Jane ever thought she would do. It goes against everything she believes in. The devil had not caused as much havoc in twenty-eight years as he has in the last couple of months. An occasional visit every now and then, but never this extreme.

After Jane is done with her shower, she starts up her laptop and makes a cup of coffee. She goes to the balcony to check on Blue, but he is not there. She knows he would never jump. Well, maybe if there was a canary teasing him from a nearby tree branch. She walks to the bedroom and sees Blue had moved indoors while she was in the shower. The sun was probably getting too hot for him. With Blue safely back in bed, that cat sure can sleep a lot, she grabs her cup of coffee and sits down at her desk. Jane is a planner who always likes to be prepared for whatever may come her way. She opens the website for her hotel. She knows it is pretty much sold-out for Friday, which is why she picked it as the day to meet, or rather to see, Tim in person. If things go bad, there will be plenty of guests around as witnesses.

As she checks the availability on the hotel's website, she sees there are only four rooms left. Jane wastes no time. She makes a reservation for the cheapest room of the four available under the name Mona Roberts, leaving the three more expensive rooms for actual guests to reserve. If Tim replies that he cannot make it on Friday, she will just cancel the reservation. But if he can make it on Friday, he will be putting himself in check.

Jane shuts down her laptop and gets dressed as quietly as she can. She throws on a pair of sneakers and heads for the door. Blue runs right by her feet, almost tripping her up, and sits in front of the door. She was planning on going for a jog in the park to clear her head, but it looks like it will be more of a walk than a jog. She puts Blue's leash on him, and they are on their way. It is hard for Jane to not take Blue with her when she can due to leaving him home all alone when she is at work. Spoiled check, high-maintenance check, needy check, affectionate check, loving check. The good with the not so good just like any other relationship.

Chapter 13

Jane spent the next day and a half waiting anxiously for Tim to respond to her last message. She checked her cell phone at least once an hour in case she missed the notification ping. She was getting messages from other men, but not from Tim. She was starting to wonder if she had been too forward and scared him off. After all, if he is not Steve, his cover would be blown the second Mona saw him in person. What are the chances he would show up even if he said he would? Jane has no intention of blowing her cover, that is for sure.

Shockingly, the weekend's weather forecast shows no sign of rain. The three rooms that were available have all been booked. The hotel is at full capacity, except for the room reserved for Mona Roberts. If Jane does not hear from Tim by her lunch break, she is going to cancel the reservation so a real guest can have the room. Jane has her two best staff members with her, and they are all earning their pay today. There have been guests checking in all morning long. Two shuttle buses from the airport dropped off enough guests to fill the lobby twice. Her shift is flying by so fast she did not even realize it is already 11:00 a.m. On days like this, Jane and her staff only take a half-hour lunch instead of an hour. One staff member goes from 11:00 a.m. to 11:30 a.m. The other one goes from 11:30 a.m. to noon, and then Jane goes from noon to 12:30 p.m.

Jane has not checked her cell phone since before she left her house this morning. It is the first thing she does once her lunch break starts. She opens her Mingle app and goes right to her new messages. She starts to shake even worse than yesterday as she sees a new message from Tim waiting for her. She knows this has gone too far already, but she has come too far to stop now. She opens the message and reads, "Works for me. What time is good for you?" Her palms are sweating so much she drops her phone.

Jane knows she needs to respond now, or it will be too late. She picks her phone up off the floor and hits Reply. She is shaking so much she can hardly type her response, "7:00 p.m., I booked us a room. Ask for a key at the front desk for room 872 under Mona Roberts." After a few autocorrections, she hits Send. Her shift ends at 7:00 p.m., so she will be able to leave right after she sees who shows up at the front desk. The devil is in complete control once again. Her stomach is so knotted she does not even eat her lunch. She sits down at her desk and tries to relax enough to stop shaking before going back to the front desk. In a matter of hours, she will be face-to-face with whoever is behind the Tim profile.

The early part of the afternoon is a lot slower than the morning was, but it starts picking up again a little after 5:00 p.m. A couple more shuttle buses drop off groups of guests from the airport right before 6:00 p.m. About eighty-five percent of the guest have checked in already, so the rest of the night will be a lot quieter, except for guests coming down to ask questions, which happens all the time. The most popular question the guests ask is about a good place to eat close by. If the guests ask nicely enough, Jane will go the extra mile and let them look over the menus she has for herself.

She looks over at the clock on the wall above the brochure rack and sees it is 6:45 p.m., and just like that, she excuses herself and rushes to the staff's bathroom. She makes it just in time before throwing up the little that was in her stomach. This is a whole new level of devilishness. Once Jane is done heaving, she wipes her face and cleans up the mess she made in the sink. She then walks back to the front desk. There are a few more guests trickling in, but she does not see any that could be Tim as they all seem to be in pairs. It looks like he is going to be a no-show after all.

Jane logs into the hotel's system and cancels the reservation under Mona's name. No sense keeping the reservation. It is already 7:15 p.m. and no one has asked for a key to room 872. She goes to her office, shuts down her computer, and grabs her cell phone and keys. From her office, she can hear her staff member that just came on for the evening shift talking to someone about a reservation under the name Mona Roberts. The next thing she hears is the staff member calling her name, but she cannot move. She is frozen in place. The staff member comes into Jane's office and tells her there is a man at the front desk asking about a reservation under the name Mona Roberts that was cancelled.

This is it, the moment of truth. Jane needs to snap out of it and get her shit together. She is the one that set this in motion. There is no chickening out now. She follows her staff member out of the office, and when she sees who it is that is standing at the front desk asking about room 872, she cannot believe her eyes.

Chapter 14

The third term of Jane's senior year in high school was the best and the worst of her high school years. She was at her heaviest weight and her acne breakouts would not let up. Stacey, Melissa, and Monica never missed a single opportunity to make every day as miserable as possible. Jane never once stood up to them no matter what they said or did to her. She just stood right there and took whatever they dished out. Once they felt they tortured her enough, they would walk away laughing and she would go to the girls' room and cry in one of the stalls.

One day, the three of them cornered Jane in the girls' room in between classes. Stacey, the leader of the pack, took a black magic marker out of her back pocket. Melissa and Monica pinned Jane in a corner while Stacey made circles around every pimple she could see on Jane. By the time the bell rang for the next class, Stacey had made twelve circles on Jane's face and at least ten more up and down both of her arms. They walked out of the girls' room laughing so loud all the students in the hallway turned to look at them. Jane tried to wash the marker off in the sink, but it was not working. Once all the students had gone into their classrooms and the hall was quiet, Jane snuck out of the girls' room and headed for her locker. There was no way she was going to walk into her next classroom looking the way she did.

Jane was walking as quietly and as quickly as she could in hopes of not being seen by anyone. As she turned the corner that led to the hall her locker was in, she stopped abruptly. The locker on the side of hers had been empty all year long, which Jane was very happy about. But for some reason, the locker door was open and there was someone standing at it. From where she was standing, she could not see who it was. She could only tell that it was definitely a boy.

At this point, Jane had two options. Option one, she could head for the exit doors without getting her things from her locker. Option two, she could approach as quietly as a mouse and hope by the time the boy realizes she is there her head will be so far in her locker that he would not be able to see all the circles on her face. Considering her mom had packed her a lunch and it was sitting in her locker; she went with the second option. She made it all the way to her locker without the boy noticing her. As she was spinning the knob on her lock, he closed his locker and looked right at her.

He was tall and skinny with dark brown wavy hair and hazel eyes. Jane felt her heart skip a beat the second she locked eyes with him. She had completely forgotten about all the circles on her face and arms for a hot second. She franticly turned back to face her locker, but she was so nervous she could not get her lock open. She wanted the boy to walk away, but at the same time, she wanted him to stay. Instead of walking away, he just stood there right on the side of her. No boy had ever stood that close to Jane on purpose, except in the lunch line.

Jane worked up the nerve to sneak a look in his direction, which she quickly regretted because he was looking right at her. He gave her a cute little smile before sticking his hand out and introducing himself. As she was about to take his hand into hers, she quickly pulled it back. It was bad enough he was seeing her face with all the black marker circles around her pimples. She didn't want him seeing all the ones on her arms too. That was the first time Jane met Brian Jacobs.

Brian's family had just relocated to Miami from Boston, which he was less than thrilled about. Brian wanted to stay and finish his senior year with all his friends back in Boston, but his parents would not hear of it. So here he was, transferring into a new school with only one term left to go before graduating. After a very brief introduction, Jane finally got her lock to open. She grabbed her lunch, and her books, then relocked her locker. She said a quick goodbye without making eye contact again and made her way out the exit doors. She could not wait to get home and take a shower to wash all the marker off before her parents came home and saw her. Jane never told her parents about what Stacey, Melissa, and Monica put her through every day.

Over the next couple of days, she kept seeing Brian in the halls and near their lockers. Brian was Jane's first full-on crush though she never told him or acted on it at all. It was clear to her that if anything happened between the two of them, it would only be as friends. Though Jane would have loved for it to be more than friends, she was glad to have someone that actually paid attention to her at all. As the days turned into weeks, she started noticing that Brian was always trying to be close to all three of her bullies, especially Monica. It seemed Jane was not the only one with a new crush.

Although Brian was a good-looking boy, none of the bullies paid him any attention. He would always go out of his way to say hello to all three of them, but they would not even bother to acknowledge his presence. Having good looks in Miami only gets you so far. How much money you have and what kind of car you drive are at the top of the requirements list if you live in Miami. In Brian's case, his parents did not have a lot of money and he did not even have his driver's license yet, never mind a car. He had absolutely no chance of catching the eye of Stacey, Melissa, or Monica, but that did not stop him from trying every chance he could.

Throughout the remainder of the third term and all the fourth term, Jane and Brian grew closer and closer. They met at their lockers every morning, ate lunches together, and occasionally hung out after school. Of course, all this happened out of the view of Stacey, Melissa, and Monica. Although Jane was grateful to Brian for his friendship, she was the one that did not want her bullies to know that the two of them were friends. Jane was afraid they would start bullying Brian too, and she did not want that to happen.

After graduation, Jane tried to keep Brian as involved in her life as possible, which worked for a little while. Eventually, Brian moved a few cities away, and they fell out of touch. Jane has thought about Brian many times throughout the years.

Chapter 15

Brian is the last person Jane thought she would see standing at the front desk in the hotel she works at, asking about room 872. He is not the skinny boy he was eleven years ago. Instead, he is a well-built, nicely dressed man. If it was not for his wavy dark brown hair and hazel eyes, she might not have even recognized him at all.

This is definitely not a part of Jane's plan. She starts to panic. She is hoping he will not recognize her, but the smile on his face as soon as he sees her tells her otherwise. Her thoughts are running rampant. What is Brian doing here asking about room 872? Brian is behind the Tim profile? Brian did have a crush on Monica in high school, so Mona would definitely be his type. Does he not realize that Mona is Monica, who happens to be a lesbian? Why would a man as handsome as Brian is be using Steve's photos on a dating app? None of this is making any kind of sense at all.

After a very brief catch-up, Jane's curiosity gets the best of her. She needs to know what is going on without giving herself away as Mona. Her palms are sweating, and her stomach is a mess. This time, it is more like butterflies than it is knots, like when the devil pays a visit. She tries to remain calm and nonchalant as she asks Brian what she can help him with though she already knows the answer. He wants a key to room 872. Jane is not about to make this easy for him. She is shocked when Brian does not lie to her, well, not really. Brian tells her that he is supposed to have a reservation for room 872, but he was told by one of her staff members that the reservation was cancelled.

Jane puts on a show for Brian and presses some keys on the computer's keyboard. Then she goes on to tell him that from what she can see room 872 was reserved under the name Mona Roberts and that Mona had called to cancel the reservation about ten minutes earlier. She waits to see what Brian will say or do next. He gives her a disappointed look and tells her how good it was to see her again before turning around and walking out the hotel door. Jane is left just standing there absolutely confused about what just happened. All her planning and scheming had not prepared her for this.

Once Jane is finally home after a very long and busy day at the hotel, never mind finding out that Brian is Tim, she cannot wait to see Blue. Luckily, Blue feels the same way and is waiting for her the second she walks through the door. She drops her keys on the table and scoops Blue up into her loving arms for some rubbing, kissing, and hugging. Once they are done with their love session, Jane gives Blue's litterbox a quick scooping and then makes dinner for them both. They eat side by side in silence before meeting up on the sofa like pretty much every other night. Blue gives himself a little tongue-licking bath before curling into a ball and falling asleep.

Jane, on the other hand, sits on her side of the sofa and ponders what her next move should be on Mingle. Should she delete the Mona account and pretend none of it ever really happened? What good could possibly come out of it now that she knows Tim is really Brian? So many questions with no sensible answers. Amid her thoughts, she hears the ping from her cell phone that, at one time, excited her. Now it just frustrates her. Why Brian of all people? There is no way Jane is opening her Mingle app until she comes up with yet another new plan. What was Brian hoping would happen if he went to room 872 and came face-to-face with Mona? Did he seriously not recognize her as Monica? Does he not know that Monica is a lesbian? What are you up to, Brian Jacobs?

It takes Jane forever to fall asleep with her mind racing the way it is. The sound of Blue's cute little snores can usually put her right to sleep, but tonight, even they are not helping her at all. She tosses and turns for hours before finally dozing off.

*****

When her alarm goes off, there is nothing she wants to do more than smash it into tiny little pieces. This is going to be a rough day at the hotel. Luckily, at least seventy-five percent of the guests checked in yesterday, so Jane should be able to get some quiet alone time in her office though if she puts her head down on her desk, she will most likely fall asleep. She gets out of bed, turns her coffee machine on, and jumps right in the shower in hopes of waking up enough to function. Blue has moved from his pillow on the bed to the bathroom mat as he waits for her to pay him some attention. Does his neediness ever stop?

In the next thirty minutes, Jane gets dressed, drinks her coffee while eating a bagel, freshens up Blue's litterbox, and feeds him. This morning, she actually remembers to pack a lunch for herself, then heads out the door. The shower and the coffee did not help much with her energy level. It is extremely low. Although the weatherman promised sunshine the entire weekend, it starts to sprinkle during her walk to work, which puts a little pep in her step.

She has been rushing around (at a much slower pace than usual) so much this morning that she had actually managed to forget about her dilemma regarding Brian. Jane had decided last night that she was not going to log on to her Mingle app until she had a new plan worked out, but this morning, she has changed her mind. She arrives at work about twelve minutes early and heads right to her office. She closes the door and takes her cell phone out of her purse. With sweaty palms, Jane opens her Mingle app and logs on as Mona. She needs to do this quickly before the devil has a chance to mess with her stomach again. She goes right to her new messages and sees one from Tim. She opens the message and reads it. "What happened to you last night? I showed up, but you cancelled the room." After reading Tim's message, she logs out of Mingle and shuts it down.

Now Jane has a new dilemma to deal with. Does she keep pretending to be Mona, or does she come clean with Brian? Her shift is about to start, so she pulls herself together the best she can, makes a cup of coffee, and heads to the front desk. One of the staff members that worked the overnight shift hands Jane an envelope and tells her a man dropped it off for her late last night. She opens the envelope and finds a note inside it which reads.

Jane,

I am sorry I left the way I did earlier. It is not that I did not want to talk to you more. I just had a lot on my mind. It really was great seeing you again after all these years. I would love to catch up with you. You were such a good friend to me back in the day. Please let me know if you would like to grab a drink sometime. You can reach me at 305-259-1023.

Brian

This is the last thing Jane needed first thing in the morning, especially after the night she had. How in the world did she let herself get into such a mess? She is starting to understand more and more why the damn devil has been so active since she started talking to Tim. Jane is so conflicted about what to do she can practically see the angel sitting there on her right shoulder, pointing and shaking her finger back and forth. The devil on her left shoulder is nodding his head back and forth. The right thing to do would be to come clean with Brian about being behind the Mona profile. The wrong thing would be to keep chatting with Brian on Mingle as Mona. She needs to decide between the two before she calls him about grabbing that drink. By now, the snowball is big enough to be Frosty's belly. Full speed ahead.

Chapter 16

After a very long ten-hour shift, Jane is completely exhausted by the time she walks through her door. She has been yawning all day long. Blue is not happy when she does not bend down to pick him up. She heads straight to the bathroom to take a shower, and Blue heads straight to the ficus tree pot. One more thing for her to deal with. After a nice long relaxing shower, Jane is shocked to not find Blue waiting for her on the bathroom mat. She knows right away what that means; he is pissed at her. After drying off and throwing on her usual evening attire, a loose T-shirt and jogging pants, she grabs the scooper and heads to the ficus tree.

Jane sees Blue curled up in his own bed. Talk about holding a grudge. She finds Blue's catnip-filled mouse and heads out to the balcony. By the time Jane even has a chance to sit down, Blue is right there waiting for her to throw the mouse. He is pleasantly surprised when Jane picks him up and gives him one of her gentle loving hugs. Blue softly rubs his head against her cheek, and Jane knows he has forgiven her. She then tosses the toy mouse across the balcony. Blue jumps out of her arms and dashes for the mouse. Sometimes Blue acts like a spoiled rotten child and sometimes he acts like a dog playing fetch. They play the cat and mouse game until Blue gets tired of it. Then he jumps up on his chair on the balcony with the mouse still in his mouth. Jane is happy for the distraction though it did not last long. Fifteen minutes of not arguing with herself about what to do with Brian is better than nothing.

Although Jane and Brian had not seen each other in almost eleven years, at one time Brian was her one and only friend. If it had been anyone else that showed up at the hotel asking about room 872, Jane most likely would have continued the charade, but now that she knows it is Brian, she has to stop it. She goes back into the house and grabs her cell phone. The first thing she does is open her Mingle app. Without swiping through any of the new potential matches or reading any of her new messages, she deletes the Mona profile. That was the first time she has opened the Mingle app since she started her other personas that the devil left her alone. What does that tell you?

The next thing Jane does is finds the note Brian left for her at the hotel. She contemplates calling him, but she does not have the nerve to do it, so instead, she sends him a text message.

Brian,

This is Jane. It was really good seeing you again too. I was a little surprised when you left so quickly, but I understand. I would love to grab a drink with you and catch up. I am off from work tomorrow and have no plans. Let me know if that works for you.

Jane

With that taken care of, Jane picks Blue up off his chair and carries him inside. Blue makes a stop at his litterbox and takes a leak. As usual, he makes a show of kicking some kitty litter around and then makes his way to his pillow on the bed. Jane heads over to her desk and turns on her laptop. All the times she has been on Facebook stalking Stacey, Melissa, and Monica, she never thought to stalk Brian.

Once her laptop is ready, she opens Facebook and logs on to her account. She does a search for Brian Jacobs, and after scanning through lots of Brian Jacobs profiles, it seems that her Brian Jacobs does not have a Facebook account. Bummer! How many people in their twenties or thirties do not have a Facebook profile? Even Jane has one. Not that she has many friends or family to share anything with.

After striking out on Facebook, Jane shuts down her laptop and heads to the bathroom to brush her teeth. It is not even 10:00 p.m. yet, but she is beat. Her eyes are starting to burn, and her head keeps nodding up and down like one of the dogs that people used to put in the back window of their cars.

Just as Jane is swishing mouthwash around in her mouth, she hears her incoming text message notification from her cell phone. She finishes in the bathroom and shuts off the lights. Jane grabs her cell phone and climbs into bed. She leans over and gives Blue a nice rub between his eyes and a good night kiss on his nose. Jane opens her text message app and sees the new message is from Brian. She opens the text message and reads it.

Jane,

I am also off from work tomorrow. I know it is late, so let's connect tomorrow afternoon to pick a time and a place to meet. I am really glad you reached out to me after how I acted last night.

Brian

Jane shuts down the texting app and silences her phone. The last thing she needs is another night of very little sleep. She pulls the covers up to her neck, moves around a little to find just the right position, and falls right to sleep.

*****

Jane and Blue both wake up refreshed the next morning. They get out of bed at the same time, go to the bathroom at the same time, and eat breakfast at the same time. Jane decides to spoil Blue and take him for another walk. The weather is perfect this time of day. The sun is just starting to rise, so it is not too hot out. The rain showers are not due to start until the late afternoon. She throws on some sneakers and grabs Blue's leash. He comes running over to Jane and sits right down so she can put his leash on. Jane was going to take Blue to the pet park, but she does not want to risk running into Monica and her lady friend again, especially considering she did not accept Monica's friend request on Facebook. So instead, they head in the opposite direction toward the water. There is a nice path that runs right along the water's edge.

It is only a short ten-minute walk to the path, but by the time they get there, Blue is already tired from walking. Jane finds the closest bench so they can sit down and rest for a bit. She already knows she will most likely be carrying Blue all the way back home. She really needs to get one of those ridiculous strollers they make for small pets. Jane sits down on a bench with a great view of the water. Blue, being as lazy as he is, lays half of his body on the bench and the other half across her lap. Looks like someone will be taking a catnap. Jane starts rubbing his head, and in less than a minute, he starts snoring.

Fifteen minutes later, Blue starts to rouse and is ready to go again. Blue jumps down off the bench and spots a small hermit crab walking along the edge of the path closest to the water. Blue goes down on his belly and inches his way closer to the crab. Blue's leash is just long enough for him to reach the crab unless Jane pulls him back. The crab spots Blue and starts its attempt at running away, which is really funny to watch. Blue inches a little closer and starts gently swatting the crab with his paw. He is totally confused why a shell is walking. The crab has tucked itself as far up in its shell as possible. When Blue swats it again, it goes rolling down the path out of Blue's reach.

Once Jane has stopped laughing, she gets up off the bench and starts heading back to her condo. Blue is full of energy for now and walks as far ahead of her as his leash will allow. When they get closer to the end of the path, Jane shortens the leash to keep Blue much closer to her. About half of the way home, Blue starts walking much slower, so Jane picks him up and carries him the rest of the way. As soon as they get home, Blue goes right to his water bowl and drinks every last drop of water in it. He then strolls into the bedroom, jumps up on the bed, and settles down on his pillow. They say cats sleep about twelve to sixteen hours a day. Blue is definitely closer to sixteen than he is to twelve. What a tough life. Jane finds her cell phone, and although it is not quite the afternoon yet, she responds to Brian's text message from last night.

Brian,

I know it is still early, but I wanted to let you know I will be good with meeting around 7:00 p.m. There is a nice bar in the hotel I work at. Let me know if that works for you.

Jane

Chapter 17

Brian waits until almost 6:00 p.m. before he responds to Jane's text message. She was convinced he was going to blow her off, but instead, he agreed to meet her at 7:00 p.m. at the bar in her hotel. Jane spends ten minutes just picking out something to wear, not that she has too many options. She does not want to be too casual, nor does she want to be too dressy. She is having second thoughts about suggesting the bar at her hotel. She initially thought it was a good idea because if something goes wrong, there will be people close by that she knows. On the other hand, does she really want to have to deal with staff members asking her questions about who Brian is the next time she works?

By the time Jane finally picks out what she is going to wear and takes a shower, it is already 6:45 p.m. She gets dressed, gives Blue a quick rubdown and a kiss on his nose, then she heads out the door. She wants to get there a few minutes early so she can try to sneak into the bar without any of her staff members seeing her. To save a few minutes, she drives there instead of walking. Jane is very much against drinking and driving, but she knows she will not have more than one drink, so she will be fine to drive back home later. Jane makes it to the hotel in five minutes and parks her car in her staff parking spot. She walks around the back of the hotel so she can use the side door, which will put her right near the entrance to the bar. She will be out of the view of her staff members unless they happen to look in that direction. There are a few guests at the front desk, so she sneaks in as quickly as she can without being seen.

Jane is relieved to see that Brian has not arrived yet. She wants to make sure to pick a table as far away from anyone else that may stop in for a drink. Luckily, there is an empty table way back in the corner with no one at any of the tables near it. It is a bit dark in the corner which would be good if this was going to be a first date with Brian, but it will be equally as good at hiding the sweat Jane can already feel coming on. She has no idea how Brian is going to react when she comes clean with him about being behind the Mona profile, but she is not leaving this bar until she has told him. A server stops by the table, and for the first time in a very long time, Jane says she is waiting for someone. When is the last time she was actually waiting for someone?

Brian finally shows up at 7:10 p.m. He apologizes for being late; he was stuck in traffic. Isn't that what they all say? The server comes back over to the table and takes their order. Jane orders a glass of white wine, anything fruity she says, and Brian orders a Heineken. Once they have their drinks, they take turns telling each other what they have been up to since they saw each other last. Jane talks about her time at college and her job at the hotel, and of course she talks mostly about Blue. Brian's story is not what Jane was expecting it to be. He went to college but ended up dropping out after only a couple of semesters. He started hanging out with a tough crowd and was arrested for robbing a convenience store about five years back.

He was just released from prison a few months ago. Jane is sweating even more than when the devil visits. Is this the same Brian Jacobs she met in high school? He was such a nice boy back then. What went wrong in his life? Brian tells Jane that his parents ended up getting divorced not too long after they graduated, and his life went to shit. Since his release, he has been staying with his mom while he tries to find a job, which is not an easy task when you have a criminal record.

Jane is feeling uneasy about telling Brian she is the woman he was supposed to be meeting in room 872 after finding out he spent time in prison, but she knows she has to. It is not fair that she knows he is the man behind the Tim profile while leaving him in the dark about herself. She continues milking her glass of wine while Brian orders a second beer. After the server brings Brian's beer over, Jane decides she needs to get it over with before she loses what little nerve she has. While she is trying to figure out a way to bring up the subject without it being weird, Brian ends up doing it for her, sort of. He asks her if she has seen Stacey, Melissa, or Monica at all since graduation. Jane finds it rather odd that Brian would be asking her about the three of them considering he knows they all bullied her in high school, but it is an opening for her to reveal herself as Mona.

Jane tells Brian that she had not seen any of them at all until recently. She goes on to tell Brian about her encounter with Stacey at Whole Foods and about her encounter with Monica at the pet park. She even confesses that she lied to them both about not being the person they thought she was. Jane then tells Brian about Monica being a lesbian. She watches his face very closely as she lets it sink in. Brian just starts laughing what sounds like a fake laugh. He had no idea she had come out as a lesbian. He was in prison when that happened. Neither of them has seen Melissa at all since graduation. Jane does not tell Brian that she has been stalking them all on Facebook for years.

It is starting to get late, and Jane is three-fourths of the way done with her glass of wine. She feels a little bit of a buzz coming on which is normal for her considering she hardly ever drinks anything alcoholic. Brian is already halfway done with his second beer. Jane does not want him to be wasted when she tells him her secret. She tells Brian she has something she needs to talk to him about. She asks him to listen to the entire story before saying anything and he agrees.

Jane starts at the beginning. She tells Brian about when she first joined Mingle and about never matching with any men she was interested in. From there, she tells him about how she *innocently* created three different personas using photos of Stacey, Melissa, and Monica, which she copied from Facebook. Jane is watching Brian's face the entire time she is telling him her story, and she can tell he already knows where it is leading. Brian takes bigger gulps of his beer and waves over the server for a third. Jane takes a small sip of her wine while she waits for the server to walk away again before she continues. She then tells Brian about how she had booked room 872 on Friday night under the name Mona Roberts and then cancelled it at the last minute.

She feels so relieved after confessing it all to Brian, but she is nervous about what his reaction is going to be. This time, when Brian starts to laugh, Jane can tell it is the real deal. Brian starts laughing so loud people are turning around on their stools to see who is making all the noise. Jane has not heard anyone laugh like that since her high school bullies. This was not the reaction she was expecting. It is so much better. Brian finally stops laughing long enough to hear Jane when she asks him if he is okay. Instead of saying "Me Tarzan, you Jane," he says, "Me Tim, you Mona" and starts laughing his head off again. Brian's laugh is so infectious Jane starts laughing along with him. Now everyone in the bar has turned around to see what is so funny.

Although Jane is having a good time with Brian, especially now that she has come clean with him, it is getting late for her to be out considering she has work in the morning. She was hoping Brian would tell her more about his experience on Mingle. She is dying to know why Brian is using photos of Steve, but he does not mention that at all. Why would he not be using his own photos? Brian is more attractive than Steve is, which only makes it even more confusing. Jane tells Brian she needs to call it a night to which he agrees. She leaves through the same side door she came in, and Brian follows her out. He walks her over to her car. As she is getting in, he tells her the next time they get together he will explain Tim to her. She smiles and says good night before closing her car door and driving away.

Jane drives a little slower than usual due to having finished her glass of wine, but she is still back home safely in seven minutes. Blue must be out cold because he does not meet her at the door. She closes the door and puts her keys and purse down on the table as quietly as she can. She peeks into the bedroom and sees Blue in his usual spot fast asleep and snoring. Although she knows nothing will ever happen between Brian and her, she cannot wait to see him again. Jane is definitely going to bring up the Tim profile the next time they are together. Brian already said he will tell her about it, and she is not going to let him forget. There is no way Brian made a fake profile for the same reason she did, so what was his reason? She changes into her usual sleepwear, brushes her teeth, and climbs into bed. She gives Blue a soft little kiss on his head before tucking herself in and going nighty night.

Chapter 18

Jane is not sure what the protocol is regarding reaching out to friends these days considering she has never really had any. She has been anxiously waiting to hear from Brian, but it has been three days since they met for drinks, and she has not heard anything. Maybe he is busy job hunting or maybe he is busy trying to get busy on Mingle. There is no way Jane is joining any of those apps again for quite some time. If she ever does join one again, it will not be another fake profile. She has had enough visits from the devil lately to last her lifetime.

For some reason, Blue is being more needy than usual today. Jane is trying to relax on the sofa after a long day at work, but for some reason, Blue is lying across her waist instead of in his usual spot in the middle of the sofa. Jane has moved him off her twice already, and he just keeps coming right back over. She has intentionally not been rubbing him or kissing him, but he does not seem to care. While she is channel surfing, she sees a new episode of *Catfish* that is on, but she cannot get herself to watch it.

Jane has the day off from work tomorrow and was really hoping she would have heard from Brian by now in hopes of getting together again. What if Brian is waiting for Jane to reach out to him? It is not like the night at the bar was a date. It was just too old friends getting together to catch up. Besides, it is 2021. Does it really matter who reaches out first? She grabs her cell phone from the end table and opens her texting app. She finds her last message from Brian and replies.

Brian,

I am off from work tomorrow and was wondering if you would like to get together again. The weather is supposed to be nice, so I am planning on bringing Blue (my cat) to the pet park in the early afternoon. Any chance you would like to join us? Let me know either way.

Jane

After finding nothing good on the television, Jane decides to call it an early night. She shuts the television off, picks Blue up off her lap, and carries him over to his litterbox while she goes to brush her teeth. There is no way Blue would make it the whole night without having to get up if he does not take a leak first. Every time he has tried, he made it about halfway through the night before waking up and climbing over Jane to get off the bed, simultaneously waking her up in the process. They finish at the same time, so Jane picks Blue up on her way to the bedroom. She gives him a good night hug and kiss before putting him down on his pillow. They are both fast asleep in the matter of minutes.

*****

After a good night's sleep, Jane and Blue are both well rested and excited about spending the whole day with each other. Jane checks her cell phone and finds a new text message from Brian that came in after she went to bed last night. She must have been out cold because she forgot to silence her phone, and the new text message notification did not wake her up like it usually does. She opens the text message and reads it.

Jane,

I have never been to a pet park, but it sounds like fun. Let me know where and when. I am free most of the day. I am looking forward to meeting Blue.

Brian

Jane does not want to seem too eager or desperate, so she waits a bit before responding to Brian. In the meantime, she gives Blue's litterbox a thorough cleaning. Then she prunes her ficus tree and does a load of laundry. By the time she is done with all her little household chores, it is almost noon. She grabs her cell phone from her bedside table and responds to Brian's text message.

Brian,

The pet park is at 1814 Brickell Avenue. I am planning on going at 1:30 p.m. while the kids are still in school. Blue and I both hope to see you there.

Jane

Next on the list is lunch. Jane has not been grocery shopping in a while, so her options are limited. Salad, eggs, or tuna fish in a can, which she usually keeps for Blue. She decides to get creative and use all three of her options at the same time. First, she puts some water in a pan and then she adds two eggs to boil. Next, she slices and dices her lettuce, tomatoes, cucumbers, and fresh mushrooms. Then she mixes them all together. She shuts off the burner and brings the pan with the eggs in it over to the sink. She turns the water as cold as it will go and lets it run over the eggs to cool them down enough to peel. While the eggs sit in the cold water, she opens a can of tuna fish. Jane picks up Blue's food dish and puts half of the can of tuna fish on it and then puts the other half in a cereal bowl.

Blue jumps up on one of the stools near the kitchen island for a better view. He came running from the bedroom as soon as he got a whiff of the tuna fish. Jane gets the mayonnaise from the refrigerator and mixes some in with her half of the tuna fish, along with a dash of black pepper. She then peels the eggs. The yoke is still a little runny, which is exactly how she likes it. She slices one of the eggs and adds it to her salad. The other egg she mixes together with the tuna fish she put on Blue's food dish. Lastly, she pours some French dressing over her salad before topping it off with her version of homemade tuna salad. Jane then gets a bottle of spring water from the refrigerator. She pours a third of the bottle into Blue's water bowl and saves the rest for herself. Blue jumps down off the stool and sits right in front of his placemat. He lets Jane put his food dish down before making a move for it. Jane sits down on the same stool Blue was just sitting on, and they both enjoy a healthy lunch.

After lunch, Jane grabs Blue's leash and attaches it to his collar, then heads out to the pet park. As they approach the entrance, she spots Brian sitting on one of the benches. Brian gets up from the bench and starts walking toward them. As Brian gets closer, Blue does something he has never done before, he stops walking and sits down. Jane is completely perplexed. She gives Blue's leash a little tug, but he is not having it. Normally Blue is very friendly even to total strangers. Anyone who will show Blue any kind of attention is a friend indeed. Brian says hello to Jane but when he tries to get closer to Blue, he is out of luck. Blue keeps backing up behind Jane as far as his leash will allow. Jane bends down and picks Blue up into her arms. She is shocked to feel him shaking. Jane apologizes to Brian for Blue's behavior and walks over to one of the benches so they can all sit down. Once they are seated Brian reaches over to pet Blue, but before he can even make contact Blue starts hissing at him. This is the first time Jane has ever heard Blue hiss at anyone in all the time she has had him. Blue is definitely not a fan of Brian. Brian gets the hint and pulls his hand back so Blue can relax. Maybe this was not such a good idea after all.

After a while, Blue calms down enough to take a nap in Jane's lap. As Jane continues to apologize to Brian, he assures her it is fine though he does seem a bit freaked out. Jane does not know how long Blue will nap for and does not want to miss the chance of hearing Brian's explanation for the Tim profile, so she asks, "How is Tim doing?" Brian turns a little red in the face, which Jane is hoping is a sign of embarrassment, not anger. Brian lets out a little chuckle and then he starts his story.

As Brian tells Jane why he started the Tim profile on Mingle, she is having a hard time believing him. She wants to nudge Blue to get him to wake up so she will have an excuse to cut her meeting with Brian short. This cannot be the same Brian Jacobs she met that day at her locker. Does Brian have a devil on both his shoulders? This is not the explanation she was expecting. At least when Jane created her different personas, she had limits to how far she would let it go. Brian is trying very hard to get Jane to see things the way he does, but she cannot even pretend to agree with him. Come on, Blue, your catnap should have ended at least five minutes ago.

When Brian is done explaining himself to Jane, he takes it one step further and asks her to join him in his charade. Brian even goes as far as to compliment Jane on how good she was at playing the part of Mona. He assures her that he would have never guessed it was her behind the Mona profile even after bumping into her at the hotel. No one would ever expect someone as nice and innocent as Jane Brooks to be behind anything mischievous, which is exactly what Brian is counting on.

Blue finally comes back to life and instantly backs as far away from Brian as he can. This cat may be a lot smarter than Jane gives him credit for. His intuition is spot-on. Jane jumps at the chance to get away from Brian without him knowing how freaked out she is by his story. She also makes a show of checking the time on her cell phone and telling Brian that she wants to get Blue home before all the schoolkids start showing up. Brian takes the hint and walks her to the park exit. Blue walks on the opposite side of Jane. Luckily, Brian is headed in the opposite direction. As he turns to leave, Brian tells Jane to at least think about what he told her. She says she will as she starts walking away from Brian toward her condo.

Chapter 19

Brian has certainly given Jane a lot to think about. Although she was initially freaked out by Brian's story, the more she thinks about it, the more she understands it. Of course, understanding and agreeing with are two very different things. She starts to wonder if she ever really knew Brian at all. Blue's demeanor changed completely as soon as they were away from Brian. Blue was back to being happy-go-lucky and driving Jane nuts by stopping to smell pretty much everything in sight.

Once Jane and Blue are back home, she jumps in the shower in hopes of relaxing and clearing her mind. Blue curls up on the bathroom mat while he waits for her to finish. While taking her shower, her mind is all over the place. One of the thoughts running rapidly in her head is why Blue behaved the way he did as soon as he saw Brian. Did Blue instantly pick up on Brian's negative vibe, or was it caused by jealousy of having to share Jane's attention at the park? Are cats really that intuitive?

The shower may have relaxed Jane a little bit, but it did nothing to clear her mind. It is times like this that she really wishes she had a close friend she could talk to about serious things like this. When Brian told her that he created the Tim profile using photos of Steve because he wants revenge on Stacey, Melissa, and Monica for treating him the way they did just because his parents didn't have enough money in their eyes, she could not believe what she was hearing. After seeing the doubt in Jane's eyes, Brian then added that it was also because of the way they had bullied her. The part about the bullying would have made more sense if they had bullied Brian too, but they never did. Brian wants to ruin all three of their lives just because they ignored him every time he tried to hit on them. And he now wants Jane to help him do it.

In all these years, Jane has never once thought about getting revenge on Stacey, Melissa, or Monica for what they put her through for four years. Instead, she worked very hard to put it out of her mind and move on with her life. It seems Brian did just the opposite. Instead of trying to forget about it, he let it take over his life. Jane wonders if Brian's time in prison is related to his plan for retaliation. He did tell her that he was only released from prison a few months ago. It was almost two months that she had been chatting with Tim on Mingle. Brian must have come up with his plan in prison while he was locked up, with nothing else to think about.

Brian explained that he had used photos of Steve on Mingle because he was hoping one of Stacey's friends would see them and tell Stacey about it. Brian said he could not believe his luck when he received a message to match with a woman whom he believed was Monica. He did not know that Monica is a lesbian or that Monica and Stacey are not close friends anymore. When Jane asked Brian what he was planning on doing when he came face-to-face with Monica in room 872, she did not believe his response. He said he had not planned that far ahead. If he did not have a plan, he would not have shown up at the hotel. Just how far is Brian willing to go to get revenge?

Jane has been so deep in thought she has not been paying any attention to Blue since they got back from their walk. She looks around for Blue and finds him in his own bed, playing with his catnip-filled mouse. Did he bring the mouse over to Jane so they could play together, and she did not even notice? She calls out Blue's name, and he comes running over to her. She picks him up in her arms and gives him a nice rubdown, focusing mostly on his favorite spot right between his eyes. Blue purrs the whole time. When Blue has had enough, he moves off her lap and curls up in his spot on the sofa. Nap time.

Jane again finds herself thinking about her conversation earlier with Brian. If there is one thing she is certain of, Brian was definitely lying to her when he said he did not have a plan for when he saw Monica in room 872. There is no way he would have shown up at the hotel without knowing what he was going to do when Monica opened the door. Was he hoping Monica would not recognize him and he would finally have his chance with her? That does not sound right to Jane. From the tone Brian was using when he told her his story, she definitely was not getting any hopeless romantic vibes, only sinister.

Just when Jane was starting to feel better about herself after coming clean with Brian about being behind the Mona profile, she once again finds herself in a pickle. The way she sees it, she has three options. Option one, she can remain neutral and do nothing at all. Option two, she can listen to the angel telling her that she should reach out to Stacey, Melissa, and Monica and warn them about what Brian is up to. Option three, she can listen to the devil and help Brian with his plan. After all, the three of them did ruin her life or at least four years of it. Do they really deserve to be told what Brian is up to? Before she can decide which option to choose, she wants to talk to Brian again and find out exactly what he has in mind for all three of them.

From what Brian told her in the park, his intention for Stacey is to break up her happy family by letting her think that Steve is on Mingle, trying to meet up with other women. Would that plan work? Would Stacey believe Steve would do something like that? What does he have in mind for Melissa since she is not married? Monica is a lesbian, not that Brian knew that, so how can he ruin her life? Jane knows option three is the wrong one to pick, but…

Chapter 20

After taking a few days to weigh her options, Jane is no closer to deciding what she is going to do than she was three days ago. The devil and the angel have been causing ruckus almost constantly. She has not had a good night's sleep since meeting up with Brian in the pet park. She knows she should listen to the angel this time, but thanks to Brian, she has been remembering all the horrible things Stacey, Melissa, and Monica did to her in high school. She could never understand why they singled her out to bully. Yes, she was an easy target, but what did any of them have to gain by making every day miserable for her?

*****

Jane will never forget the first time she was bullied by the three of them. It was the first day of her freshman year. She had never even met Stacey, Melissa, or Monica before. She was sitting at a table in the corner of the cafeteria by herself when she saw her bullies for the first time. As they came walking toward her, she actually thought for a second they might want to join her. That thought ended when all three of them busted out in song. Instead of singing, "Who let the dogs out? Woof, woof, woof!" they all sang "Who let the pig in? Oink, oink, oink!" They sang it loud enough so everyone in the cafeteria could hear them. To add more insult to injury, Stacey then took Jane's lunch tray and dumped it in her lap. The three of them busted out laughing as loud as they could and then walked away as if nothing had happened. Some of the other students started laughing along with them, but most were horrified by what they had just witnessed. One of the cafeteria ladies came over and helped clean her off.

*****

Jane grabs her cell phone and opens her texting app. She finds her latest text from Brian, and as her palms start to sweat and her stomach starts to tighten, she responds.

Brian,

Before I can give you an answer, I need to know exactly what you have in mind for Stacey, Melissa, and Monica. Let me know when we can meet up again.

Jane

After sending the text to Brian, Jane puts her cell phone back in her purse. She gives Blue a kiss goodbye and heads out the door on her way to work. The hotel is once again almost completely booked for the weekend, so today, being a Friday, will be crazy busy. Jane makes it to the hotel with just enough time to make a nice hot cup of coffee before she needs to relieve the overnight staff. One week ago today, she was waiting to hear from Tim on Mingle about meeting in room 872. Today, she is waiting to hear from Brian about his plan to ruin the lives of her three high school bullies.

A part of Jane wishes she could go back in time a few months, to a time when her life was dull, quiet, and boring. Another part of her is enjoying the thrill and excitement of doing something completely out of character. When she goes to the front desk, she is relieved that the staff member who is the same one that was working when she snuck in and out of the side door last Friday does not bring it up. The less people that see her and Brian together, the better. At this point, she has no idea what she could be getting herself into.

Before she knows it, the day is half over. There have already been three shuttle buses from the airport full of guests. The hotel lobby has been full of guests checking in for most of the morning. Jane was so distracted this morning she forgot to pack a lunch. It is too busy for Jane to leave the hotel for lunch, so she orders lunch from her favorite sushi place, Kone Sushi. She orders a magic dragon roll and a cup of miso soup. Once her lunch is delivered, she takes it into her office instead of the staff room so she can keep an eye on the lobby in case another rush comes in. She decides to check her cell phone while she eats her lunch and sees a new text message from Brian.

Jane,

That sounds reasonable to me. Let me know when you have some free time, and I will make it work on my end. They deserve everything they have coming to them. You know it as well as I do.

Brian

Her hands start to sweat, and she starts shaking just from reading Brian's text message. What is it exactly that he thinks they deserve? Jane does not respond. She puts her cell phone away and realizes she has suddenly lost her appetite. She wraps the rest of her magic dragon roll in its wrapper and puts it in the staff refrigerator. At least she ate the miso soup before reading Brian's text message, so she has something in her stomach. She goes back out to the front desk just in time to help with another shuttle bus. Staying busy is exactly what she needs right now. Anything to keep her mind off Brian and his plan. Just how far is Brian willing to go? Just how far is Jane willing to go?

By the time her shift is over, she is completely beat. Luckily, she remembered to grab her sushi roll so she can eat it for dinner. Blue is waiting for her as soon as she walks in the door. He gets a whiff of the shrimp in Jane's sushi roll and stretches up her leg, trying to get at the bag. She lifts the bag higher so Blue cannot reach it and walks to the kitchen. She does not like giving Blue tuna fish too often, and he just had some with Jane the other day, but it is the only way she will be able to eat her sushi roll in peace.

After dinner, Jane turns on her laptop and opens Facebook. She logs on and scrolls through Stacey's, Melissa's, and Monica's profiles. All three of them have added new photos since her last stalking. How is it possible to always look so damn happy in every photo? Is it all for show, or is it all legit? From the new photos on Melissa's page, it seems she has a new man in her life. A lawyer from the Brickell area. Husband number three? On Stacey's page, Jane sees photos from Stacey and Steve's oldest son's birthday party. According to the new photos on Monica's page, she just got engaged to the woman Jane saw her with at the pet park. Three perfect lives for the three meanest bullies. Sometimes life is just not fair.

After seeing all the new photos on Stacey's, Melissa's, and Monica's Facebook pages, Jane grabs her cell phone and responds to Brian's text message from earlier. The devil has taken notice and makes his presence known. With sweaty palms, Jane responds.

Brian,

I am working at the hotel tomorrow from 7:00 a.m. until 5:00 p.m. We could meet in the bar again or somewhere different. Let me know what works for you.

Jane

This is not a side of Jane that she is very comfortable with. She has never done anything vindictive in her life. Throughout all four of Jane's high school years, she was bullied daily by Stacey, Melissa, and Monica. Not once did she ever do or say anything back to them. In an extremely messed-up way, Jane had convinced herself that she deserved to be treated the way they treated her. After all, most of the things they said about her were true. She owes it to herself to at least hear what Brian has to say. How bad can it really be?

Jane and Blue get comfortable on the sofa. As she is channel surfing, she comes across an episode of *Dateline* she has not seen before. The episode is about a serial rapist who raped five very beautiful women in the Miami Beach area back in 2016. The rapist was never caught. He stopped his attacks as far as the authorities know. They are guessing he moved out of the area when the press got too heavy. None of the women were able to give a description of their rapist because he wore gloves and a mask. He blindfolded them and tied them to their beds. He never spoke a word. None of them could even say if he was black or white, young, or old, American or foreign.

For some reason, as Jane watches the *Dateline* episode, she cannot help but think about Brian. He did tell her that he was hanging with a tough crowd and that he had been in prison for a few years. Maybe the rapist did not move away. Maybe he was in prison for robbing a convenience store. Calm down, Jane. You are letting yourself get all worked up. The rapist could be anyone. Why would a handsome man like Brian need to rape women? It does not add up. Is she making plans to meet up with the Miami Beach rapist after work tomorrow? So much for getting a good night's sleep tonight. She finishes watching the episode. When they show a tip hotline number right before the credits, Jane copies it down just in case.

Chapter 21

After a very restless night's sleep, Jane and Blue crawl out of bed. Jane struggles through her morning routine. At least today she remembers to pack a lunch. Blue walks her to the door to ensure she will not leave without his goodbye rub and kiss on his nose. Even though it is still early, it is already eighty-one degrees outside. Jane is going to be dripping sweat by the time she gets to the hotel. Good old Miami. The worst part about the heat is that it makes the scent of urine from all the homeless people that much more pungent.

During her walk to the hotel, Jane realizes she did not check her cell phone for a new text message from Brian. She stops walking for a second to get her cell phone out of her purse. Sure enough, she has a new text message from Brian. She reads it as she walks.

Jane,

I can meet you at the bar again when you are done with work, or you can come to my place where it is quieter. If I do not hear back from you before 4:00 p.m., I will plan on meeting you in the bar at 5:00 p.m.

Brian

The devil is loving this. Jane's palms are so sweaty she almost drops her cell phone. There is no way she is going to the house of a man that may or may not be the Miami Beach rapist. Jane puts her cell phone back in her purse. She will not be responding to Brian's text message. She tries to calm her nerves before she walks through the hotel doors. The hotel lobby is empty when she arrives, except for the staff member at the front desk who is playing on his cell phone. He looks up when he hears the hotel doors open and puts his cell phone away as soon as he realizes it is Jane.

Saturdays are very unpredictable at the hotel. Some weeks they are busy and some weeks they drag by as slow as molasses. It is usually due to how many of the guests check in on Friday though sometimes it depends on how many guests have issues with their rooms or questions about neighboring attractions. This is one of the slower ones. Jane was hoping it would be busy so she would not have time to think about seeing Brian again. She has also been thinking about the *Dateline* episode. Once she hears what Brian has in mind for revenge, she will need to decide whose side she is on, the devil or the angel.

Jane has been watching the clock for the last hour. As her meeting time with Brian gets closer and closer, she starts feeling nervous. She is almost to the point of being nauseous. How did she ever let herself get into this situation in the first place? Is she really entertaining the idea of helping Brian with his plan of revenge? With only fifteen more minutes left of her shift, she heads to her office where she has a view of the front desk and the side door near the bar. She is secretly hoping Brian will not show up at all. She checks her cell phone for a new text message, but she does not have one. Five minutes before her shift ends, Brian walks through the side door and enters the bar. Jane is relieved he did not come over to the front desk to ask for her. The less people that see them together, the better, especially if things go horribly wrong. Jane says good night to her staff members and walks out the front doors. She then reenters through the side door in hopes of not being seen entering the bar by either of her staff members.

Jane finds Brian at the same table they sat at last time in the corner of the bar. There are only a couple of other people in the bar, which is normal for this time on a warm sunny Saturday. As Jane approaches the table, she notices Brian is already on his second beer.

When the server comes by, she orders a Diet Coke instead of anything alcoholic. She wants to have a clear mind so she can stay focused as Brian explains his plan for revenge on Stacey, Melissa, and Monica.

Jane starts out by explaining to Brian that she was a bit freaked out by the things he told her about the other day in the pet park. She tells Brian she had no idea he was so affected by being rejected and ignored by the three girls. The more she thinks about it, the less sense it makes. Brian was only in school with them for around eight weeks. She was bullied by them for her entire four years of high school. Brian then tells Jane that he is surprised she is not the one with a plan for revenge. To which she replies, "So what do you have in mind?"

As Brian starts to explain his plan, Jane cannot stop scanning the bar to make sure no one can hear what he is saying. The more beer Brian drinks, the louder his voice keeps getting. So far, Brian's plan is not what she was expecting. She is starting to doubt he is being honest with her in hopes of getting her to agree to help him. Brian is sticking to his story about the Tim profile on Mingle. He assures Jane that his plan of revenge for Stacey is only to break up her happy family. Though the thought of shattering Stacey's perfect marriage does sound tempting to Jane, she is certain there is more to it than that. For all she and Brian know, Stacey and Steve may have an open marriage. Stacey hearing that Steve has a profile on Mingle would be meaningless. If Jane is going to agree to help Brian, they would need a plan for all three women that would be guaranteed to get results.

Brian admits that he does not have a plan for Monica now that he knows she is a lesbian. He then tells Jane that his plan for Melissa fell apart once he heard she is in another relationship. Brian tells Jane he had matched with whom he believed was Melissa on Mingle under another one of the profiles he had created. Unfortunately, her profile just vanished before he had a chance to chat with her. Jane cannot help but chuckle to herself. It seems she and Brian were chatting with each other more than she knew. Even more than the devil knew. Jane again asks Brian what he planned on doing in room 872 if it had been Monica who had opened the door. Brian reassures her he had not planned that far ahead. Jane is now convinced Brian is lying to her. Can she really be sitting across from the Miami Beach rapist?

The server comes by again, and Brian orders a third beer for himself and a second Diet Coke for Jane. Seems Brian plans on being here awhile. Jane checks the time on the clock over the bar and starts calculating how long Blue has been home alone. After the server drops off their new drinks, she tells Brian she needs to leave in the next thirty minutes. Blue must be starving by now, and if he has not already used the ficus tree pot again, he will be soon. Brian nods in agreement. Jane then tells Brian that if she is going to agree to help him, she needs to be involved in all the plans and decisions. Brian agrees with her, but again, she is not believing him. There is something about Brian's tone that sounds condescending. It is apparent that Brian is starting to get pretty drunk. He is starting to slur his words, and his body is starting to sway. One thing is clear to Jane; Brian has a drinking problem. Is her life so boring and unfulfilling that she needs to be making revenge plans with a drunk who has a criminal record and is possibly the Miami Beach rapist? Strangely, the devil has not been bothering Jane in the slightest.

She is leaving in ten minutes, and nothing has come of this meeting at all. She offers Brian an ultimatum. She tells Brian she will only agree to help him, one bully at a time. They agree to start with Stacey considering she was the leader of the pack. Jane tells Brian he needs to delete his Tim profile on Mingle right away. If something bad happens, the Tim profile could possibly point toward Brian, and that would not be good. Brian takes out his cell phone and opens the Mingle app. Jane feels a little bit of excitement for some unknown reason.

Brian deletes the Tim profile without reading any of his new messages, then shuts his cell phone down. What started out as a revenge plan initiated by Brian seems to be turning into a revenge plan executed by Jane.

Jane and Brian agree to take the weekend to come up with a plan regarding Stacey. They will both come up with a few different ideas and then compare them together and agree on the one that will get the best results. Jane takes a ten-dollar bill out of her wallet and puts it on the table to pay for her two Diet Cokes. Brian is only halfway through his third beer, and there is no way he is leaving it behind, so

Jane stands up and says good night. Brian tells her he will text her in a couple of days to see what she has come up with. Jane nods and heads out the side door.

Chapter 22

When Jane walks through her door and Blue is not there to greet her, she is not surprised. It is exactly what she expected. She knows Blue as well as he knows her. Blue will be sleeping in his own bed, and he will have left Jane a present in the ficus tree pot. Sure enough, she was correct about both of her predictions. She is pretty sure she just saw Blue open one of his eyes to make sure it is her that is now scooping out his mess. How this ficus tree is still alive is a mystery. Once Jane is finished cleaning up after Blue, she fills his water bowl with fresh bottled water and gives him one of his favorite salmon dinners.

As Blue plays hard to get, Jane realizes that she has not eaten in quite some time. It is too late for a big dinner, so she settles for a bowl of Froot Loops and a banana. When she is about halfway through her banana, Blue finally decides to grace her with his presence. Leave it to Jane to have such a temperamental cat. Blue has not made eye contact with her once since she walked through the door. When she has finished her dinner, she decides to take a quick shower. She has the lingering scent of cigarette smoke on her person from being at the bar. Blue has not fully forgiven Jane for leaving him home alone for so long.

When she gets out of the shower, she is expecting to see Blue waiting for her on the bathroom mat, but he is not there. Jane heads to the bedroom to put on her sweatpants and T-shirt to relax in. She is once again surprised to not find Blue in the bed. Jane grabs a notebook and a pen from her desk and settles in on the sofa. The ever-familiar feeling of sweaty palms and a stomach being tied in knots starts creeping in. Here comes that damn devil making himself known once again.

Jane opens the notebook and writes the name Stacey at the top of the page. Never in her wildest dreams did she ever think she would be sitting here preparing to make a list of ways to seek revenge on Stacey. After hearing everything Brian said about all three of the bullies, maybe it was not Jane's fault they bullied her after all. They made her feel bad so they could make themselves feel good. Did they all have insecurities they were dealing with too?

Blue finally makes his way from his bed to the sofa and curls up in his spot right in the center. He looks up at Jane while she reaches over and rubs him between his eyes. When he is satisfied that she loves him again, he drops his head into the curl of his body and goes right back to sleep. If only Jane's life were that simple. She refocuses back on the task at hand. She is pretty sure whatever Brian comes up with will be much more severe than what she comes up with. Jane cannot help but wonder if Brian will tell her all the ideas he thought of. Why did she have to watch that damn episode of *Dateline*?

After twenty minutes, Jane's page is still blank, except for the name *Stacey*. Even though she keeps replaying some of the bullying memories over and over in her mind, all she can hear is the angel telling her she does not want to do this. Judging by the photos on Stacey's Facebook page, her life went on as normal after high school as it did for Melissa and Monica. As Jane reflects on her own life, she realizes her life went on pretty normally too. Granted the love of her life is a Russian Blue cat and she is still a virgin at twenty-eight years old. On the other hand, she does have the job she had always wanted and a nice place to call home in sunny Miami. Things could have turned out much worse. As Jane decides what she is going to do, the knots in her stomach dissipate and her palms dry up.

Jane bends over and gives Blue a kiss on the top of his head. His nose is buried too far to reach. For her new plan to be successful, she is going to have to be very sneaky and conniving. If this backfires, her life as she knows it will be over. So much for a dull and boring existence. Jane puts making the revenge list on hold for tonight. Instead, she goes over to her desk, puts her notebook away, and wakes up her laptop. It is time to put the first part of her new plan in motion. When her laptop is ready, she opens Facebook. Once she is logged in, she clicks on her notifications. She opens her friend request from Stacey and clicks on Accept. Next, she clicks on the friend request from Monica and clicks Accept on that one too. Lastly, Jane searches for Melissa's profile and sends her a friend request. With phase one of her plan complete, she shuts down Facebook and her laptop.

It has been a long day for Jane and for Blue. Jane goes to the bathroom to brush her teeth. Blue makes a pitstop at his litterbox this time before climbing into the bed. Jane shuts off the lights and gets into bed. She gives Blue his good night rub between his eyes and a kiss on his nose. She is feeling much better now that she knows what she is going to do. Considering Brian and Jane agreed to take the weekend to come up with revenge ideas, Jane is going to spend it spoiling Blue and figuring out the next part of her plan.

*****

As Jane pries one eyelid open to look at her alarm clock, she cannot believe what time it is. She turns her head in the other direction and sees Blue with his head propped up on his paws, just looking at her. She reaches over and rubs him between his eyes as he purrs away. When Blue has had enough good morning lovey-dovey, he jumps over Jane and off the bed. Jane musters up the energy to do the same though instead of jumping she is practically crawling. She follows Blue out of the bedroom and straight to his placemat with his empty water bowl and food dish. Subtlety is not one of Blue's strong points.

Jane goes to the bathroom to take care of her morning business. When she comes back out, Blue has not moved an inch. She picks up Blue's empty dish and bowl and gives them a quick cleaning in the sink before starting on their breakfasts. As part of spoiling Blue today Jane makes an omelet for him and then an omelet for herself. She likes to add in a bunch of different vegetables, but Blue is too picky to eat them. Jane makes Blue's omelet with just egg, a little cheese and a little ham. She always makes Blue's omelet first, so it has a chance to cool down enough for him to eat while she makes one for herself.

Timing is very important when it comes to sharing mealtimes with Blue. In between finishing Blue's omelet and starting her own, Jane turns on the coffee machine so it will be ready to go right before her omelet is ready. Once both of their omelets are ready, she fills Blue's water bowl a little more than halfway with bottled water and then adds a little bit of milk. She fills a glass with orange juice for herself and prepares her coffee. Blue has been pacing back and forth between Jane's legs the whole time she has been preparing their breakfasts. As she places her drinks and omelet in front of her stool at the kitchen island, Blue goes back to sitting in front of his placemat as he waits patiently for Jane to bring his breakfast over. They both start eating at the same time.

Once they are done eating and Jane has cleaned all the dirty dishes, she turns her laptop on. She is anxious to see if she has any messages on Facebook. This may be the very first time Jane is excited to log on to Facebook. Unfortunately, her excitement is short-lived. She has no new messages, but she does have a notification, letting her know that Melissa has accepted her friend request. What a strange twist of events. Jane is now friends on Facebook with the three women that bullied her for four years in high school.

Jane grabs her notebook and pen and heads out to the balcony. Blue is one step behind her. She sits down in her chair, and Blue jumps up onto his. Before she even has the chance to write down one thing in the notebook, Blue is already snoring. How in the world can he go right back to sleep so soon? Jane wants to have as much of her new plan figured out before she talks to Brian again. She knows she is smarter than Brian is, but he is the one with a criminal record. One small slipup is all it would take for the whole thing to blow up in her face.

The first thing Jane does is turn to the page with Stacey's name at the top of it. It is time to come up with her three options for revenge. For her plan to work, she needs her list to be as extreme as she is expecting Brian's list to be. There is a chance that Jane could be wrong about Brian. Maybe he really did not have a plan for what he would have done in room 872 if Monica had opened the door for him. It could just be a coincidence that the devil reacted the way he did every time she had any kind of interaction with Tim and then with Brian. Also, the way Blue reacted when Brian was close by. Then add in that the Miami Beach rapist stopped attacking women right around the time Brian went to prison. Of course, Jane hopes she is jumping to the wrong conclusion, but she needs to know one way or the other. She will be putting herself in a dangerous position if she is right, but how could she live with herself if she is, in fact, helping a rapist target more victims? No matter what Stacey, Melissa, and Monica did to Jane in high school, no one deserves to be brutally raped while tied to their own bed. She has to do the right thing.

Jane was going to make a separate list just for Stacey, but instead, she is going to make one list for all three women. Adding murder to the list is something she will not do. She thought about suggesting they kill a pet and leave it on a doorstep, but one look at Blue and she just could not write the words. The first thing on her list is stealing their identities and bankrupting them. This would not work for Melissa considering it is her father that has all the money, and Jane is not about to involve anyone else in this. The second thing on her list is somehow causing them to be disfigured. She leaves the best for last; paying one of Brian's old buddies to rape all three of her high school bullies. Just writing the words on paper makes the hairs on the back of her neck stand up.

Jane spends the rest of the afternoon working out the next few details of her plan. She cannot decide if she should try to talk to Stacey, Melissa, and Monica together or separate. Other than denying who she is to Stacey at Whole Foods and Monica at the pet park, she is pretty certain she has never spoken to any of them before. Though Stacey was the worst of the three in high school, she did seem genuinely friendly in Whole Foods. Maybe Jane should start with Stacey alone and see how it goes. Before she reaches out to Stacey, Jane needs to talk to Brian again. She needs to know where his head is at before involving Stacey, Melissa, and Monica in her plan.

Chapter 23

The rest of the weekend was pretty uneventful for Jane. She did her semi-usual household chores, laundry, grocery shopping with Blue, vacuuming and giving Blue's litterbox a good thorough cleaning. She even grilled some extra chicken breasts so she will have some ready for her dinner salads. Blue had a great weekend. Jane took him to Whole Foods with her where he was paid a lot of attention by the other shoppers, and she took him for a nice walk by the water. Blue kept looking around for his friend, the walking shell, but he could not find him anywhere.

It is Monday again, and Jane is at work doing some paperwork in her office. She has her cell phone out on the desk so she will know as soon as Brian sends her a text message. Jane is very anxious to see what Brian came up with for his revenge list. He did say they would text on Monday, but he did not say what time of day. Jane does not want to seem overly eager, so she holds back on texting him first. With the way he drinks beer, there is a very good chance he is still fast asleep.

After Jane's two staff members finish their lunch breaks, she decides to walk to La Granja. The streets are busy for a Monday afternoon. If you are a people watcher, Miami is definitely the place for you. Some of the sites you might see in Downtown Miami may leave you puzzled, disgusted, or, very possibly, both. Pretty much anything goes. It is only a quick five-minute walk for Jane to get from the hotel to La Granja. She holds her breath for as much of the walk as she can. Thanks to letting her staff members take their lunch breaks first when Jane arrives at the restaurant, there is no one in line. If she had come an hour earlier, the line would be out the door. All the 9:00 a.m. to 5:00 p.m. office workers taking their noon lunch hours fill all the good places to eat. La Granja is good and cheap. Exactly what Jane looks for in a restaurant.

Jane orders the quarter chicken lunch special with rice, but no beans. She has her food in less time than it took to walk to the restaurant. Most of the tables are empty, so she takes one at a window. Jane is not a fan of soda from a soda fountain. There is always too much syrup, so she gets a bottled water instead. When she is about halfway done with her lunch, she hears her text message notification go off. She takes her cell phone out of her purse and opens her texting app. The new message is from Brian.

Jane,

Hope you had a good weekend. Let me know when you want to get together to compare our ideas for the bitches.

Brian

From the tone of Brian's text message Jane is even more certain that she is right on the money about Brian's intentions for Stacey, Melissa, and Monica. He definitely has a lot of pent-up anger against them that he is ready to let out. Jane will need to stay one step ahead of Brian at all times. She finishes her lunch and walks back to the hotel. She does not want to leave Brian waiting too long for a response. Who knows what he might do without Jane to keep him in line? Brian did tell Jane during their last meeting in the bar that he was starting a new job this week and was hoping to have his own place by the weekend. Living with his mother was a drag.

With so many unanswered questions, Jane is not sure how to respond to Brian's text message. She knows one thing for sure; she does not want to meet him at the bar again. Though she does feel safer meeting Brian in a public place, she is uncomfortable with it being connected to her place of work. She also does not want to invite him to her place. Blue would not be okay with Brian being in his space. She would however, like to go to Brian's place so she can hopefully have a chance to snoop around a bit when Brian goes to the bathroom. If Brian does turn out to be the Miami Beach rapist, Jane is pretty sure he would not rape her. The five previous victims were a lot more Brian's type than Jane is, judging by the schoolboy crushes he had on Stacey, Melissa, and especially Monica.

Jane wants to play it cool with Brian. She does not want him to catch on to what she really has in mind. If he is the Miami Beach rapist, then he is a very dangerous man. He may not rape Jane, but there are plenty of other ways he can hurt her. Jane takes her cell phone out of her purse and opens her texting app. She reads Brian's newest text message again and responds.

Brian,

I know you said you are starting a new job this week. Let me know when you have time to meet up and we can take it from there.

Jane

The rest of Jane's shift drags by. Mondays are always slow days at the hotel. By the time she walks through her door, all she wants to do is crash on the sofa and chill. Blue, on the other hand, wants just the opposite. He wants attention, and he wants it now. Jane walks over to the sofa and sits down. Before she even has a chance to take her shoes off, Blue is up on her lap with his face just inches away from hers. Jane knows ignoring Blue would be a losing battle. If she tried to move him off her lap, he would just climb right back on. Jane caves in like she always does and gives Blue a good long rubdown from head to paw. She, of course, finishes with a kiss on his nose.

Once Blue's neediness is over, he jumps off Jane and works his way over to his placemat. He sits down right in front of his empty food dish and stares at Jane. If it is not one thing, it is another. At least today the poor ficus tree pot holds no new presents. Jane takes her shoes off, then heads to the kitchen. Tonight, she will have one of her healthy salads with one of the chicken breasts she grilled on top of it. Blue's dinner is a can of chicken in gravy and a little of Jane's chicken breasts diced up and mixed in it.

After they are both done eating, they get cozy side by side on the sofa. Blue curls up into one of his balls. Jane turns on the television and surfs the channels. She finds an episode of *Catfish* but does not stop surfing. That show will never be the same for Jane again. As luck would have it, Jane finds a rerun of the *Dateline* episode she just watched the other night about the Miami Beach rapist. Jane stops surfing. When she watched it the other night, she missed the beginning of the episode. This time, it is just starting. She watches the entire episode and looks for any signs that may point to Brian.

The only description any of the women could give of their attacker is an estimated guess of his height and weight. They all said he was between five feet, eight inches to six feet tall and weighed between one hundred and seventy pounds to one hundred and ninety pounds. They also all said that his weight could be a bit higher or lower. He was wearing a loose-fitting hoodie which he did not take off until he had them blindfolded. Jane is not sure how much Brian weighs or how tall he is, but she is almost certain he fits both estimates given by the victims.

Unfortunately, Jane does not learn much more after watching the *Dateline* episode the second time than she did the first time she watched it, except for the very similar height and weight estimates. No wonder the cops got nowhere with the case. After almost five years, it sits as an unsolved cold case. The rapist wore gloves and used condoms all five times. No fingerprints or DNA was left behind. Not a single hair or skin cell was found at any of the scenes. All five victims were asleep in their beds when they were attacked. The rapist gained access to their homes through a sliding glass door on a balcony. Jane gets up off the sofa and walks over to her balcony door to make sure it is locked. Blue wakes up just enough to pop his head up to see what Jane is up to. When he realizes Jane is not actually going out onto the balcony, he puts his head back into his ball and goes right back to sleep.

This is insane. Brian cannot be the Miami Beach rapist. There are thousands of men in Miami that could fit the descriptions given by the victims, especially considering none of them could even say what race or ethnicity he is or give an estimation of his age. Jane is just being overly paranoid. Or is she? Jane jumps a little bit when her text message notification goes off. Watching the *Dateline* episode again and possibly meeting up with the man behind the five attacks has her a little on edge. She has, however, noticed that the devil has not made an appearance since she decided what she was going to do. Jane gets up from the sofa and walks over to the kitchen island to get her cell phone. She knows the text message is going to be from Brian. Who else could it possibly be from?

Jane,

I started my new job this morning. I can meet up with you any weekday after 6:00 p.m. or anytime on the weekend if that is easier. I moved into a studio apartment over the weekend so we can meet there if you are okay with that. Let me know.

Brian

Well, he sure did not waste any time moving out of his mother's place. He did not even wait until he received his first paycheck before getting out of there. Jane had only met Brian's mother a couple of times back when they were hanging out in high school. She does remember Brian and his mother being pretty close back then. Something must have happened to change that. Jane cannot help but wonder if Brian became abusive toward his own mother when he was hanging out with the tough crowd.

Jane decides to not respond to Brian's new text message right away. She puts her cell phone back on the kitchen island before heading to the bathroom to brush her teeth. Jane has another early morning tomorrow and she was already starting to doze off during *Dateline*. Knowing Jane as well as he does, Blue moseys on over to his litterbox while she finishes in the bathroom. After kicking some of his kitty litter over the top of the litterbox, he meets Jane in the hallway to the bedroom. Blue jumps up on the bed first and circles around on his pillow before curling up nice and tight in just the right spot. Jane shuts the light off and climbs into her side of the bed. Sleep will not come as easily for Jane as it will for Blue. Her mind is racing faster than Mario Andretti in his glory days.

Chapter 24

The next morning, Jane and Blue are out of bed bright and early. Jane turns on her coffee maker while she takes a quick morning wake-up shower. For breakfast, Jane has a slightly toasted cinnamon bagel with her cup of coffee. Blue is less than satisfied with his dry cat food even though Jane mixed in a little bit of milk for him. If cats could pout, that is exactly what Blue would be doing right now. On her way out the door, Jane gives Blue a few of his favorite treats to which he is very grateful.

There is a slight chill in the air as Jane walks to the hotel. Of course, for Floridians, a slight chill is anything below eighty degrees. As soon as Jane gets to the hotel, she heads to the staff room to make a second cup of coffee. Jane seems to have built up too much of a tolerance to caffeine over the years. When she first started drinking coffee, she would feel wired for hours. These days, Jane can drink a cup of coffee right before bed, and it would not keep her awake. She drinks it more out of habit than any other reason.

Jane spends the morning in her office, working on the staff schedule for the next week. She has been so preoccupied lately she had completely forgotten that she put in vacation time for the upcoming week. It takes some doing, but with the help of her supervisor, they manage to borrow enough staff in supervisory roles from neighboring sister hotels to cover all her shifts. Jane does not have any plans for her week off as usual. She will have a lot of quality time with Blue if nothing else. Jane is pretty sure Blue looks forward to her vacations more than she does.

Jane once again did not have enough time to pack her lunch, so she heads out to Pizza Rustica again for their delicious shrimp pesto pizza. The last time she opted for pizza, things did not turn out so well. Fingers crossed she does not have a reason to lose her appetite again today. When she arrives at the pizzeria, all the inside tables are taken, so she sits at one of the outside tables. Luckily, it has warmed up a bit back into the eighties. What would these people do if it ever snowed in Miami? A server brings out her huge slice of pizza and her bottled water in no time at all. Jane decides to respond to Brian's text message from last night.

Brian,

I have tomorrow off from work so I could meet you tonight or tomorrow night around 6:00 p.m. if you are free. I will be on vacation all next week so I will have plenty of free time then too. I am okay with going to your place. Let me know which day is better for you.

Jane

While Jane finishes enjoying her pizza, she spots a copy of the *Miami Herald* someone left behind on one of the tables. From the angle of where she is sitting, she cannot make out all the headline on the front page, but she does see the word *rapist* in bold letters. She instantly goes into a state of panic. Maybe from where she is sitting Jane cannot see the whole word. It could actually say *therapist*. At least this time she ate almost all her pizza. Jane gets up out of her seat and walks over to the table with the newspaper on it. She looks around to see if whoever the newspaper belongs to is still around. By now, there are only two other outside tables with people sitting at them. No one else is nearby, so Jane grabs the newspaper and walks back to her table with it.

She sits back down and unfolds the newspaper. What she reads is so much worse than what she had thought. This cannot be real. Jane has never been a believer in coincidences. Even if she was a believer, this is too much to take in. Her head is starting to spin out of control. So many details to consider and they are all adding up to one thing. Jane folds the newspaper in half, then rolls it up like a tube. She then takes her tray with the last couple bites of her pizza and throws it in the trash can. With the newspaper in one hand and her bottled water in the other, she makes her way back to the hotel.

Jane heads to her office with the rolled-up newspaper. She tells her staff members to let her know if they need any help before closing her office door. Jane sits down at her desk and unrolls the newspaper. The headline on the front page reads Miami Beach Rapist Returns. Jane cannot believe what she is seeing. She starts reading the article, and all her suspicions are starting to look like reality. The victim was attacked in her own bed. She was blindfolded and tied to the bed posts. The rapist entered through the sliding glass door on her balcony. He was wearing all black and a face mask.

The article does say that it could be a copycat. They are not ruling anything out. Why would there be a five-year gap in between attacks unless he was just released from prison? Another detail floats into Jane's mind. This new attack happened right after Brian moved out of his mother's house. As Jane continues to read the article, she notices they do not say the victim's name. They do, however, say that her husband was away for work at the time of the attack. When Jane reads the next sentence, she starts to freak out. It says that the woman's two sons were home in their beds during the time of the attack. This cannot be happening.

Jane has never once logged in to Facebook on her work computer, but there is no way she can wait until she gets home from work. She has to know if she is right. One of the other managers already has Facebook downloaded on the computer, so Jane opens it and enters her log in information. As soon as it is ready, she clicks on her friends list and then clicks on Stacey's name. When Stacey's profile opens it is obvious from the comments on her page that Jane was correct. The victim they are talking about in the *Miami Herald* is Stacey. There are so many comments from Stacey's friends saying how sorry they are to hear what happened to her over the weekend. Jane logs out of Facebook and goes into a state of panic.

No matter what Stacey may have done to Jane in high school, she definitely did not deserve to be raped. No one deserves to be raped. Jane cannot help but feel a little guilty. Maybe just maybe if she had connected with Brian sooner about their revenge plans, this would not have happened. But then again there is no proof that Brian is the Miami Beach rapist. Brian could be completely innocent. This could all be a case of Jane's imagination running wild. She does her best to stay busy for the rest of her shift to hopefully keep her mind off Stacey and especially off Brian.

Jane has not heard back from Brian about when he wants to meet up again. Maybe he cannot text when he is at work. Come to think of it, Brian did not say where he got a new job just that he was starting it this week. Does his new boss know he has a criminal record for robbing a convenience store? Jane walks out the hotel doors at exactly 5:00 p.m. on the dot. She has been in a frantic state since she read the article. She tried staying away from her staff members as much as possible to prevent them from picking up on her vibe. Jane cannot wait to be home. She practically sprints all the way. By the time she walks through her door she has sweat dripping down her back.

As per the norm, Blue is waiting for Jane at the door. Though she is sweaty, and her nerves are on edge, Jane picks Blue up in her arms and gives him a very gentle loving hug. Blue tries to push away when he has had enough, but Jane is not ready to let him go. She holds him against her chest for another thirty seconds before loosening her hold of him enough to be able to kiss him on his nose. Jane then carries Blue into the kitchen with her. She pulls one of the stools away from the kitchen island and puts Blue down on it. Tonight, Blue will definitely be getting one of his favorite salmon dinners.

After dinner Jane takes a nice hot shower to calm her nerves a bit. Blue follows her to the sofa after she gets into her sweatpants and T-shirt. Right after they both get into comfortable spots on the sofa, Jane hears her text message notification go off. So much for being calm. Jane gets back up and grabs her cell phone from her purse. She knows before even checking that the new text message is from Brian. She opens her texting app and sees she was right.

Jane,

Sorry for responding so late. I guess tonight is not going to work. I can definitely meet up tomorrow after work. Let me know what time is good for you and I will send you my new address.

Brian

Jane notices that her hands are actually shaking from just reading Brian's text message. How in the world is she going to be with Brian in his studio apartment tomorrow night without him sensing how nervous she is going to be? Though the devil is a pain in the butt, Jane would rather be sweating and feeling sick because he was visiting. She must be losing her mind. In less than twenty-four hours Jane will be alone with Brian at his place. She is trying very hard to hold on to the hope that Brian is not who she thinks he is. Was she so wrong about the kind of person he is when they met in high school? Only time will tell. Somehow, Jane musters up the courage to hit respond to Brian's text message.

Brian,

No worries. I can meet you at your place tomorrow at 6:00 p.m. Send me your address when you have a chance. Looking forward to seeing you.

Jane

Just writing those words makes Jane want to vomit. The last thing she wants to be doing is seeing Brian, never mind seeing him alone in his studio apartment with nowhere to run or hide. She walks over to her balcony door and checks the lock. When Jane was looking for a condo to buy, she purposely picked one on the second floor due to her fear of heights. Considering recent developments, Jane is now wishing she had bought one much higher up. With the balcony door securely locked, she heads to the bathroom to do her nightly routine and Blue follows right behind her.

Chapter 25

When Jane wakes up the next morning, she is very happy that she has the day off from work. She tossed and turned for what felt like hours last night before she was finally able to fall asleep. Her mind was running rapidly. She feels as stiff as a gym sock. How did she get herself into such a mess? Let us not forget that Jane does not have one single bit of proof that Brian is actually the Miami Beach rapist. The cops cannot even say for sure one way or the other if this new attack was committed by the same man that committed the other ones five years ago. At this point the cops and newspaper reporters are only guessing it is the same man because of all the similarities in the M.O.

Once Jane and Blue are finished with their breakfasts, she brushes her teeth and takes a quick shower. Blue curls up on the bathroom mat while he waits for her to finish. Feeling refreshed, Jane is ready to start her day. She checks her cell phone to see if Brian has responded back to her text message from last night. She sees that she does, indeed, have a new text message from Brian. It came in after she went to bed last night. Luckily, she had left her cell phone on the kitchen island. The text message notification did not wake her up.

Jane,

My address is 1500 NW North River Drive, Unit 12 in Miami. Text me when you are on your way, so I know when to expect you.

Brian

The next thing Jane does is sit down at her desk and bring her laptop back to life. Blue is in another one of his needy moods today. He jumps up onto her lap and makes himself comfortable. Jane opens Google and types *Miami Beach rapist* in the search bar and then hits Enter. She wants to see if there are any new developments in the recent case before meeting up with Brian at his house. The only new information available at this time is that there were no DNA, hairs, fingerprints, or skin cells found at the scene. They had not released that information in the *Miami Herald* article. The cops are more convinced now that this new attack was, indeed, committed by the same rapist from five years ago. The victim, Stacey, gave the same description of her attacker as the other five women gave back when they were attacked.

After reading everything she could find about the new attack, Jane needs some fresh air. She shuts down her laptop and moves Blue from her lap to the floor. Blue is not happy about being awakened during his canary-chasing dream. He was finally going to catch that damn canary midflight. Of course, once he sees Jane putting her sneakers on and heading for his leash, his whole attitude changes. Blue runs over to the door and sits down so Jane can put his leash on before they head out the door.

The weather is perfect for a nice walk. Today, Jane heads to the pet park. It is a weekday, so all the kids should be in school at this time. When they arrive at the pet park, there is only one other person there. He is an older man with what looks like a very old English bulldog. They are a matching pair. Blue pays them no attention at all. Jane and Blue do their usual lap around the outside perimeter of the park. Blue stops and smells pretty much everything in sight. Sometimes Blue acts just like a baby, but most times he confuses himself with a dog. The next thing you know, Blue will be lifting his leg to take a leak.

By the time they are done with their lap around the park, the old man and his dog are heading to the exit. It is quite amusing watching the two of them walk from the back. If they were in a race to get to the exit, Jane would put her money on the old man. That poor dog should be in one of those doggy buggies. Someday, someone will be saying the same things about Jane and Blue.

After their lap, they head over to the same bench they always sit at. Jane likes this specific bench because it faces the gate, which is the only way in or out of the pet park, so she always knows if any large dogs will be joining them. The last thing she needs is to have a huge mastiff off his leash charging at Blue. Jane sits down first, and then Blue jumps up on the bench. Blue is really tired from all the walking, so he puts his head in Jane's lap and lies down. He will be counting mice in no time at all.

Jane tries her best to relax. Her nerves have been on edge since she looked at Stacey's Facebook page. She rubs Blue gently between his eyes until she can hear his cute little snores. She has been so lost in her own thoughts that she has not been paying attention to the gate for the park. It is not until she hears a little yapping noise that she notices they have company in the park. There is a woman with a little chihuahua about halfway between where Jane and Blue are sitting and the gate. From the way the sun is shining, Jane cannot see the woman well enough to be sure, but that yapping chihuahua certainly looks familiar. Jane turns and looks the other way in hopes of not being recognized. The next thing she knows, the damn chihuahua is at her feet, yapping away. Blue wakes up and sees his little playmate. Jane puts Blue's leash back on him before letting him jump off the bench. The chihuahua has grown a little bit since she saw him last. Blue is still much larger and stronger, but he plays nice. It is actually adorable the way they play together.

Jane is very relieved when the voice she hears speaking to her is not Monica's voice. When Jane looks up, she sees Monica's fiancée standing there, looking down at her. Jane really did not pay much attention to her last time. She was in too much of a rush to get away from Monica as quickly as she could. This time, she notices that the woman engaged to one of her high school bullies is drop-dead gorgeous. Jane is not very familiar with the labels in the lesbian world, but she thinks lipstick lesbian sounds about right. The woman asks Jane if she wants her to separate her chihuahua from Blue. Jane tells her it is fine. They seem to be having a lot of fun together. The woman sits down on the bench with Jane and introduces herself as Samantha.

As Blue and the chihuahua continue to roll around and jump on top of each other, Jane and Samantha start chatting. It is both awkward and nice for Jane at the same time. Samantha tells Jane that Monica mentioned she knew Jane from a long time ago, but she did not get into any details. Jane cannot help but wonder if Samantha thinks she is an ex-girlfriend of Monica. Who is she kidding? Like Monica would ever have a girlfriend that looks like Jane no matter how desperate she may have been. Jane tells Samantha that she and Monica went to the same high school. She does not mention anything about the bullying. That will be up to Monica to tell her.

They continue chatting about nothing important until Samantha suddenly asks Jane if she remembers Stacey, one of Monica's other friends from high school. Like she could ever forget Stacey. Again, she does not mention the bullying though it is on the tip of her tongue. Instead, she just tells Samantha that the name sounds familiar. The next thing out of Samantha's mouth makes Jane very uncomfortable. Samantha asks Jane if she heard about what happened to Stacey last weekend. Jane starts sweating, and her stomach starts turning even though the devil is nowhere to be found.

Jane decides to play dumb and just says she has not been in touch with anyone from high school in a long time. Jane cannot help but wonder if Samantha can see the sweat that she can feel. It is not hot outside, so Jane cannot use the weather as an excuse. Blue and the chihuahua have tired each other out. They are now lying side by side on the ground, panting away. Samantha goes on to tell Jane that Monica heard from her friend Melissa that Stacey was attacked in her own bed while her sons were sleeping in their rooms. The more Jane hears, the more she sweats. She is also finding it hard to control her breathing. Jane is trying her best to keep it together in front of Samantha, but on the inside, she is in turmoil. Could Brian really have done this to Stacey and to those other five women?

Blue gets up off the ground and walks over to Jane. She can tell he has had enough and wants to go home. Jane bends down and picks him up. At the same time, Samantha gets up from the bench and picks up her chihuahua. Samantha tells Jane she has to get going to which Jane concurs. They walk across the pet park together both with pet in hand. Jane is relieved when they say goodbye and part ways in different directions. She is certain Samantha must have noticed her body's reactions when she brought up the attack on Stacey. It is a miracle she did not go into a full-on panic attack.

As soon as they walk through the door to Jane's condo, Blue heads right to his water bowl and laps up every drop of water in it. Jane, on the other hand, heads over to the sofa and drops down on it like a sack of potatoes. Not only did she meet the fiancée of one of her high school bullies today, but she also had a brief conversation with her about another one of her bullies being raped. Jane's thoughts and emotions are all over the place. She then checks the time and sees that it is almost noon already. In six hours, she will be meeting up with the man that she believes is behind Stacey's attack. Jane's stomach starts turning again and the hairs on the back of her neck are standing straight up. The snowball is picking up speed. It is only a matter of time before it crashes.

Chapter 26

Jane cannot put it off any longer. She gets dressed in the most unflattering clothes she can find in her closet. How exactly should a woman dress when she is heading out to a possible rapist's apartment? She picks up Blue and gives him a goodbye hug and kiss on his nose. She grabs her keys and her cell phone. She enters Brian's address into her Google maps app and heads out the door. According to the Google maps app there is a little bit of traffic along the route. It will take Jane thirteen minutes longer to get to Brian's place than she had planned on.

Jane pulls up in front of the building Brian lives in and suddenly wishes she owned a can of mace. She had heard this part of Miami was a bit shady, but shady may be a bit of an understatement. Jane is pretty certain she can see two drug dealers standing on opposing corners out her car window. Most of the buildings have graffiti painted all over them, and most of the windows have bars on them. No wonder Brian was able to get an apartment so easily. From the looks of it, Brian's neighbors were probably his neighbors in prison.

Although Jane's car is, by no means, new or worth much, she would still like it to be where she parked it when she leaves Brian's place. When she gets out of the car, she makes sure to close the door as quietly as possible. The last thing she needs is to draw any attention to herself. No woman should ever be alone in a neighborhood like this one. Of course, once she hits the button to lock the doors the beep that goes off, letting her know the car is locked is loud enough for anyone close by to hear. Jane walks as quickly as she can from her car to the door of Brian's building. She presses the button for his apartment number and waits to be buzzed into the building. Luckily, Brian is quick to hit his buzzer and the door unlocks for her to enter.

Jane is relieved to see that Brian's apartment is on the first floor considering there is a sign on the elevator saying it is out of order. Before Jane has the chance to make it to Brian's door, he pops his head out into the hallway and waves to her. Brian has a smile on his face, but Jane cannot tell if it is friendly or mischievous. She cannot help but wonder if he is gloating about raping Stacey and not leaving a clue behind for the cops. As she walks down the hall to Brian's door, she can feel herself start to sweat again and her stomach is starting to do major somersaults. *Hold it together Jane. Do not let him see you sweat.*

Brian holds the door open for Jane. As she walks by him into his apartment the hairs on the back of her neck once again stand at attention. Considering the outside of the building looks like it is ready to be demolished Brian's apartment is actually very nice inside. Granted it is very small as most studio apartments are, but everything looks brand-new. All the appliances are stainless steel, and the floors are a very nice ceramic tile. Brian does not have much in a way of belongings, which is good considering the limited space he has. There is a small table with two chairs in the kitchen area and a futon couch which he must also use as his bed. Jane opts for one of the chairs at the small table to sit at. Brian offers her something to drink, and she goes with a bottle of water. There is no way she is drinking anything alcoholic tonight, especially not in an unsealed bottle.

Brian joins Jane at the small table. He hands her a bottled water, then pops the top off a beer bottle for himself. Jane is trying her hardest to not act nervous. Brian does not waste any time. He takes a piece of paper out of his back pocket and unfolds it. As Jane watches him, she realizes that she left the list she had made of revenge ideas on top of her laptop. Brian now has a devilish smirk on his face. What in the world does he have on his list? Jane tells Brian about forgetting her list at home but assures him that she remembers what her three ideas are. Jane is waiting for Brian to mention something about Stacey being raped, but he has not said a word about it yet. He could just be waiting for Jane to bring it up first.

It seems they must have both suffered from a case of miscommunication. They had initially agreed to come up with three ideas for Stacey, but instead, they both made lists that would or could involve all three women. They agree to take turns revealing their ideas. Jane is so uncomfortable she may need a bathroom break to vomit. Brian goes first with his first idea. When Jane hears what his idea is, she is shocked. Brian's first idea is for Jane to seduce Monica's fiancée into an affair, thus leaving Monica devastated. Brian has obviously never met Monica's fiancée. Even if Jane was a lesbian, there is no way she could ever get Samantha to give her a second look, especially when she has Monica waiting at home for her. That was not at all what Jane was expecting as one of Brian's ideas. She was sure they would be much more severe and possibly even violent. It is Jane's turn to tell Brian about her first idea. The look on Brian's face as Jane tells him about her idea of stealing their identities and bankrupting them as much as possible is a mix of shock and surprise. This is not going at all as Jane had thought it would.

Hopefully, Brian's next idea is much better than his first. Jane has still not had a drink from her water bottle. It looks as if the cap has not been tampered with. But as we all know, looks can be deceiving. Brian excuses himself and heads for the bathroom. The first thing Jane does is check to see if the cap on her water bottle has any signs of being previously opened. She is relieved to see that it is completely intact.

Jane then gets up out of her chair as quietly as she can and starts heading toward the only closet in the place. She has no idea what she is looking for, but she will know if or when she finds it. Just as she is about to slide the closet door open, she hears Brian flushing the toilet. Jane knows she will not be able to make it back to her seat before Brian emerges from the bathroom. Instead, she makes a beeline to his sliding glass doors and pretends she has been admiring the view. Brian's view leaves a lot to be desired. His apartment faces the back of his building where they store the trash dumpsters. There are even a couple of old beat-up couches piled on top of one another.

They meet back at the little table. This time, Jane opens her bottle of water and takes a drink. Brian tells Jane that considering he went first last time with his idea; it is her turn to go first this time. This is exactly what Jane did not want to happen. Both of Jane's other ideas, though not real, are much worse than her first one. Is Brian playing a game with her, or are all three of his ideas going to be tamer than Jane's ideas? She is still on the fence about Brian being the Miami Beach rapist. Is she really expecting Brian to tell her about it if it is him? She has to keep going with her plan. She needs to see Brian's facial expressions, especially when she tells him her last idea.

Jane tries to make her second idea sound a little milder than she originally intended to. She does not use the word *disfigure* like she had written down. Instead, she says her second idea is to find a way to make all three of them less desirable. She leaves it up to Brian to fill in the blanks. Brian is not saying much of anything, which is making Jane even more nervous than she was. Brian tells Jane that he did a little research on Facebook, and he noticed all three of their targets have a dog. Jane's mind goes into overdrive. If Brian was on Stacey's Facebook page, then he must know about her attack. So why is he still not saying anything about it? Unless, of course, he went on Facebook before Stacey was attacked. Brian tells Jane his second idea is to kidnap their dogs one at a time and collect a ransom before letting them go. Jane cannot help but think about the other fake idea she had about taking their dogs, killing them, and leaving them on their doorsteps. Again, Brian's idea is much milder than Jane's idea. Maybe she was wrong about Brian all along.

The anticipation of hearing Brian's third idea is causing Jane much anxiety. Her palms are sweaty, and her nerves are jumping. It is like the devil is claiming victory once again even though Jane's ideas are not things she would ever go through with. It does seem the devil has been a fan of Brian's ever since Jane messaged him as Tim on Mingle. Jane knows she is a good person, so having the devil around so often these last few months is causing chaos in her life. Again, Jane finds herself wondering why Brian is not mentioning anything about

Stacey's attack. It has been all over the television news and all the newspapers, not just the Miami Herald. Granted they have not mentioned Stacey's name or shown any photos of her, but one of the local news channels did announce her address.

Brian finishes his beer and gets up to get another one. He is calm, cool, and collected. Is this how a man who recently raped a woman he knew from high school acts? Did he attack the other five women as practice for the three he really wanted to rape, or is Jane's imagination leading her down a dead-end street? Wouldn't a woman know if she is sitting face-to-face with a rapist? Jane cannot wait to get out of Brian's apartment, but there is no way she is leaving without hearing Brian's third idea. Brian comes back to the table and sits down. Only then does Jane realize that he had left his piece of paper with his list on it right there on the table. She could have easily leaned across the small table and read hiss last idea.

Brian seems oblivious to the fact that Jane is sweating from every part of her body. Jane takes a few sips of her water in hopes of cooling down though she knows it will not help. It is not that kind of sweating. Brian takes a big chug of his beer before setting it down on the table. He then picks up the piece of paper with his revenge list on it. Jane cannot take it much longer. She needs to know what his third idea is. In a strange way, Jane is hoping it is much worse than his first two. She is very glad she is not going first this time. She is also very glad she forgot to bring her list with her. Jane can say anything at all for her third idea, and Brian will be none the wiser.

Jane feels a little bit better after Brian tells her his third idea although there is nothing to feel better about. Brian's third idea is very similar to Jane's third idea except Brian is serious about his and Jane is not. Brian does not use the word *rape* probably out of fear of what Jane's reaction would be. Instead, he says his third idea is to have some of his friends from the tough crowd he got mixed up with either attack Stacey, Melissa, and Monica or attack their partners. Jane is hesitant about telling Brian the third idea on her list. When they discussed making separate lists to compare, they did not say how they would decide which idea they would go with. If Jane now tells Brian her idea about having one of Brian's old friends rape the three women, wouldn't the logical choice be the ideas they have in common? That was the reason Jane put it on her list in the first place, but that was before she heard that Stacey was actually raped.

Jane excuses herself to go to the bathroom. She does not really need to go she just wants some time to think this through. Her thoughts are all over the place. She cannot even tell up from down or right from wrong. If Jane pretends to be shocked or horrified by Brian's third idea, he may never open up to her about possibly raping Stacey. On the other hand, if she tells Brian what her third idea is, he may be more comfortable talking to her about raping Stacey. If that is the case, maybe Jane can find a way to prove that Brian is the Miami Beach rapist and stop him before he has a chance to attack Melissa and Monica, not to mention how many other women he may rape after he is done with these three. Another thought that is dancing around in Jane's head is if she should bring up knowing about Stacey's attack or pretend she has not heard about it. She could really use a good strong drink right about now.

Jane does a little snooping in Brian's medicine chest before flushing the toilet even though she did not use it at all. She takes her time washing her hands in the sink and drying them off before returning to the small table which seems even smaller now. Brian has managed to finish off his second beer and started a third. He definitely has a serious drinking problem. Once Jane is settled back in her chair, Brian asks her what her third idea is. Jane cannot tell if the devil is fast approaching or if her nerves are shot. Her hands are starting to clam up, and her stomach is twisting ever so gently.

Jane decides at the last minute to tell Brian the idea she wrote down. If there is any chance Brian is the Miami Beach rapist, Jane will have a much better chance proving it if he thinks she is on his side. She doesn't get into too many details, only that, like his idea, she thought they could get one of Brian's old friends to attack Stacey, Melissa, and Monica. Jane also decides at the last minute to mention her meeting with Samantha in the pet park. She tells Brian what Samantha told him about Stacey being raped over the weekend in her own bed. She did, however, leave out the part about seeing all the comments posted on Stacey's Facebook page. She only decided to tell

Brian about her meeting with Samantha so she could watch his facial expressions while she talked about it. Jane is pretty sure Brian's eyes lit up when she said the word *raped,* but then again, he is almost done with his third beer since she arrived. Who knows if he had others before she showed up? His eyes could just be glossed over from being intoxicated.

According to Brian, he had no idea Stacey had been raped. He says he has not watched the news or read a newspaper in weeks. Jane finds it odd that Brian does not ask any other questions. Nothing about a suspect or any clues. He does not seem shocked or upset. Jane just sits there looking at Brian, unsure what to say. What Brian says next sends shivers down her spine. In a very calm voice, Brian simply says, "One down, two to go." Is that a confession?

Suddenly, Jane is not so sure this is a good idea. Brian starts to notice a change in her and asks if she is okay. She tries her best to assure him she is fine. She tells him she is tired from a long busy day and needs to be heading home. She needs to be up early in the morning for work. Luckily, he does not question her any further. He is pretty wasted and hopefully won't even remember all her sweating and shaking in the morning. They both get up from the table and head toward the door. Brian opens the door for her, and while they stand in the doorway, they agree to text in a day or two and then they say good night. It takes all the self-control she has to not run down the hall away from Brian.

Jane is ecstatic to see her car is still where she parked it. All the tires ae still on it, and none of the windows are broken. She unlocks the door, gets in her car, and drives as fast as she can on a city street. When she makes it back home, she does not even stop to show Blue any attention. She goes directly to the bathroom and hops in the shower. She has never felt so dirty in all her life.

Chapter 27

After another night of very little sleep, Jane is a tad bit grumpy when she walks through the doors to the hotel at 7:00 a.m. Getting caught in a rain shower without a raincoat or an umbrella halfway between her house and the hotel definitely did not help. Being stuck at work for ten hours in soaking wet clothes is enough to put a damper on anyone's day, not to mention what the rain does to her frizzy red hair. She grabs some elastics from her desk drawer and does the best she can with her hair. If she just lets it air-dry loose, she will end up looking like Bozo the clown. Just the thought of it brings back a very bad memory.

*****

When Jane was younger, she loved Halloween. It was the one time of the year that she could dress up any way she wanted to without anybody making fun of her. Most times, her parents would buy her any costume she wanted. When she first started going trick-or-treating, her dad would take her around to the neighborhood houses. It was one of the few things they actually did together as father and daughter. Jane's mother would stay at home to give out candy to any kids that would come knocking at their door. As Jane grew older, she preferred to go by herself. She was pretty sure her father would follow her at a distance just to make sure she was safe.

The last time Jane went trick-or-treating was when she was a freshman in high school. She had just turned fourteen years old. She had decided she was not going to go, but her dad talked her into it. He knew how much she loved going every year. Because she agreed to go last minute, she did not have a chance to buy a costume, so she improvised. She wore one of her old one-piece sleepers which was dark blue with white polka dots. Her father painted her face white and drew big eyebrows on her face and a huge red smile. He then found an old red clown nose they had used a few years back as part of a different costume and stuck it on over her nose. The only thing left was to stretch her red hair out on both sides of her head and spray it with enough of her mother's hairspray to keep it in place.

Before she even walked out the door, she knew it was a bad idea. She was in high school now. Kids in high school don't still go trick-or-treating. All her neighbors knew who she was when they opened their doors. A couple of them even went as far as to comment on her being too old to be asking for free candy. She always did the same route every year. She knew who always had the best candy and who gave fruit instead of candy. Her favorite house was next. A sweet little old lady lived there by herself. All her kids had grown and moved far away. She had no grandkids, so she loved when all the neighborhood kids came trick-or-treating. She always had tons of candy, and she would let you take up to five pieces each. Needless to say, her house was all the kids' favorite.

Jane had decided that after she went to her favorite house, she was going to head back home. Did her father really think she needed all this candy? With an acne problem like the one she had; chocolate was one of the last things she should be eating no matter how much she loved it. The little old lady let her take as many candies as she wanted to that year. Jane only took three and said thank you before moving out of the way for the next kids.

As she started heading back to her house, she was caught completely off her guard when she heard three very familiar voices calling out "Bozo the clown!" followed by laughter and loud footsteps.

Jane started walking faster in hopes of making it safely home before they could catch up with her. That was not what happened. With only three more houses to go, she felt something hit the back of her head. She was not sure what had just happened, but she had a good idea. She stopped walking and turned around just in time to be hit in the face with a second egg. This one had been thrown by Melissa. Monica's hands were empty, so Jane guessed her egg was the one that was running down her back. Stacey walked right up to Jane and said, "Aren't you a little too old to be out trick-or-treating Bozo?" Then she took her egg and cracked it on the top of Jane's head. As the yolk ran down Jane's face, her three bullies stood there laughing their heads off. She did not say a word. She simply turned around and walked as fast as she could to her house. She could still hear the three of them laughing as she closed her house door. She has not gone trick-or-treating again since that night. Stacey, Melissa, and Monica called Jane by her new nickname, Bozo, for the rest of their freshman year.

*****

It takes one of Jane's staff members calling out to her to bring her back to the present. She needs to cover the front desk so they can start their lunch breaks. Being a good person can be a lot of work. Not allowing the devil sitting right there on your shoulder to run and ruin your life is not an easy task. This is especially true for those that have been bullied. Can I get an amen?

Retaliation is what most people seek, want, and need after living through being bullied. Jane is a very rare exception to the norm. On average, there are one hundred and eighty days in a school year, which means there are roughly seven hundred and twenty days to make it through in high school. If Stacey, Melissa, and Monica only bullied Jane three quarters of those days, that is still five hundred and forty separate times she was bullied. Not once out of all those times did she ever say or do anything back to them. Jane is certain that number is higher, especially considering some days they cornered her more than once. The three of them most definitely let the devil run their lives at least for their high school years. Jane cannot help but feel sorry for them.

When it is Jane's turn to take her lunch break, she is happy to see the rain has stopped and the sun has made an appearance. She heads out to Raja's for some Indian food. This is another one of her favorite places to eat. It is a small little hole-in-the-wall family-owned Indian restaurant. The inside could definitely use a makeover, but the food is delicious. She is not one for spicy food, which most Indian food is, but they do offer a mild curry chicken that she loves! Jane always plans her trips to Raja's on the days they offer pumpkin as a side dish. Throw in some yellow rice and an order of their incredible naan with a little extra butter and she is a very happy camper.

With still a half hour left of her lunch break, Jane decides to make a quick stop at the Marshalls a couple of blocks away. This is a very dangerous place for her to visit. She has never gone to Marshalls and left empty-handed. Window-shopping can be very expensive for Jane at Marshalls. You never know what you might find from one day to the next. She heads to the bed and bath section to check out the bed sheets and towels. Not that she needs any new ones, but it is hard to say no sometimes with their discounted prices. As she is looking though the selection of bathroom towels, she hears a man and a woman talking in the next aisle over. They are in the aisle with the bed sheets. Jane can hear the woman telling the man she is with that she would never buy bed sheets that have less than a five hundred-thread count. The man chuckles mostly to himself and says, "You really are a prima donna."

It is the woman's voice that Jane remains focused on. She knows she has heard that voice before, but she cannot put a face to it. She walks as quietly as she can to the end of the aisle she is in. Hanging from the ceiling is one of those huge round security mirrors. It is hard to make out any of the woman's features in the mirror, but Jane can tell the woman is facing the opposite direction. Her back is to the mirror. Jane walks to the other end of her aisle and creeps around to the endcap. She does not want to just walk into the aisle in case the woman is someone she does not want to bump into.

Jane stands right at the edge of the endcap and pretends she is looking at something on the top shelf. She is actually trying to see the woman's face, but the man is blocking her view. She goes up on her tippy-toes and almost falls into the endcap. As she steadies herself, the man bends down to look at some of the bed sheets on a lower shelf. She has a direct view of the woman with the familiar voice. They make eye contact for a brief moment before Jane walks as quickly and quietly as she can away from Melissa.

Even though Jane and Melissa are now Facebook friends, that, by no means, makes them instant friends in the real world. Bumping into Melissa in a Marshalls while she is shopping with her new lawyer boyfriend is not something Jane is ready for. What in the world are two wealthy people like them doing shopping in a Marshalls in the first place? Jane is pretty certain she has never owned any five hundred-thread count bed sheets. Blue would be in heaven sleeping on a five hundred-thread count pillowcase. Maybe someday, Blue, but today is not that day.

Jane hurries through the smelly streets of Downtown Miami back to the hotel. She makes it back with a few minutes to spare. Stacey in Whole Foods, Monica at the pet park, and now Melissa in Marshalls. What is going on in Miami these days? Jane heads to her office. She wants to go over the hotel reservations for the coming weekend. Her vacation starts in two days. She always gets anxious when she is away from the hotel for so long. She makes sure to tell her entire staff to call her on her cell phone if any issues arise. So far, the hotel is seventy percent booked. Though it is much more profitable for the hotel to be completely booked, Jane feels better that it isn't. Check-in and check-out days can be extremely stressful when the hotel is at full capacity. With her on vacation, she would be worried about the level of customer service in her absence.

The sound of Jane's text message notification startles her a little bit. She was so focused on making sure she has enough staff scheduled especially on Friday and Sunday that the beep made her jump in her seat. She gets her cell phone out of her purse and opens her texting app. As she suspected, her new text message is from

Brian. At first, she thinks about not reading it while she is at work, but she caves in rather quickly.

Jane,

Just checking in to see when we can meet up again so we can select which idea or ideas we are going to go with. Let me know what works for you. Talk soon.

Brian

Jane is not in the mood to deal with Brian right now. She needs to stay focused on the staff schedule so she can leave work on time. She will respond to his text message later. She needs to find a way to confirm one way or the other if Brian is the Miami Beach rapist or not. She has a lot more thinking and planning to do in the days coming up. It is starting to look like her vacation will not be as boring as usual.

Chapter 28

When Jane gets home from work, she is surprised to not be greeted by Blue at the door. The only times he does not greet her the second she walks through the door is when she has been stuck late at work or when she forgets to clean out his litterbox for him. Blue definitely has abandonment issues. She looks in her bedroom first, assuming Blue will be sleeping on his pillow, but he is not there. As she starts taking her work clothes off, she notices her closet door is not closed all the way. For most people, finding a closet door slightly open would be no big deal, but for her it is alarming.

One time, about a year ago, Jane had left her closet door open while she was taking her morning shower before heading to work. For some reason, Blue had decided to go snooping in the closet. When she got out of the shower, she got dressed and closed the closet door, unaware that Blue was inside the closet. When she returned home from work later that day, she could not find Blue anywhere. When she finally opened the closet door, she couldn't believe her eyes. Blue was curled up in a ball on the closet floor, fast asleep. He must have been exhausted after destroying most of her clothing.

Jane never had Blue declawed when he was a kitten. She thought it was a horrible thing to do to a cat. Blue certainly made use of his claws that day in her closet. Though most of her clothes were still on their hangers, the majority of them now had tears in them from Blue's claws. He must have been going crazy trying to find a way to get out of the closet. Ever since that day, she always makes sure her closet door is shut before she leaves the house, and that Blue is not on the other side of the door.

Jane looks inside the closet and is very thankful to not find Blue in it. She is also very thankful that none of her clothes need to be replaced again. Next, she looks under the bed. She finds Blue's catnip-stuffed mouse and some dust balls, but no Blue. Satisfied Blue is not in her bedroom, she moves on to the bathroom. A few times, Jane has found Blue sleeping in the shower. For the life of her, she could not figure out why he would go into the shower in the first place considering how much he hates being wet. She pulls back the shower curtain, but once again, Blue is nowhere to be found.

Jane's condo is not that big, so she is quickly running out of places Blue can be. She does a quick scan of the kitchen before moving on to the living room. Blue is not in his bed, and he is not on the sofa. Next, she looks on her desk chair. Nothing. Where in the world is Blue? The sofa is too low to the floor for him to be under it. She is starting to panic. What is she missing? She goes back into the kitchen. Did Blue somehow get into one of the cabinets and get stuck inside it? She starts frantically opening all the bottom cabinet doors, but again no Blue. She even takes the lid off the trash can in case Blue somehow managed to fall in looking for something to eat and could not get back out. No Blue.

As Jane stands there, scrambling her brain, trying to think of where she has not checked, she hears Blue's meow. It is very faint, but it is definitely Blue's meow. She would know that sound anywhere. It is so low that Jane cannot tell where it is coming from. Though she is still freaking out, she is a bit calmer just knowing Blue is here somewhere and he is alive. She starts calling out to him, hoping he will meow again when he hears his name, but all she hears is the sound of her racing heart. Where the hell are you, Blue? She goes back into her bedroom and looks in every place Blue could possibly squeeze himself into, but again, no luck.

There is only one thing left that Jane can think of. She goes back to the kitchen and opens the side cabinet where she keeps all of Blue's things. She takes out the can of his favorite treats from the top shelf. She goes into the living room with the can and starts shaking it as hard as she can. If Blue is here and he hears the sound of her shaking his can of treats, he will come flying out at her. Through the sound of the treats banging around in the can, she again hears Blue's meow. She stops shaking the can so she can focus on where the sound is coming from. Then she hears it again, but she is still having a hard time figuring out where it is coming from. It is definitely louder here in the living room than it was in the kitchen. Jane does another quick shake of the can as hard as she can and then stops. Sure enough, Blue starts meowing again. This time, she thinks she knows where it is coming from, but it does not make sense.

Jane walks over to her sliding glass door. She grabs the little hanging wand and pulls the shade open. Sitting there in his balcony chair is Blue. She opens the slider and rushes out to Blue. There does not seem to be anything wrong with him. She picks him up into her loving arms and gives him the biggest hug she has ever given him. She is so overcome with emotions she starts crying without even realizing it. She turns around and walks back into her condo. She closes the sliding glass door and locks it. She grabs the wand and closes the shade. Blue starts getting antsy, so she puts him down. He runs right over to his water bowl and laps up every drop. Jane was so happy and relieved when she found Blue that she did not even think about the most important thing other than Blue being safe. How in the world did Blue get locked out on the balcony? It is not like Blue can open the sliding glass door to get out on the balcony by himself. Never mind that the door was locked from the inside.

Jane starts to panic again. The only way Blue could end up locked outside on the balcony is if someone put him out there and then locked the door. That means someone was in her condo while she was at work. How is that even possible when no one has a set of keys except her? She goes back into her bedroom and starts looking around to see if anything is missing. Nothing looks touched or out of place. Then she remembers the closet door being open. Whoever was in her condo today locked Blue out on the balcony and was definitely looking through her closet. She knows for a fact she closed that door before leaving for work this morning. Her intruder must have forgotten to close the door when he was done looking for whatever he was searching for. She checks her jewelry box next. She really does not have anything of value in it, but she looks anyway. Nothing is missing in there either.

Jane contemplates calling the cops and reporting a break-in, but with nothing missing what can they really do? Blue seems unaffected by being locked outside on the balcony. He probably spent most of the day watching birds fly by. Luckily, he did not try to swat at one and lose his balance. They say cats have nine lives, but do they really? She cannot help herself. She picks Blue up again and holds him tight against her chest. What would she have done if he was hurt or gone for good? Tonight, Blue will be eating a can of solid white tuna fish and drinking a nice bowl of warm milk for dinner.

After dinner, Jane and Blue take their usual spots on the sofa. Blue does his usual circling in the center of the sofa before ending up in the same exact spot he always does. He starts wrapping himself into a ball but stops halfway and looks up at Jane. She knows exactly what Blue is waiting for. She reaches over and gives him a nice gentle rub between his eyes to which he purrs in appreciation. Once he is satisfied, Blue tucks his head into the center of his ball. Unfortunately, she is not as unfazed as Blue is about having an intruder in her condo today.

There are so many questions running through Jane's mind that she is having a hard time focusing on any of them. Who would break into her condo? Why would an intruder break into her condo? What would an intruder be looking for in her condo? How did an intruder break into her condo? Why would an intruder lock Blue out on the balcony? Then her mind wanders over to Brian's text message from earlier. She still has not responded to him. Jane gets up from the sofa and grabs her cell phone from her purse. She sits back down as gently as she can so she does not wake Blue from his catnap.

She opens her texting app and clicks on the newest message from Brian. From the time stamp on the text message, Jane can tell Brian sent it at 2:35 p.m. while she was in her office at work. With so much going on in her head, she cannot remember if Brian told her he is not able to text while he is at work or if she just thought it herself. She is certain Brian told her he works Monday through Friday and has weekends off. If that is the case, why would Brian not be at work at 2:35 p.m. on a Thursday? Jane starts to wonder if Brian could be her intruder, but it does not make any sort of sense. Why would Brian break into her condo? It would, however, explain why Blue was locked outside on the balcony. Blue's reaction when he was close to Brian was something Jane had never witnessed before. If Brian had broken into her condo Blue would have gone crazy. Blue would have gone into attack mode. She needs to meet up with Brian as soon as possible. If Brian is her intruder, he will definitely have scratch marks on his arms from when he picked Blue up to put him on the balcony. She hits Reply on Brian's text message.

Brian,

I have a long day at work tomorrow, but then I am on vacation the following week. I can make time to meet up with you any day. Let me know what works best for you.

Jane

She gets up once again from the sofa and heads over to her desk. She pulls her chair out as quietly as she can which turns out to not be quiet enough. Blue pops his head up, and when he sees where Jane is, he jumps off the sofa and lazily makes his way over to her. If she did not know better, she would think Blue is sleepwalking. She bends down and picks Blue up, then places him in her lap. He gets comfy and goes right back to sleep. Blue's quiet little snores have their usual calming effects on Jane though tonight it does not last long. She was planning on doing some Facebook scanning, but instead, she is sitting here frozen in place.

When Jane looked around earlier to see if she could find anything that is missing, she was only thinking about anything of value. She was not thinking about something that had no value at all. Sitting at her desk now, she does notice something that is missing. Her piece of paper with her list of revenge ideas is gone. She had left it right on top of her laptop. She has not used her laptop since that day, so the piece of paper should still be sitting right where she left it, but it is not there. Why would someone break into her condo and leave with a piece of paper with three fake revenge ideas written on it? Of course, the intruder would not know the ideas were fake. This newest revelation is making it look more and more like Brian is the intruder. But why would he take her list with him? There is no way she will be getting any sleep tonight.

Chapter 29

It takes all the energy Jane can muster up to get out of bed the next morning. She tossed and turned pretty much the entire night. Getting up not once but twice to make sure she had locked the sliding glass door definitely did not help with her sleeping. She was sure she kept hearing someone creeping around. When Blue got up in the middle of the night to go to his litterbox, she jumped up in her bed. Saying she got two hours of sleep is most likely an exaggeration. Luckily, today is Friday, so it will be busy enough at work with most of the guests checking in to keep her focused and awake.

Before Jane heads out the door, she again checks the lock on the sliding glass door. She also double-checks her closet door. Once she is sure everything is how it should be, she gives Blue his goodbye rub and kiss on his nose, then heads to work. It is a beautiful morning outside. The sun is still on its way up. The mourning doves are louder than usual. Living in Miami does have some perks. Just being able to see palm trees out her window every day makes up for having to smell urine every time she walks to work.

When Jane arrives at work, one of the first things she does is check to see if any new reservations came in for the weekend. They are now at eighty percent of capacity. She does not feel as guilty about going on vacation as she would if it was completely booked. Besides, Fridays are always the busiest days, and she is working during the busiest times. By the time she leaves for the day, almost all the guests will have checked in already. The next thing she does is make herself a nice big cup of strong Cuban coffee. She will take any help she can get to keep her eyes open today.

Two shuttle buses from the airport show up with the first mob of guests checking in. With the help of her other two staff members, they managed to check in all the guests in less than an hour with no complaints. The next shuttle bus should arrive in about ninety minutes, which is too long of a wait for Jane. She needs to stay busy to stay awake. The Cuban coffee is not helping very much. When Jane first started drinking it, it was like being on crack. Not that she has ever done crack. These days, it does close to nothing to her energy level. She knows if she sits down at her desk, she will end up putting her head down to rest and fall right to sleep. So instead, she busies herself by straightening up and restocking the brochure display in the lobby. Normally, she would have one of her staff members handle the task, but today it is all her.

Almost exactly ninety minutes later, Jane sees the next shuttle bus from the airport pull up outside the hotel. It is one of those double-decker shuttle buses. They usually only use these if there were too many people for one regular shuttle bus but not enough for two. She watches as the people start getting off the shuttle bus and suddenly starts to feel a little bit jealous. Jane will be on vacation starting tomorrow, but unlike all these people, she is not going anywhere that would require a plane or a shuttle bus or a room at a hotel. She will not even be packing a suitcase for that matter. Now is not the time for her to start feeling sorry for herself. There are enough new guests to fill the lobby. Time to get them checked in. There will be enough time for self-pity later.

If today is going to be like every other Friday, Jane knows the next rush will not be until after lunch, so she sends her two staff members on their lunch break. They know they cannot leave the hotel in case she needs help. While Jane is alone at the front desk, she gets her cell phone out of her purse. She is not certain, but she thought she heard her text message notification go off during the last rush of guests. She opens her text message app, and sure enough, she has a new text message from Brian. Although thinking about Brian is the very last thing she needs right now, she cannot stop herself from reading the new text message.

Jane,

I have no plans for this coming weekend. Say when and where and I will be there.

Brian

Just seeing Brian's name on her phone gives her the creeps. Is she seriously texting the Miami Beach rapist? Is Brian the man that broke into her condo and locked Blue out on the balcony? For so long, Jane was unhappy about her boring life, but with everything that is going on now, she would welcome her boring life back with open arms if she could. If only she had been stronger and not given in to that pesky devil so many times. Jane wants to meet up with Brian as soon as she can. She does not want to give the possible scratches from Blue on Brian's arms enough time to heal. She responds to Brian's text right away before he has a chance to make other plans.

Brian,

The weather is supposed to be nice tomorrow, so I am planning on taking Blue back to the pet park. How about meeting there again around noon? Let me know.

Jane

Meeting Brian at the pet park with Blue will serve two different purposes. The first purpose being Jane does not want to be alone with Brian again until she figures out if he is her intruder. She will feel much safer in a public park. The second purpose being she wants to see if Blue will react the same way he did the last time Brian met them in the pet park. It is possible that Blue only reacted the way he did toward Brian because he was jealous Jane was paying more attention to Brian than she was to him. Though it is a possibility, she does not think it is probable. Typically, when Blue meets anyone new, he goes right up to them in hopes of getting pet or rubbed. He loves the attention! Blue did not do that with Brian. He was not a fan of Brian's from the very instant they met.

When her two staff members finish their lunch break, they offer Jane the rest of the pizza they had ordered. It is not shrimp pesto pizza, but as they old saying goes, "If it's for free, it's for me." She takes the two slices of pizza and warms them up in the toaster oven in the staff room. While the toaster oven works its magic, she goes out to the lobby and gets a bottled water from the vending machine. When the timer goes off, she gets the pizza slices out of the toaster oven and goes into her office. Jane likes being able to see the front desk and lobby when she is on break just in case she is needed. But today she also has a second reason for wanting to eat her lunch in her office.

Jane closes the office door and turns on the computer. Once it is ready, she opens Facebook and enters her log in information. The first thing she notices it that she has a new message. The only messages she ever receives are junk or spam messages. She clicks on the message tab, and her inbox opens. The new message is from Melissa. Jane clicks on the message and reads it.

Jane,

I think I saw you in Marshalls in Downtown Miami. Was that you? I would really like to apologize for the way I acted toward you in high school. Let me know if you would be okay with that.

Melissa

PS: Did you hear about what happened to Stacey?

Never in her wildest dreams did Jane ever think she would get an apology from any of her bullies. It was weird enough getting friend requests from Stacey and Monica on Facebook, never mind Melissa saying she wants to apologize. Miracles really do happen. Jane does not respond to Melissa's message; instead, she closes it and goes onto Stacey's profile page. This is what she had planned on doing last night until she realized her paper with her fake revenge list on it was gone. Jane scrolls through all the new messages, looking for any new information Stacey may have posted. There are lots of messages from Stacey's friends, asking how she is doing and sending their prayers along to her. The only post Jane can find from Stacey herself is one from two days ago. It is a generic message to all her friends, thanking them for their prayers and their support during a trying time.

Next, Jane closes Facebook and opens the website for the *Miami Herald*. She starts scanning all the newest articles, trying to find any updates about Stacey's attack. The most recent article she comes across is from four days ago. Jane reads the article only to learn that the cops have no new information. They still cannot say one way or the other if this new attack was carried out by the same rapist from five years ago. They have no new leads to follow up on. They are asking the public to please contact them if they have any new information that may be relevant. At the end of the article, there is a phone number for another tip line, and Jane writes the number down.

Just as Jane is about to eat her last bite of pizza, she sees two more shuttle buses from the airport pull up in front of the hotel. These should be the last two for today. After all these guests are checked in, there will only be a few stragglers left to check in. She chews the last bite of pizza as fast as she can and washes it down with a mouthful of water. She wipes her face with a napkin and heads out to the front desk. The hotel doors open, and within seconds, the front lobby is full of guests once again. She puts a smile on her face and starts welcoming them all to the hotel.

Though this may be the most stressful part of Jane's job, it is also her favorite part. She loves trying to guess where the guests are from by their accents. When she first started working at the hotel, she would always guess Cuba for everybody. Over time, she has picked up on some small differences from country to country. In all honesty, she still guesses Cuba most of the time. Once they are done checking in all the newest guests. Jane checks how many guests are left to check in. There are only six more reservations left to check in. She was hoping for ten or less, so seeing only six makes her feel much better about leaving for her vacation in less than an hour.

When Jane arrives at her condo, she pauses before putting her key in the lock. She flashes back to yesterday when she opened the door and Blue was not there to greet her. Suppose the intruder came back. Instead of putting her key in the lock, she squats down and jingles her set of keys at Blue's level. If he hears the keys and is not locked on the balcony, he will be at the door. She jingles them again as loud as she can. Then she hears it. Blue starts meowing on the other side of the door. She opens the door and whisks Blue up into her arms. She gives him a hug, a rub between his eyes, and a kiss on his nose. Getting Blue is definitely that best thing that has ever happened in Jane's life.

Chapter 30

When Jane wakes up the next morning, she is feeling much better. She ended up taking some melatonin last night to help her relax, and it made her pass out for a solid eight hours of sleep. She looks over at Blue and sees him wide-awake, just lying there, looking at her. She reaches over and gives him a little morning rub before he springs up and jumps off the bed. Jane knows exactly what that means: Blue is hungry. She gets up out of bed and makes her way to the bathroom. Blue, of course, follows her in. He wants to make sure she has not forgotten about him as if she ever has.

Jane has not been grocery shopping in a while, so her options for breakfast are once again pretty bleak. She goes to grab the box of Froot Loops, but she remembers that she gave Blue the last of the milk with his dinner after his ordeal on the balcony the other night. She contemplates making oatmeal, but she has to really be in a mood for oatmeal, and that is not the case this morning. Eggs it is. She does not have any fresh vegetables to make an omelet with, so she settles on some scrambled eggs. She grabs her last four eggs and a couple slices of cheese from the refrigerator. Normally, she would add a little bit of milk, but that is not an option today.

Jane cracks the eggs in a bowl and whips them up. She melts some butter in the frying pan and lets it heat up a little bit before pouring the eggs in. As she mixes the eggs around in the pan with a spatula, she cuts the two slices of cheese into small little strips. While the eggs are still a bit wet, she scoops out a third of them and sets them aside for Blue. Jane does not like her scrambled eggs wet at all, but Blue prefers them a little mushy. She then adds the strips of cheese to the remaining eggs in the frying pan and lets the cheese melt into the eggs. Once the eggs start to get a little browned, she shuts off the burner and scoops her eggs onto a plate. She puts Blue's eggs on his food dish, and they both dig in at the same time.

After breakfast, Jane puts a load of laundry in the washing machine and gives Blue's litterbox a good cleaning. While the laundry is in the dryer, she does some light dusting and vacuuming. Blue hates when Jane vacuums. The second he sees her take the vacuum out of the closet, he runs and hides under the bed, which explains why she found so many dust balls under the bed the other night when she was looking for Blue. When she is done with all her household chores, she flosses and brushes her teeth. She has just enough time for a quick shower before she has to leave to meet Brian at the pet park.

The second Jane gets Blue's leash off its hook, he comes running out of the bedroom. He was just snoring away on his pillow less than two minutes ago. She hooks his leash on his collar, and they are out the door. They have a few minutes to spare, so Jane lets Blue do his usual stopping to smell pretty much everything he sees. When they walk through the gate of the pet park, she sees Brian sitting at her favorite bench. She was not sure he was going to show up considering he never replied to her last text message. As Jane and Blue start making their way across the park, her palms start to sweat, and her stomach starts to tighten. She cannot tell if this is the work of the devil or just her nerves overreacting. Maybe the two are more in sync than she ever realized.

When Brian sees Jane and Blue approaching, he gets up from the bench and starts walking toward them. Blue stops dead in his tracks. When Jane looks back at Blue, he has his back arched up and he is making a low hissing sound. Maybe this was a bad idea. Brian stops a few feet away from them, unsure how to proceed. She bends down and tries to soothe Blue with gentle rubs. Blue stops hissing, but his back stays arched as high as he can get it. Jane picks Blue up in her arms and holds him to her chest with his head over her shoulder, facing away from Brian. She can feel how stiff Blue's body is. This is not an act of jealousy; this is an act of fear.

Jane and Brian decide to do a lap around the park. Jane keeps Blue tight against her the entire time. It is the only way Blue feels safe enough to relax his back. Brian walks on the opposite side of Jane, so Blue cannot see him at all. They walk and talk at the same time. Brian is being a bit more aggressive than he was the last time they met. Maybe being drunk calms him down. He continues asking her which revenge idea they are going to follow through with. He wants to get started right away. Jane reminds Brian that Stacey was just tied to her own bed and raped two weeks ago. Brian does not even acknowledge hearing what she is saying. He is wound up pretty tight today. Maybe that is what Blue picked up on: Brian's negative energy.

Jane was so concerned about Blue that she did not even notice that Brian is wearing a long-sleeved shirt even though it is almost eighty degrees outside. How can she see if there are any scratches from Blue on his arms if he has them covered? The better question is, why is he wearing a long-sleeved shirt today? Brian continues to push Jane for an answer. She knows he is not going to let up until she gives him what he came here for. Instead, she turns the table and asks him the same question. Which idea does he want to follow through with? Brian does not even hesitate. He had his mind made up before he even made it to the pet park. There is no way he is going to change his mind no matter what Jane says. Brian is insistent they follow through with their third ideas. He uses the excuse that they were the only ideas that they had in common. What about the fact that they are the only ideas where people will get hurt?

There is absolutely no way Jane is going to assist Brian in attacking Melissa and Monica. She is positive now that he is the Miami Beach rapist. She is also positive that Brian is the man that broke into her condo and locked Blue out on the balcony. There is nothing she wants to do more than to pull the sleeves on Brian's shirt up so she can see the proof she knows is there. Jane is getting more and more uncomfortable being this close to Brian. If she was a cat, her back would be arched and she would be hissing.

Jane starts to act like Blue is getting too heavy for her to continue carrying him. She hates to use Blue as an excuse, but she cannot think of another way to get away from Brian without him getting suspicious. She tells Brian she needs to head back home. He does not seem pleased, but what can he do? Jane tells Brian that if they are going through with their third ideas, she needs time to think things through. She makes Brian promise to not do anything until they agree on what it is they are actually going to do. He says he already has some thoughts, but he will wait to hear from her again before acting on any of them. Although Jane is sure she would be horrified, she wishes she could read Brian's mind if only for a minute.

They make their way back to the exit gate. Brian holds the gate open for them. Blue catches a glimpse of Brian as Jane walks past him, and Blue's entire body tenses right back up. Jane says goodbye and starts walking toward her condo. She waits until she is a couple of blocks away from Brian before putting Blue back on the ground. That is the last time she will ever let Brian anywhere near Blue.

Considering Blue did not get to enjoy even a minute of their visit to the pet park, Jane decides to walk with him to the waterfront instead of heading home. It is a beautiful day outside and she is on vacation, so no sense rushing back home right away. Surprisingly, there are not many people around when they get to the waterfront. Jane stops at the first empty bench so Blue can rest a bit. She sits down on the bench, and Blue jumps up next to her. She is happy to see that Blue is back to his normal self. Any signs of fear have vanished. He lies down on the bench with his head in her lap, and within minutes, he starts snoring.

While Blue naps, Jane's mind wanders to her meeting with Brian. The vibe he was throwing off today was very different than any other time they have met. It is hard to believe he is the same Brian that she met back in high school. It is like he is a completely different person. They say spending time behind bars can do that to a person. Jane cannot even understand how he went from being the nice, friendly, polite boy she met that day at her locker to a man hanging out with a tough crowd and robbing convenience stores, never mind turning into the Miami Beach rapist. Something went terribly wrong in his life after high school.

Blue wakes up about fifteen minutes later and is ready to go. Jane walks with Blue about halfway along the pier before turning back and heading home. She needed the outing as much as if not more than Blue did after her meeting with Brian. Being by the water always makes her feel relaxed and alive. By the time they make it back home, they are both parched. Jane grabs a bottle of water out of the refrigerator. She pours a third of it in Blue's water bowl before chugging the rest of it down all at once. She is feeling a bit sticky after walking that much in the hot Miami weather, so she heads to the bathroom to take another quick shower.

When Jane opens the shower curtain to get back out of the shower, she is surprised to not find Blue curled up on the bathroom mat. She instantly starts to panic. After she finishes drying off, she goes to her bedroom and is relieved to find Blue asleep on his pillow. He must be tuckered out from all that walking. Jane is not really a napping kind of person, but maybe Blue is on to something. She closes the shade and climbs back into bed with Blue. She is on a staycation after all.

Chapter 31

Jane is awakened by a noise she cannot place. She had not even realized that she had fallen asleep. She looks over at Blue's pillow and sees that it is empty. How long has she been asleep? She hears the noise again, and this time it makes her jolt up in her bed. Her first thought is to call out to Blue, but what if her intruder is back and he has Blue? She slowly and quietly makes her way to the edge of the bed. She says a silent prayer that the bed does not make the awful squeaking noise it makes sometimes. Jane puts her feet on the floor and gently rises from her bed.

Instead of hearing the bed squeak, she hears the noise again. She cannot even tell where in the condo it is coming from. Jane shimmies from her bed to the doorway, trying to not make a sound. She is in her own home, yet she is afraid to stick her head out into the hallway. This is no way to live. Jane pauses for a moment and wonders if this is how Stacey is feeling after what happened to her in her own bed. Jane creeps ever so slowly into the hallway. She is starting to sweat and feel nauseous. She should have never laid down to nap in the first place.

Jane makes it to the end of the hallway. The bathroom is directly across from her. The kitchen is diagonal to where she is standing, and the living room is to her right. She stays as still as she can while waiting to hear the noise again before deciding on her next move. All she hears is silence. She leans forward and peeks around the corner.

She can see most of the kitchen but does not see anything out of the ordinary. Nothing that would be causing the noise. As she goes to lean a little farther around the corner, she hears the noise again and stops mid-motion. This time, she can tell it is coming from the bathroom.

She pokes her head out so she can see the rest of the kitchen and the living room. Nothing looks out of place in either room. Then it dawns on her that although everything looks normal, she does not see Blue anywhere. Is he locked out on the balcony again? Jane has two options. She can either make her way over to the sliding glass doors and look for Blue on the balcony or she can head toward the bathroom. What are the chances she could make it all the way to the sliding glass doors without whoever is in the bathroom hearing her? Jane glides her way across the floor to the bathroom. It is eerily quiet. This is what they mean when they say you could hear a pin drop. Her heart is racing out of control. She tries to take a step forward, but it is like she is frozen still. Then the noise happens again. It is definitely coming from the bathroom. She puts both hands on the doorframe and leans forward on one leg. She does a quick scan of the bathroom, but she sees nothing that can be causing the noise. Did she imagine hearing the noises?

The next thing she knows, Blue jumps out from behind the shower curtain with his catnip-stuffed mouse in his mouth and drops it at her feet. She wants to laugh. She wants to cry. She wants to scream at Blue for scaring her half to death. Instead, she picks up Blue's toy and throws it into the living room. Is that what Blue gets up to when she is at work all day? The noise she was hearing was not that of an intruder. It was Blue playing with his catnip-stuffed mouse in the shower, of all places.

Jane makes her shopping list and heads to Whole Foods. She wants to be in and out as quick as possible, so she leaves Blue at home. He is not happy about that decision, but he did already have an outside adventure earlier today. It takes her longer to get into the parking garage than it does for her to get from her condo to the store. Granted it is very convenient to have a grocery store so close, but traffic was already bad enough before they opened their doors.

Once Jane finally makes it inside the store, she grabs a shopping cart and starts working her way through the aisles. When she gets to the pet aisle, she is happy to see the salmon dinners that Blue loves is fully stocked. She grabs every can they have on the shelf and puts them in her cart. She also grabs a bunch of the chicken with gravy to mix it up a little bit. She finds everything on her list, plus a few extras, a result of going grocery shopping without eating first. The checkout lines move quickly. Once she is done paying, Jane heads for the elevator to the parking garage. This may be the slowest elevator ever made. It takes longer for the elevator to come than it did to stand in line.

By the time the elevator dings to let her know it is finally on its way to her, there are four other people standing behind her, waiting for it. As the elevator arrives Jane squeezes over so the people that are on it can get out before she gets in. When the elevator doors open, she finds herself face-to-face with Steve. She automatically looks to see if he is alone. Although she does not see Stacey close by, she does see one of their boys holding Steve's hand. She cannot help but wonder if Steve feels guilty for not being there when Stacey needed him the most. Once everyone is out of the elevator, Jane gets in first, followed by the other four customers, which makes for a tight fit considering they all have shopping carts with them. Jane ends up squished against the back wall. First in, last out.

By the time Jane is back home and puts her groceries away, it is already time to make dinner. She bought a rotisserie chicken that was fresh out of the oven. The scent coming from the chicken is making her stomach growl and it is making Blue meow. Blue knows that scent. He also knows when he smells it, he will be eating like a king. Jane starts by carving the chicken. Though the skin is absolutely delicious, she only allows herself one small piece before flushing the rest of it down the toilet. One time, before she knew better, she threw the skin out in the trash can. When she came home from work the next day, Blue had knocked the trash can over to get at the skin and left an awful mess for her to clean. Luckily, she had not thrown any of the chicken bones out with the skin, or Blue would probably have choked to death on one.

Once she is done carving the chicken, she puts some aside for Blue's dinner and some aside as a topper for her salad. The rest she puts on a plate and covers with aluminum foil before putting it in the refrigerator. She likes giving the chicken a little time to cool off before feeding it to Blue. While the chicken cools, Jane cuts up her lettuce, a perfectly ripe tomato, a quarter of a cucumber, and some fresh mushrooms. She pours some French dressing over it, then adds the chicken pieces she set aside for herself. With her dinner complete, she dices up the chicken for Blue into bite-size pieces and puts them on his food dish. She grabs a bottled water and shares it with Blue. Jane cannot get much healthier than tonight's dinner unless her salad dressing was diet French, which it is not. Diet salad dressings have an awful aftertaste.

Once she has cleaned up her mess in the kitchen, she joins Blue, who is already snoring away in the center of the sofa. She turns on the television, but after doing a channel search and finding nothing she wants to watch, she shuts the television back off. Jane's mind is working overtime once again. Why in the world did she have to create those damn fake profiles on Mingle? Ever since that day, her life has been turned upside down, not to mention her frequent visits from the devil. Something good has got to come out of this mess.

Everything revolves around Brian. Jane can feel it in her gut, or did she just eat too fast? There are three questions Jane needs answers to. The first question, is Brian her intruder? The second question, did Brian rape Stacey? Last but certainly not least, is Brian the Miami Beach rapist? She needs to find a way to get the answers to these questions as quickly as possible. She can't live her life being afraid to get out of bed if she hears a noise. She needs to come up with yet another new plan, presumably a plan that will work this time.

Blue wakes up and jumps off the sofa. He heads straight for his litterbox. Blue is definitely a creature of habit. Jane knows his next stop will be his pillow. Blue is calling it a night. Jane takes the hint and heads to the bathroom to brush her teeth. Even though he was just taking a leak a couple of minutes ago, Blue is already snoring away by the time Jane finishes in the bathroom and climbs into bed. She leans over and gives him a gentle good night rub, followed by a good night kiss on his head.

Jane knows it will be a while before she is able to fall asleep. Her mind is racing way too much. The next thing she knows, she is sitting up in bed. Two similar yet very different thoughts just popped into her head at the same time. She climbs back out of bed and makes her way over to the sliding glass doors. She forgot to double-check that they are locked before going to bed, which is the connection to her second thought. By being inside Brian's place the other night, Jane knows that his studio apartment faces the back of the building. She also knows he lives on the first floor. Though this will be the scariest and, most likely, the stupidest thing she will ever do in her life, Jane has a plan. How does that old saying go, "What's good for the goose is good for the gander"?

Jane grabs her cell phone from her purse and opens her texting app. She clicks on Brian's name and sends him a new text message.

Brian,

Sorry to text you so late, but I was wondering if you are free tomorrow to meet up again. I want to discuss our options in person. I will leave Blue at home this time. Let me know.

Jane

She cannot believe she is doing this, but what other option does she really have? Jane climbs back into bed, gives Blue another kiss on his head, and lets his quiet little snores drift her off to sleep.

Chapter 32

When Jane wakes up the next morning, the first thing she does is check her cell phone for a response from Brian. She is a bit disappointed when she does not find one. He never bothered to respond to her previous text message either. Instead, he just showed up at the pet park. In the text message she sent last night, she did not specify a time or a place to meet, so Brian will need to reply to this one. She needs for this to happen as soon as possible before she has a chance to chicken out.

Blue comes strolling out of the bedroom and heads right for his litterbox. Jane makes a mental note that she needs to do some scooping or Blue will be visiting the ficus tree pot again. Jane is not in the mood to make a big breakfast this morning. She gives Blue his dry cat food with a little bit of milk mixed in, which he is not overly excited about, and she has a bowl of Froot Loops. After their boring breakfasts, Jane jumps in the shower. She is hoping to hear back from Brian soon and wants to be ready to go right away. Blue follows Jane into the bathroom and gives himself a tongue bath.

As Jane is drying off, she hears her text message notification go off. She nearly trips over Blue as she rushes to get to her cell phone. She opens her text message app and sees that the new text message is indeed from Brian. She opens the text message and reads it with water still dripping off her.

Jane,

Sorry for the delayed response. I had a busy night last night. I can meet up with you in the late afternoon today if that works for you. Let me know when and where.

Brian

Just the thought of what Brian got up to last night makes Jane feel instantly nauseous. She returns to the bathroom and finishes drying off. Blue has since made his way back onto his pillow. Once she finishes in the bathroom, she goes over to her desk. She sits down in her chair and brings her laptop back to life. Timing is a very important element of her plan. Once her laptop is ready, Jane opens Google and clicks on maps. She types in Brian's address as her destination, and then she types in her address as the starting point. During normal driving conditions they are twenty-one minutes away from each other. Jane makes a note of that on a post-it.

She needs more time than that. Next, she changes the destination address from Brian's address to the address for P.F. Chang's in Brickell. According to Google maps it is a ten-minute drive from her place to the restaurant. Perfect. Jane then grabs her cell phone and responds to Brian's text message.

Brian,

I don't know if you like Chinese food, but how about meeting at P.F. Chang's in Brickell at 5:00 p.m.? Let me know either way.

Jane

She has no intention of meeting Brian at P.F. Chang's for dinner. If Brian agrees to meet Jane at the restaurant at 5:00 p.m. he will need to leave his place by 4:30 p.m. to arrive on time. At the same time Brian is leaving his place, Jane will be arriving at his place. That means Jane needs to leave her condo by 4:00 p.m. the latest. If she gets there right as Brian is leaving, that should give her an hour to do what she needs to do. She still has not figured out what excuse she is going to use for not being at the restaurant when Brian gets there. Hopefully, he will not just head over to her place from the restaurant instead of calling or texting her first.

Why is it taking Brian so long to respond to her text message? The waiting is excruciating. Jane tries to find things to do to stay busy instead of checking her cell phone every five minutes. She empties the old kitty litter out of Blue's litterbox and washes it out in the bathtub before refilling it with new kitty litter. As soon as she puts the litterbox back in its place, Blue runs over and christens it. Then she does some minor pruning of her ficus tree. The poor tree has seen much better days. Between Blue using it as a second litterbox and swatting at the lower hanging leaves like piñatas, it is a wonder it is alive at all.

Blue wakes up, jumps out of bed, and comes running out of the bedroom. He spots Jane at the computer desk, but instead of heading over to her, he goes over to his placemat and just sits down. Very subtle, Blue, very subtle indeed. With the way her nerves have been jumping today, she did not even notice her stomach has been growling at the same time. She shuts down Google and lets her laptop go back to sleep. Considering she has so much chicken left over, she decides to spoil Blue once again. He will be much happier with his lunch option than he was with his breakfast. Jane grabs the plate with the leftover chicken on it out of the refrigerator and carries it over to the counter. She grabs Blue's food dish and washes off the remnants of his breakfast before dicing up some more chicken for him.

Blue has moved into the kitchen to get a better view. Once she is done with Blue's lunch, she dices up some more of the chicken and puts it in a bowl. She rewraps the rest of the leftovers with the aluminum foil and puts it back in the refrigerator. She then grabs the jar of mayonnaise, checks the expiration date, and then scoops two tablespoons of it on top of the diced chicken. Next, she gets the pepper shaker out of the cabinet and gives it a few shakes over the mayonnaise. After putting the pepper shaker back in the cabinet, she mixes the diced chicken, mayonnaise, and pepper together in the bowl. Voilà, homemade chicken salad for one. Jane's plan was to make a sandwich with half of the chicken salad and save the other half to put on top of a salad for dinner later, but she forgot to buy bread when she went grocery shopping. So instead, she just eats all the chicken salad right out of the bowl while Blue devours his lunch. Blue gives his compliments to the chef by licking his lips and even his nose.

The sound of Jane's text message notification is like music to her ears in more ways than one. When she grabs her cell phone, she notices the time. It is already 3:45 p.m., which is almost the time she needs to head out. She is so anxious her palms start to sweat. When she touches the home button on her cell phone, there is so much sweat on her thumb and the scanner cannot even read her thumb print. She wipes her hands on her pants and tries again. This time, the scanner reads her thumb print, and her cell phone unlocks. She opens her text message app and sees a new message from Brian. She clicks on his name to open the message.

Jane,

I love Chinese food! I will see you there at 5:00 p.m.

Brian

Chapter 33

Thanks to watching pretty much every episode of *Dateline* that has ever aired, Jane knows what she will need for her outing tonight. With only thirteen minutes to spare, she does not waste even a second. She runs to her bedroom and grabs her backpack, which she has not used in years. In the backpack, she puts everything she can remember people using to break into places. She grabs a couple of very small screwdrivers, a pair of tweezers, a playing card, a paperclip, a paring knife, and a safety pin. Next, she gets a pair of latex gloves and a black hairnet. She is already all dressed in black. She puts on her black trainers and heads out the door.

Jane drives the speed limit all the way to Brian's place. The last thing she needs is to get pulled over by the cops with her backpack filled the way it is. How would she explain its contents to the cops? As she turns the corner onto Brian's Street, she can see his car is still parked in front of his building. She pulls over and parks. Brian's car is facing away from her, so hopefully he will not do a three-point turn and come toward her when he heads out. Jane ducks down as low as she can go while still being able to see out the window. The last thing she needs is for Brian to drive by her car and see her crouching down in it.

At 4:35 p.m., Jane sees Brian walk out the door of his building. He walks over to his car and gets in. He starts his car, revs the engine a couple of times, and then drives away. Jane waits in her car a couple of minutes just in case he forgot something and comes back for it. She does not want to waste any more time, every minute counts. She leaves her car parked where it is and walks casually toward Brian's building. Strangely, there are no drug dealers on the corners today. Maybe they don't work on the Lord's day.

Jane walks past the entrance to the building and stops when she gets to the corner. If anyone is watching her, they are most likely wondering why someone is all dressed in black when it is almost eighty degrees outside. Black attracts the sun, which is one of the reasons she can already feel sweat dripping down her back. The other reason also accounts for why her stomach is tight and she feels like throwing up. To hell with you, devil. Throwing up in Brian's apartment would not be a good thing.

Jane tries to act as cool and nonchalant as possible as she leans against the building. Across from her is a vacant lot where druggies usually go to shoot up. On the side of her is a building which looks like it is all boarded up. It is most likely home to quite a few squatters. After doing a couple of scans up and down the street, she makes her way down the side of the building to the back. She remembers from her visit that there was only one other apartment after Brian's. She creeps as quietly as she can up to the sliding glass door of the first apartment. Luckily, it is closed tight. As she keeps going, she wonders if anyone is home and if they can see her shadow through the shade. Next up is Brian's apartment.

As Jane gets closer, she can see that Brian's shade is slightly open. If she looks at just the right angle, she can see directly inside. She takes her backpack off and takes out the black hairnet. The last thing she wants to do is leave any of her red frizzy hair behind for Brian to find. Next, she puts on the latex gloves. She will not be leaving any fingerprints behind either. Jane moves closer to the door so she can get a good look at the lock she needs to pick. She puts one hand on the door handle to steady herself and cannot believe it when the door moves. Brian left his place without locking the sliding glass door in this neighborhood. What is he insane? As if we do not already know the answer to that question.

Jane does a quick scan of her surroundings before sliding the door open and slipping into Brian's apartment. Her stomach tightens even more. The devil is showing no mercy. Jane puts her backpack down near the sliding glass door so she cannot forget it when she leaves. She would literally trip over it on her way out the door. She opens the backpack and takes her cell phone out. She double-checks that it is on silent mode, then she clicks on the camera app. She makes her way to the bathroom. She is pretty sure there is nothing worth finding in there considering she did a little snooping the last time she was here, but a quick second look cannot hurt.

It is a small bathroom with very limited places to put or hide anything. There is a small medicine cabinet above the sink which she looked in last time, but she slides the doors open anyway. She does not find anything in Brian's medicine cabinet that shouldn't be in any man's medicine cabinet. Next, she opens the doors to the cabinet under the sink. The only things in the cabinet are a plunger, one thing of bathroom cleaner and a few rolls of toilet paper. As she starts to leave the bathroom, she has a flashback to an episode of *Dateline* she watched a few months ago. In the episode, the cops found a gun hidden in the tank of the toilet. She walks up to the toilet and takes the cover to the tank off and looks inside. Again, she comes up empty. The tank could definitely use a good scrubbing.

Jane checks the time on her cell phone. She wasted too much time in the bathroom. Brian's place is so small he does not have room for a dresser, so there are no drawers to look through except in the kitchen. Opening all the drawers in the kitchen and going through them seems very time-consuming. Instead, she heads over to the closet. She wanted to look in the closet the last time, but she did not have enough time. The doors are the metal-folding kind. She opens both doors at the same time so she can see every part of the closet at once. There is one bar going across the closet which Brian has mostly full of T-shirts and some pairs of jeans. Across the floor of the closet Brian has a few pairs of sneakers, a couple pairs of shoes, and a pair of flip-flops. There is a shelf above the bar holding Brian's clothes. Jane is not tall enough to see what is up on the shelf, so she grabs one of the chairs at the table and carries it over to the closet.

She steps up on to the chair and scans the contents on the shelf. One side of the shelf has folded bath towels and facecloths. The other side has folded bed sheets and pillowcases. She moves the chair into the closet so she can check behind the towels just in case Brian has something stuffed behind them. She climbs back up on the chair and reaches behind the towels. She slides her arm back and forth, but she does not feel anything. Jane does, however, get a whiff of something foul with her head so far in the closet. She gets down off the chair, feeling frustrated. There must be something here that proves Brian is the Miami Beach rapist.

Jane checks the time again and starts getting nervous. Brian should definitely be at the restaurant by now so why has he not called or texted to see where she is? Did he head right over to her place? Five more minutes is all she is willing to spend looking for something she may not find before getting out of here. What is that gross smell? Is that coming from Brian's sneakers? She bends down close to the floor, but the lower she goes, the fainter the smell becomes. While she is down near Brian's shoes, she puts her gloved hands inside every sneaker and shoe. Good thing she wore the latex gloves. She does not find anything once again. As she starts getting back up, the smell intensifies. What is that awful smell, and where is it coming from?

When Jane is standing straight up and moves deeper into the closet, the smell is the strongest. Is the smell coming from Brian's clothes? Does Brian hang his dirty laundry in the closet? She reaches over and grabs a pair of jeans. She pulls one of the legs up to her nose and sniffs. Although the smell is a little bit stronger, she is also smelling fabric softener. These clothes have been washed recently. They are not the cause of the smell. Where the hell is that smell coming from? Losing her patience, Jane starts pulling on all the clothes and smelling every one of them. She then finds the hanger with the last T-shirt on it and pushes all the hangers to that side of the closet. She does the same thing with the last hanger holding a pair of jeans.

With the clothes separated, she can now see the wall behind all the clothes. At first, she is not sure what she is looking at, but she knows it is what she has been looking for. She raises her cell phone and starts taking pictures. She takes lots of pictures, most of which are close-ups. One of the times she zooms in with the camera lens, she notices something she had not noticed before. It takes every ounce of self-control to not vomit right in Brian's shoes. That's it. She has seen enough. She pulls the hangers back to where they were and closes the closet doors. She carries the chair back over to the table, making sure to put it exactly how she found it. Then she walks over to the sliding glass door and grabs her backpack. She slowly sticks her head between the slats of the vertical blind and out the door to see if anyone is around before she walks out the door. Other than a big fat rat that just ran toward one of the trash bins, the backyard is empty.

Jane makes her way outside and readjusts the vertical blind to how Brian left it, then she closes the door. She creeps past the neighbors' sliding glass doors and to the end of the building. She sticks her head around the corner of the building, looking for anyone who might be passing by. The coast is clear. She creeps along the side of the building and stops at the next corner at the front of the building. She scans the street both ways. The only person she sees is an old man getting into his car. She makes her way to the sidewalk and heads for where she parked her car. She hurries across the street, fearing the old man may not see her and run her over.

Jane gets in her car and starts it up. Just as she is about to pull away from the curb, she hears a familiar sound. The sound is that of Brian's loud engine. She quickly puts the car back into park and kills the engine. Then she once again ducks down as much as she can in her seat. Brian is coming down his street the same way Jane had, so he will not be passing her face-to-face. The chances he will look in her direction and see the hunch of her back is very slim. As the sound of Brian's engine gets louder, she starts sweating more. Then the sound passes by her and gets lower until it stops. Jane raises her head just enough to see out the window. She spots Brian's car in front of his building. She watches until Brian gets out of the car and walks toward his building. When she sees Brian open the door to his building, she starts her car again. As soon as the door closes behind Brian, Jane pulls away from the curb and drives away.

162

Chapter 34

When Jane gets home from Brian's place, she is happy to see Blue waiting at the door for her. She drops her backpack down and picks Blue up. She gives him a nice long hug before rubbing him between his eyes and kissing his nose. Blue fusses to get down. He has something else on his mind, dinner. He walks over to his placemat and sits down. He looks up at Jane and lets out one loud meow. Message received. Jane goes to the kitchen and gets Blue one of his cans of salmon from the cabinet. Not as good as rotisserie chicken, but it will do. Her stomach is still not feeling right, so she skips dinner.

Only now does the realization of what she did today start to hit her. Breaking into Brian's apartment is a crime that could send her to prison. What was she thinking? Jane also realizes that she did not find the piece of paper that she wrote her revenge ideas on at Brian's place. Maybe he has it in his wallet for safekeeping, or maybe it was not him that took it in the first place. Then her mind wanders to what she saw on the wall in Brian's closet behind his clothes.

She walks over to her laptop and wakes it up again. While she waits for it to do its thing, she gets a glass of wine. She needs something to steady her nerves. She grabs her cell phone and sits down in her chair. She is not surprised at all to see Blue waiting at her feet. Once she is situated, Blue jumps up and makes himself comfortable. Jane opens her cell phone and e-mails the photos she took at Brian's place to herself. She then opens her e-mail on her laptop and downloads the photos. She wants to be able to see them better than she could on her cell phone screen. Or does she?

Once the photos are done downloading, Jane clicks on the first one. She cannot believe what she is looking at. As she starts to zoom in on the photo, she relives another high school flashback in her mind.

*****

There are not many things that are more frightening to an overweight teenage girl that is already being bullied by the three most popular girls in school than gym class. Jane hated gym class. She used every excuse possible to get out of participating. Just the thought of having to change in the girl's locker room was horrifying enough. Jane spent more time in the nurse's office than she did anywhere else in that school. She is pretty sure the nurse knew what she was up to, but as a heavy woman herself, she never denied Jane a pass for gym. Most times, she would just spend gym period in the nurse's waiting room. If there were any students that were actually sick, the nurse would make Jane go to the gymnasium and sit on the bleachers instead.

Sometimes gym class would be outside on the field, depending on how hot it was. Jane cannot be in the sun for too long due to her fair skin. Instead of sitting on the bleachers, she would hang out underneath them to avoid the sun. On one such day, Jane had used an excuse of a sore ankle to get out of running track outside. As the rest of her class made their way to the track, Jane found a spot to sit in the shade under the bleachers. She brought one of her textbooks with her so she could do some extra studying for one of her upcoming quizzes.

Jane was so enthralled in her studying that she did not hear Stacey, Melissa, and Monica as they climbed the steps of the bleachers. They climbed until they were directly over where Jane was sitting. At the same time, all three of them dropped a condom full of water on the top of Jane's head. Jane was completely soaked and so was her textbook. Her bullies thought it was the funniest thing they have ever seen. They laughed so loud most of the gym class heard them all the way over at the track. Jane simply got up from where she was sitting, pushed her wet frizzy hair out of her eyes, and walked back to the nurse's office. She had convinced herself that if she never let them see her cry and never did anything to let them know they got to her they would eventually stop. That never happened until after graduation day.

*****

Jane snaps back to the present time and zooms in on the photo she opened on her laptop. Brian is definitely a very disturbed man. The more she looks at the photo, the more nauseous she becomes. Blue senses something is not right and looks up at her. As she pushes the chair back, Blue jumps off her lap. Jane gets up as quickly as she can and makes a mad dash to the bathroom. She gets down on her knees in front of the toilet and proceeds to vomit. Salad is not very appetizing the second time around. She stays bent over the toilet until she is sure there is nothing left in her to come out. Blue is so intuitive he did not even follow Jane into the bathroom. Instead, he headed to the bedroom to take a nap on his pillow.

She makes her way back over to the desk and sits down. She takes a sip of her wine to get rid of the awful taste in her mouth. She then turns her focus back to her laptop screen. The reality of what she is looking at is so disturbing she has to look away. After regaining her composure, she zooms back out on her laptop so she can see the whole picture. This time, she notices something she had not noticed before and she starts freaking out even more.

The photo on Jane's laptop screen which she took while she was searching Brian's closet shows seven, not six like she had previously thought, but seven, used condoms pinned to the wall behind Brian's clothes. He had used them and then hung them on the wall without emptying them out. That was the foul odor she had been smelling. As if that is not bad enough, each of the condoms have a woman's name written on them. Jane had not noticed the names until she zoomed in on one of the condoms.

She grabs a piece of paper and a pen. Then she prepares herself as she zooms in on the picture again. She starts with the first condom all the way to the left. She zooms in until she can read the name written on it. On the piece of paper, she writes the name Amanda. Then she moves on to the second condom and then the third and fourth and fifth. Under the name Amanda, she now has Stephanie, Marie, Linda, and Vanessa.

Jane knows before even moving on to the sixth condom which name is going to be written on it. She is hoping she is wrong because, if she is right, that means Brian has raped another woman very recently. She looks back up at the laptop screen and moves over to the sixth used condom hanging on Brian's closet wall. She can tell the writing on this one is much newer than the first five she looked at. She does not even have to zoom in as much as she did for the others to be able to read the name Stacey. Jane writes Stacey's name under the name Vanessa on the piece of paper.

There is one more condom to go. It is obvious it is the most recent one because its contents had not had enough time to dry up. Jane starts to feel nauseous again, and it is not the devil visiting. Who in their right mind would save used condoms as trophies after raping all these women? Jane cannot help but wonder what Brian did with them while he was in prison and then again when he was living at his mother's house. What if his mother had found them like she did? How would Brian have explained them to his mother if she had asked him about them?

She scans all the way to the right so she can see the last used condom. Although it is exactly what she was expecting, when she reads the name on the condom, she starts dry heaving. She now knows what Brian was so busy doing last night. The name written on the last used condom is Melissa. Jane cannot take anymore. She needs some fresh air, and she needs it now. She gets up from her chair and walks over to her sliding glass doors. She pulls the blind open, unlocks the door, and steps out on the balcony. Within seconds, Blue is right there by her side. She walks up to the railing and leans over it. There is a slight breeze which is exactly what she was hoping for. Blue jumps up on his chair and gets comfortable. Does this cat ever get enough sleep?

What are the chances that Brian raped a different Melissa? Not that it would make a difference. Brian agreed he would not do anything until they had a chance to discuss their options in person together. Granted Jane did not show up at P.F. Chang's, but that was after he attacked Melissa. Come to think of it, how come Brian has not called or texted her to find out why she did not meet him at the restaurant? Considering what Jane now knows about Brian, the last thing she wants is to be on his shit list. She goes back inside and gets her cell phone. She opens her texting app and sends Brian a new message.

Brian,

I am so sorry I did not make it to the restaurant. Blue started throwing up all over the place. I rushed him to the vet and completely forgot to let you know.

Jane

Okay, so it was Jane that was throwing up, not Blue, but it was the first thing that came to her mind. Although she is certain the Melissa that Brian was referring to when he wrote the name on the used condom is one of her high school bullies, she wants confirmation. She sits back down at her desk. She looks over at Blue's chair on the balcony and sees he has not moved at all. Seems she is not the only one that wanted some fresh air. Jane opens Google and goes to the *Miami Herald* website. As soon as the website loads, her heart starts racing. The main headline right there for her to see in big bold letters, THE MIAMI BEACH RAPIST STRIKES AGAIN. She starts reading the article word by word. Again, they do not list the victim's name. Jane never once thought she would think of Melissa or Stacey as victims, but that is what they are now. She was a victim of theirs for four years, and now they are victims of Brian.

As she continues reading the article, it is as if she is rereading the first one she read about Stacey. The rapist broke in through the sliding glass door. He attacked Melissa in her own bed. He tied her to the bed and blindfolded her. He never said a word. He wore a black mask to hide his face and all-black clothes. Not a single hair or skin cell was left behind. He wore gloves the entire time, so no fingerprints were found anywhere. He used a condom, as Jane knows all too well, so no semen was left behind either. That is because it is hanging in Brian's closet.

The only description Melissa could give the cops of her attacker was an estimated height and weight, which was very similar to the estimates all six of the other women gave. It was, without a doubt, the same man. The Miami Beach rapist has definitely returned, and he has picked up where he left off. As Jane finishes reading the article, it dawns on her that they did not mention a connection between Stacey and Melissa. Was that on purpose, or have they not made the connection yet?

Jane closes the *Miami Herald* website and opens Facebook. She enters her log in information. Once it is open, she goes right to her friends list. It is not a long list. The entire list fits right there on the laptop screen. She does not even need to scroll down. She sees Stacey's name and Monica's name, but Melissa's name is not in the list. Jane could swear she sent Melissa a friend request and Melissa accepted it. She clicks on the search bar and enters Melissa's name. The search shows a few different Melissa Miller in Miami, but none of them are the one she is looking for. Did Melissa block her for some reason?

Jane goes back to her friends list and clicks on Stacey's name. When Stacey's profile page opens, Jane goes to Stacey's friends list. When she clicks on See All Friends, she is not surprised at all how long the list is. According to Facebook, Stacey has almost five hundred friends. Luckily, she can scan through them alphabetically. She scrolls and scrolls and scrolls until she finally gets to the letter *M*. She scrolls slower now and is surprised to not see Melissa listed as one of Stacey's almost five hundred friends. Having no luck on Stacey's profile page, she goes back to her own page and clicks on Monica's name from her friends list.

When Monica's profile page opens, Jane does the same thing she just did on Stacey's page. According to Facebook, Monica only has close to three hundred and twenty-five friends. Jane does notice while she is scrolling through them that most of them are women. Some of them she is not quite sure if they are women or men. Butch lesbian is the correct term she thinks. When she gets to the letter *M,* she is again surprised to not see Melissa's name listed. The only conclusion Jane can come to is that Melissa must have deleted her Facebook profile most likely right after she was raped.

Without Melissa's name being listed on the *Miami Herald* website and without being able to find her on Facebook anymore, Jane does not have any concrete proof that she is the one Brian used that condom with. There is a very slim possibility that it could be a different Melissa. That is too much of a coincidence for Jane to even consider. She knows without a doubt they are the same Melissa. Jane shuts down Facebook and her laptop. She grabs her cell phone and joins Blue back out on the balcony. He is still snoring away.

What is Brian thinking? Does he not realize that Jane is going to piece everything together? He is the one that shared his revenge idea about attacking all three women with her, and then ironically two of the three have been raped in less than a month. The sound of her text message notification startles her for a second. She knows the new message is going to be from Brian. Did he believe her lie about taking Blue to the vet?

Jane,

I thought you were a good girl, but good girls do not tell lies. When you did not show up at P.F. Chang's I went by your place. I knocked on your door and heard Blue meowing, but you were not home. I looked for your car, but it was not there either.

Brian

Jane starts shaking so much from reading Brian's new text message that she drops her cell phone. The noise of the cell phone hitting the floor wakes Blue from his sleep. He picks his head up and looks around for what caused the noise. Watching him reminds her of how she was the other day when she could hear Blue playing with his toy in the shower. Jane picks up her cell phone and is relieved to see the screen did not crack. She walks back inside with Blue right behind her and heads right for her glass of wine. This time, she does not just take a sip, she downs the rest of what was left in the glass.

Jane shuts and locks her sliding glass door. She walks over to her broom closet and grabs an old mop. She brings the mop over to the sliding glass door and puts it in the bottom track. If the lock gets picked, there is no way the door will be able to be opened from the outside. She may be acting paranoid, but she is not taking any chances. There is no way she will be getting any sleep tonight.

Chapter 35

When Jane wakes up, she is very glad she is on vacation. Last night's sleep was one of the worst night's sleep she has ever had. Every time she fell asleep, she would wake right back up, thinking she heard a noise. She needs to get control of her life again. The only way she will be able to do that is to get Brian out of her life. Unfortunately, that may be a lot easier said than done.

She could just show the photos she took of the wall in Brian's closet to the cops. If she did that, how would she explain what she was doing in Brian's apartment when he was not home? That would be like confessing to breaking and entering. She could make an anonymous call to one of the tip lines they had posted in the *Miami Herald* or at the end of the *Dateline* episode. If they decided to trace the call, it could lead them right back to Jane. She is a very smart woman though you would not know it by the mess she has let herself get involved in. She just needs a little more time to think things through.

Today is a Monday, so Brian should be at work until 5:00 p.m. if he has not been fired yet. That gives Jane some time to come up with (you guessed it) yet another new plan. How much time does she have before Brian comes knocking on her door if he even bothers to knock? This is totally insane. Jane has always stayed out of trouble. She was a straight A student all through school, except for gym class. She has never even received a speeding ticket. She was pulled over by the cops once for driving too slow instead of too fast. They let her go with just a verbal warning.

It takes all the strength and willpower Jane has to get herself out of bed. She walks directly over to the coffeepot and makes some extra strong Cuban coffee. She already knows it is not going to do much to wake her up, but maybe it can at least help her focus enough to conjure up a way to deal with Brian. Blue follows her out of the bedroom and makes a pitstop at his litterbox before joining her in the kitchen. Blue walks over to the cabinet with his food in it and sits down right in front of it. Again, subtlety is not one of Blue's strong points. Jane never has to wonder if Blue is hungry. He may not be able to speak in a language that she can understand, but his actions speak very clearly and very loudly.

Considering she has a lot of nice fresh vegetables and eggs that are not expired, she and Blue will be having one of her world-famous omelets for breakfast this morning. By the time Jane is done making their omelets, she is already on her second cup of Cuban coffee. One thing is for sure; she will be spending some quality time on the toilet today. The thing about Cuban coffee is that, until your body gets used to it, you can plan on making extra visits to the bathroom.

When she is done eating and cleaning up after herself, she sits down at her desk. She wakes her laptop up and then goes back to the *Miami Herald* website. She wants to see if there are any new articles about Melissa's attack online. The attack is front-page news once again. Even though the cops have no evidence at all linking these two recent rapes to the other ones from five years ago, they are still saying it is the same man. They do say there is a very small chance it could be a copycat. About halfway through the article, the reporter states that he tried to get a comment from the victim but all he could get was a "no comment" from the family's lawyer. How does the reporter know the name of the victim? Jane could not find Melissa's name anywhere on their website. With the kind of money Melissa's father has, he would definitely have a very good lawyer at his beck and call. Jane does some more searching on Google for other articles about the attack, but none of the ones she finds lists Melissa's name.

The reporter at the *Miami Herald* must have a connection with the cops.

Jane suddenly realizes that she somehow forgot all about the piece of paper with the list of women's names from the used condoms. She changes her search efforts to the other women from five years ago. She remembers hearing about the rapes, but she cannot remember any of the victim's names. In the search bar, she types in *Miami Beach rapist* and hits Enter. There are hundreds of results found. If the cops did a search history on her laptop, they would be very suspicious.

The story became national news very quickly. Jane does not want to spend her whole day looking through all these articles. She scans through them looking at the date they were posted online. She is looking for one of the last ones that was written after the fifth attack. This would be so much easier if Jane could sort the articles by dates. She finally finds one with the headline MIAMI BEACH RAPIST STRIKES A FIFTH TIME and clicks on the link. Strangely enough, it is an article from the *Miami Herald* that was written by the same reporter that tried to get a comment from Melissa. Jane scans the article, looking for the women's names. There are no photos of any of them and no last names, but she does find their first names. She compares the names Brian wrote on the used condoms to the names in the article and they match perfectly. She now has all the proof she needed to be absolutely sure that Brian is the Miami Beach rapist.

Enough of that for now. Jane shuts down Google. She heads to the bathroom to floss and brush her teeth. Once she is done with her dental hygiene, she hops in the shower. She does her best thinking in the shower. Blue comes waltzing into the bathroom. He does his circling routine on the bathroom mat, then curls into one of his tight balls. He must be exhausted after eating his breakfast. Considering she does not have to rush off to work this morning, she takes an extra-long relaxing hot shower. She lets the water calm her down and clear her mind. She should have tried this last night right before climbing into bed. Maybe she would have been able to sleep at least a little bit more than a few minutes here and a few minutes there. It could just be my imagination, but the steam does seem to be melting the rolling snowball ever so slowly.

Jane gets out of the shower, making sure to not step on Blue in the process, and dries off. She gets dressed in her baggy sweatpants and loose T-shirt, then heads to the kitchen. She fills her coffee cup with the rest of the Cuban coffee that has been sitting in the coffeepot. Three cups of Cuban coffee in just as many hours. Her stomach is not going to be happy with her. She takes her cup of coffee and heads to the balcony. She opens the blind, takes the mop out of the bottom track, unlocks the door, and slides it open. Before she even has a chance to step out onto the balcony, Blue is running through her legs, almost tripping her up.

Blue jumps up on his chair. Instead of lying down to take yet another nap, he actually sits up and starts scanning the sky for low-flying birds. It is nothing less than a miracle that he has not fallen over the railing trying to catch one. Jane sits in her chair and tries her best to just relax. She has so many things going around in her head she is finding it difficult to focus on just one. Her main objective is to stop Brian before he has a chance to attack Monica or any other woman ever again. There is no way she could live with herself if she did nothing now that she knows what she knows. The question is what she can do without getting herself into any trouble. She does not want to end up spending time behind bars for breaking into Brian's apartment.

There is also the matter of Brian having the list of revenge ideas that Jane wrote in her own handwriting. Did Brian break into her place just so he could get his hands on that list? Jane never found anything else to be missing. If she alerts the cops about Brian being the Miami Beach rapist and he shows them the list it would not look good for her at all. Brian could easily tell them that Jane was his accomplice, and they just might believe him. What would happen to Jane? More importantly, who would take care of Blue?

Somehow, she needs to be able to stop Brian before he rapes anyone again without incriminating herself in any way. Jane looks over at Blue, as if he can help her figure out a solution, but he is too busy birdwatching to pay her any attention. It looks like she will have to deal with Brian all on her own. Maybe, just maybe, the answer lies in the question itself. Maybe she does not have to deal with Brian by herself. What would happen if she got Stacey, Melissa, and Monica together and she told them everything she knows about Brian, including showing them the photos on her phone as proof? What if the four of them came up with a plan together?

Jane spends the next hour going over just how much she is willing to share with Stacey, Melissa, and Monica. She has no idea how they will react once she confides in them. Jane is certain that if she was one of Brian's victims, she would either want him locked up for the rest of his life or dead. If Brian gets sent to prison as a convicted rapist, he will end up being raped more times than he could have ever raped anyone else. That just might be worse for him than being dead.

Just the thought of talking to any of the three women makes Jane very anxious, never mind trying to talk to all three of them at the same time. Maybe she should start with Monica considering she is the one that needs to be on guard. Once she gets Monica on her side, the two of them together can then talk to Stacey and Melissa. That sounds like a much better idea. Monica did send Jane a friend request on Facebook, so she must be willing to at least talk to her. Then again, she could be just trying to get more Facebook friends than Stacey or Melissa. There is only one way to find out.

She goes back inside and opens Facebook on her laptop. She clicks on Monica's name from her friends list. Just seeing Monica's name under the words *friends list* is bizarre. When Monica's profile page opens, Jane clicks on send a message.

Chapter 36

Jane's nerves are shot. As she puts Blue's leash on him, she starts questioning if she is doing the right thing. Deep down, she knows that she is. She has never taken Blue to the pet park at this time of day before. She is hoping there will not be a lot of large dogs around. Although it is late afternoon, the sun is still shining. It has cooled down to a pleasant seventy degrees. Perfect weather for a nice walk outside. Blue is up to his usual shenanigans all the way to the park. Luckily, they left early enough, so Jane just lets him do his thing.

As they approach the gate to the entrance of the pet park, Jane only sees two dogs. One of them is the old English bulldog with the even older man she saw a couple of weeks ago. The other dog is the one she is looking for. Here goes nothing. She opens the gate, and Blue walks in ahead of her leading the way. She closes the gate, and they head over to Blue's playmate, the yapping chihuahua. The closer she gets, the more she sweats. Doing the right thing is not always easy.

Blue tries to sneak up on the chihuahua, but right before he is about to pounce, the chihuahua turns and sees him. Playtime begins for the two of them, but not for Jane. She is relieved to see that Monica brought Samantha with her. It is Samantha that gets up from the bench to greet Jane. They shake hands and exchange pleasantries. Jane is feeling a bit uncomfortable being in such close proximity to Monica, but she manages to make eye contact with her, and they both nod their heads. Jane has no idea what to expect from this meeting. She could be wrong, but Monica seems just as nervous as she is.

Dragging this out is not going to do any of them any good. The sooner she gets down to business, the sooner she can be back home alone with Blue. While Blue and the yapping chihuahua take turns jumping all over each other, Jane and Samantha join Monica on the bench. Never in her life did she ever imagine she would be sitting in a park on a bench with one of her high school bullies, at least not of her own free will.

Samantha is definitely the talker in their relationship. She is the one that starts asking Jane all kinds of questions. Monica has hardly said two words. After messaging Monica on Facebook, Jane decided she was going to tell her everything she knows about Brian being the Miami Beach rapist. The only part she is going to leave out is the part about using Stacey, Melissa, and Monica's photos on Mingle to talk to men. Monica does not need to know that part. Instead, Jane tells them that she bumped into Brian at the bar in the hotel she works at. She also accidentally forgets to mention the revenge lists she and Brian made.

Jane was not going to tell them about the breaking and entering part either, but she cannot figure out another way to explain what she found in Brian's closet. It is not like he would just show her his display of used condoms hanging on the wall in the back of his closet. Jane is not a good liar. She has always tried to be as honest as possible. When she does lie, it is never very believable. Jane tells Monica and Samantha that she went over to Brian's place for a drink one night and ended up forgetting her cell phone at his place when she left. Without her cell phone, she did not know Brian's cell phone number, so she could not call him to find out when he would be home. She tells them that she just stopped by again the next day. When she got there, Brian was not home, so she checked his sliding glass door, and it was unlocked. She did not actually break in considering the door was left unlocked. It sounds almost believable to Jane as she hears herself trying to sell the lie to Monica and Samantha.

As Jane tells them everything she knows about Brian, they continue to look at her in disbelief. It is a damn good thing she kept those photos on her cell phone. Jane takes a second to check on Blue and the chihuahua. They are being a little too quiet for a cat and a dog playing together. She is not at all surprised when she sees the two of them fast asleep, cuddled together. She cannot help herself. She takes her cell phone out of her pocket and takes a photo of Blue and the chihuahua sleeping together. It is one of the cutest things she has ever seen. It is definitely a post-worthy photo if Jane was the posting type, which she is not.

While she has her cell phone out, she starts showing the photos she took at Brian's place to Monica and Samantha. Their reactions are the same as the ones she had when she slid the hangers apart. At first, they both look very confused. They are not sure what they are looking at even though Jane already told them beforehand. Who in their right mind would expect to see used condoms hanging on someone's wall? As Monica scrolls through the photos, she looks like she may vomit at any second. When she gets to the photo of the used condom with Stacey's name written on it, she has had enough. Monica hands Jane's cell phone to Samantha. She does not want to see anymore. Samantha takes the cell phone from Monica and zooms in on the last photo she was looking at. Like Jane, Samantha can tell this used condom is a lot newer than the previous ones. Then Samantha moves on to the last photo Jane had taken that day. It is the one with Melissa's name written on a used condom. Samantha again zooms in on the photo, which is a huge mistake on her part. The next thing Jane knows, Samantha is vomiting all over the ground near their feet. She did not even have enough time to get up from the bench before letting it out. Jane knows exactly how Samantha feels. Seeing that photo of the used condom with the semen still in it had the same effect on her. Monica never made it to the last photo, and she has no interest in seeing it now.

Luckily, Blue and the chihuahua were off to the side of the bench, so they did not get a vomit shower. The horrific sound Samantha made while vomiting did manage to wake them from their naps, but once they knew everything was okay, they both went right back to sleep. If only Jane's life was so easy. Monica started dry heaving when she saw Samantha vomiting. Fortunately, she managed to keep everything down.

Jane finds herself wondering why in awkward times like this the strangest thoughts enter her mind. While she sits there watching Samantha trying to pull herself together, Jane cannot help but wonder if, like her, this is the first time Samantha has ever seen a used condom. Although their reasons would be totally different, Jane being a virgin and Samantha being a lesbian, it could be something they have in common. Jane notices that Monica does not try to comfort Samantha at all. She wonders if it is because she is there with them or if the cold meanness is still there inside Monica. Once a bully always a bully.

Samantha is completely embarrassed. She is grateful that she had not eaten very much earlier in the day. Most of her vomit was just liquid. The stench from it is still pretty damn foul. Samantha cannot even make eye contact with Jane as she hands her cell phone back to her. In hopes of making Samantha feel better, Jane confides that she had just made it in time to her toilet when she had zoomed in on the same photo. Monica has not even asked what was in the photo that caused such a reaction. When she has had enough, she has had enough.

The grossness of the lingering odor has made their meeting even more uncomfortable than it was before. None of them know what to say. Jane finds herself wishing she was Dorothy so she could click her heels, or rather her sneakers, three times and be back at home with Blue. In the message Jane sent Monica on Facebook, she really did not get into many details. She only said enough to get Monica's attention.

Monica,

Do you have time to meet up with me today? I think you might be in danger.

Jane

She was very surprised to get a response in only five minutes. It was Monica's idea to meet at the pet park. Jane has not told Monica about Brian wanting revenge on all three of them because he felt rejected by them back in high school. It is Samantha who asks the questions that allows Jane to make the needed connection. "Who is this Brian guy and why do you think Monica might be in danger?" Before Jane has the chance to answer her Monica interjects, saying she was just about to ask the same questions. If Jane had to pick between being shocked, appalled, or unsurprised that Monica does not remember who Brian is; unsurprised would win by a long shot.

At this point, Jane has no idea if Monica has told Samantha that she bullied Jane all through their high school years, along with Stacey and Melissa. It is probably not something most high school bullies brag about ten years later to their life partner. Then again, Jane is thinking like a victim. To prevent the situation from getting any more awkward than it already is, Jane dances around the bullying subject, which Monica seems grateful for.

Jane explains to Samantha that she and Monica ran in different circles in high school. During their senior year, a boy named Brian transferred to their high school from out of state. She explains how her locker was right next to Brian's locker. She omits the part about how they met the very first time. Or that Jane was leaving school early because Stacey had drawn circles on her face and arms with a black marker while Melissa and Monica held her still in the girl's bathroom. Jane goes on to say that she and Brian became pretty good friends for the rest of their senior year and for a short while after. She also tells them that Brian had a crush on all three girls. Monica actually turns a little red in the face when Jane adds that Brian tried hitting on them pretty much every day, especially Monica. Jane is curious if Monica is this nice shade of red because she is embarrassed that her lesbian partner is hearing a boy was hitting on her or because she is embarrassed that she does not even remember the boy.

Monica is the one that makes the connection and spells it out for Samantha. Brian had crushes on Stacey, Melissa, and Monica. Stacey and Melissa have both been raped in the last month. Brian now has used condoms hanging on the wall in his closet with their names written on them, along with five others from years ago. It is only logical to think that Brian would target Monica next. Though she would probably not admit it, Jane is certain she sees fear come over Monica. No woman, straight or lesbian, would be okay after hearing everything Jane has told Monica and Samantha today.

As Blue and the chihuahua finally come back to life, it is Samantha that asks just the right question once again. "What do we do to stop him?" Thank God Monica brought Samantha along for their meeting. Jane admits that she has not been able to come up with a way to stop Brian without getting herself in trouble with the cops for the way she found the used condoms in Brian's closet. She just knew she had to warn Monica about the potential attack on her. Monica then asks Jane if she has already talked to Stacey and Melissa about all this to which Jane says she has not.

As Blue and the chihuahua start getting a little too hyper, the three women get up from the bench to pick them up. It is only a matter of time before Blue starts sniffing around Samantha's vomit. As they all walk toward the exit gate, Monica asks Jane if she would be willing to meet up again, along with Stacey and Melissa, so she can share everything she knows including the photos with them as well. Before Jane can answer, Samantha says she wants to be there too. Knowing Samantha will be there with them is a huge relief to Jane. Hopefully, with Samantha there, none of the others will bring up their high school days. Sometimes it is best to let sleeping dogs lie. Jane tells Monica she will meet up with all of them, and hopefully together they can come up with a way to stop Brian.

As they are walking out of the exit gate, Monica tells Jane she will reach out to Stacey and Melissa to set up a time that works for all of them as soon as possible. Monica then asks Jane for her cell phone number so she can let her know when and where the meeting is. After they exchange cell phone numbers, Jane and Blue head toward their place while Monica, Samantha, and the yapping chihuahua head in the opposite direction. Jane feels herself take a deep breath and release it. She cannot believe that just happened. Jane Brooks just sat down on a bench in a pet park with Monica Roberts and her lesbian lover and had an adult conversation. Who would have ever thought that would happen in this lifetime?

Chapter 37

After her meeting with Monica and Samantha, Jane is completely exhausted physically, emotionally, and mentally. She is also overwhelmed with a sense of relief. What she just did was a very brave thing to do. She just admitted to breaking and entering which could land her behind bars to one of her high school bullies. There is nothing stopping Monica from contacting the cops and telling them everything she has just shared with her. Hopefully, if Monica does choose to do that, it would be out of fear, not in hopes of getting Jane in trouble. No matter what the outcome, she knows she did the right thing. At least now if Brian does attempt to attack Monica, she will be ready for him. Jane is also relieved she is not the only one that knows the truth about Brian. Who knows what he will do to her if he figures out what she is really up to?

Even though Blue just had an exhausting playdate with his chihuahua friend, he is not ready to call it a day. He finds his catnip-stuffed mouse and drops it in front of Jane. She is not really in the mood to play right now, but how can she say no to Blue when he is just sitting there, looking up at her with those beautiful eyes of his? She picks up the mouse and throws it across the room. Blue makes a mad dash to retrieve it, but he cannot seem to find where it landed. He is going crazy looking all over the living room for the mouse. Jane walks over to help him find it. As she stands in the center of the room, looking for the mouse, Blue stands near her feet, just waiting for her to spot it.

There is only one place it can be: under the sofa. Jane gets down on her hands and knees in front of the sofa and slides one of her arms under it, hoping she will be able to feel the damn mouse. Within seconds, Blue is doing the same thing. His paw does not reach quite as far as her arm, but that does not deter him. Having no luck, she realizes there are only two other options. She can either try moving the sofa by herself or she can lie down on the floor so she can see under the sofa. Considering she is already on her hands and knees; she decides to go with the second option and lies down on the floor. She cannot help but laugh when she looks over at Blue and he has copied her again. He is flat on his belly with his back legs and tail stretched out behind him. Blue looks over at Jane as if to say, "Now what?"

Because the sofa is so low to the floor, Jane has to lay one side of her head flat on the floor to be able to see anything at all. This was not a good idea at all. The saying "Out of sight, out of mind" works its way into Jane's head when she sees the results of never vacuuming under her sofa since the day she moved in. The dust balls under her bed were nothing compared to what she is looking at right now. In her defense, the sofa is too low to the floor for the vacuum to fit under it and it is too heavy for her to move by herself.

Jane gets up off the floor and walks over to the sliding glass doors. She grabs the old mop from the bottom track, then gets back on her hands and knees in front of the sofa. Blue is looking at her in total confusion. He has no idea what she is up to. She starts on one end of the sofa, shoving the old mop under it and pushing it all the way to the other side. She keeps doing this until she makes it to the other end of the sofa. Once she has gone the whole length of the sofa, she pulls the old mop out from under the sofa. She is utterly disgusted by what it looks like now. It is completely covered with huge dust balls.

She drops the old mop and gets up off the floor. She walks around the sofa to the other side and is shocked by how much more dirt and dust is waiting for her to clean up. She thought most of the dust balls were stuck to the old mop, but that is not the case. Blue comes walking around the sofa behind her. He stops right near her and looks at the mess she just made. Then he spots his dust-covered mouse in the middle of it. He will not be picking that mouse up in his mouth until Jane has a chance to wash it.

She goes and gets the vacuum cleaner out of the closet so she can clean up the mess. Blue's reaction is something you would see on *America's Funniest Videos*. Blue is scared shitless of the vacuum cleaner, but he wasn't done playing cat and mouse. Suppose Jane accidentally vacuums up the mouse. As Jane gets closer with the vacuum cleaner, Blue moves into the mess so he can get closer to his mouse. He contemplates picking it up in his mouth, but he cannot get himself to do it with all the dust covering it. He looks back in Jane's direction, and she is closing in on him. He looks back at the mouse and then back at Jane. What to do, what to do? With only seconds to spare, he starts swatting the mouse with one paw and then the other paw. He looks like he is playing hockey with the mouse as his puck. Blue does not stop until he makes it to the bedroom. As Jane turns on the vacuum cleaner, Blue makes his way under the bed with his dust-covered mouse right next to him.

Jane had no intention of doing any housework today, but she does feel a lot better knowing the floor under her sofa is now free of dust balls. After she puts the vacuum cleaner back in the closet, she goes into the bedroom. She knows exactly where she will find Blue. She gets down on her hands and knees and grabs the dust-covered mouse from under the bed. She brings the mouse into the kitchen and does her best at washing it off in the sink. The dust turns into nasty gray clumps that make it easier for her to pick off. With the coast clear, Blue emerges from under the bed and stealthily makes his way into the kitchen. He jumps up on to the kitchen counter to get a better view of what Jane is up to. With the sound of the running water, Jane did not even hear Blue approach or jump up onto the counter. When she shuts the water off and turns around, the surprise of Blue's appearance startles her. She has been very jumpy since she came home from work that day and found Blue locked out on her balcony.

She knows it is going to be a waste of time, but she throws the mouse into the living room anyway. Blue jumps down from the kitchen counter and runs after the mouse. She sprays the counter with kitchen cleaner and wipes it down with paper towels. When she is done cleaning the counter, she goes into the living room and is not surprised at all by what she sees. The wet mouse is right where it landed, and Blue is balled up in his spot on the sofa. Before Jane even threw the mouse, she knew there was no way Blue would put it in his mouth while it is still wet. She makes a mental note to buy Blue a new toy the next time she goes shopping.

Jane hears her text message notification go off, but she cannot remember where she left her phone when they got home from the pet park. She stands there, waiting for it to go off a second time, but it does not happen. She tries to mentally retrace her steps, but she comes up blank. She has so much going on it is no surprise she is a bit frazzled. She checks the table near the sofa, the desk, and the kitchen island, but she does not find it. Then she remembers she went into the bedroom to take her sneakers off. She walks into the bedroom and finds her cell phone on the bedside table. Typically, she only puts her cell phone there when she is going to bed.

She picks up her cell phone from the bedside table and opens her text message app. She was expecting to see a new message from Monica about their meeting, but instead, it is a new message from Brian.

Jane,

We need to talk.

Brian

Her hands start to sweat, and she instantly feels nauseous. There is definitely a strong link between the devil on her shoulder, her nerves, and Brian. She had purposely not responded to Brian's last text message, but maybe that made things worse. Jane lied to Brian. Brian knows Jane lied to him. Brian called Jane out on her lie. What is she supposed to do now? Should she admit she lied and tell another lie to cover for the first lie or should she embellish the first lie in hopes of Brian believing it? Honesty is always the best policy, or at least sometimes.

There is nothing she wouldn't do to be able to go back in time and never join Mingle in the first place. Was her boring life really that bad? Instead, Jane finds herself in a state of panic. She grabs the old mop and removes the dust-covered mophead. She puts the mophead near her washing machine so she can give it a good washing before using it again. Then she puts the mop handle back into the bottom track of her sliding glass door. She double-checks the lock on the sliding glass door and her front door. She cannot go on living like this. Jane knows she needs to respond to Brian's new text message, but she has no idea what to say. What is taking Monica so long to text her?

Embellishing the first lie seems like the better option. If Jane admits that she lied, what will she use as her reason for telling the lie in the first place? Telling Brian, the truth about wanting to get him away from his place so she could break into it, is definitely not an option. Here goes nothing.

Brian,

Sorry I never responded to your last text message. I did not lie to you. I rushed Blue to the vet that night. If you did stop by my place and heard meowing through the door, that would have been from my neighbor's cat that I am watching while she is away. How do you know where I live?

Jane

It had not occurred to Jane until she was writing her text message that she never gave Brian her address. She does not have a landline, so he could not have found her in a phone book, if they even make those anymore. She does not have her address in her Facebook profile. Brian must have followed her home from work one day without her knowing. It will be interesting to see Brian's answer. Will he lie, or will he admit that he followed her home without her knowledge?

Jane heads to the bathroom to floss and brush her teeth. While she is in there, she also pops two Tylenol PM. They are her only hope for getting any sleep tonight.

Chapter 38

The thing about taking Tylenol PM is, yes, they will knock you out, but they will also leave you feeling drowsy for hours after you finally wake up. That is how Jane is feeling right now as she eats her bowl of Froot Loops and drinks her second cup of coffee. Spoiled Blue only ate half of his dry cat food breakfast before he made a visit to the ficus tree pot. His way of reminding Jane that she forgot to scoop out his litterbox yesterday. as if she did not have enough on her mind already. The ficus tree is looking sadder and sadder.

*****

Jane made the mistake of putting up a Christmas tree for her and Blue's first Christmas together in her new place. Blue sat still in one spot the entire time she decorated the tree. She was so impressed with Blue for not going after any of the decorations or getting tangled up in the lights as she hung them. She spent almost two hours decorating that damn tree. When she woas finally done, she slowly inched it into just the right space at just the right angle. She shut the blind and turned on the Christmas lights. If she could have patted herself on the back for a job well-done, she would have. The tree looked beautiful. It was definitely photo ready.

Jane went into her bedroom to get her cell phone so she could take a photo she could send to her mom. That is when it happened. The angelic Blue that had just sat still for almost two hours made his move. Jane could hear low clinking noises, but she did not think much of it. She grabbed her cell phone, and just as she was walking back into the living room, her beautifully decorated Christmas tree came crashing down. Blue tried to make a run for it, but as he was attempting to crawl out from under the ruins, his back paw got stuck in a wire from one of the sets of lights. He was caught in the act, you might say. Ever since then, Jane puts a few small Christmas balls on the ficus tree and calls it a day.

*****

After she finishes her breakfast, Jane scoops out Blue's real litterbox and then his backup litterbox otherwise known as her ficus tree pot. She really needs to buy some new potting soil and try to save the ficus tree before it is too late. Jane adds potting soil to her mental note list, along with more post-its. Blue is predictably napping in his own bed. His way of letting Jane know he is not happy with her for forgetting about his dirty litterbox. Jane suddenly realizes that she has not checked her cell phone since last night. She gets her cell phone and can see from the home screen that she has one new text message. As she clicks on the icon for her text message app, she says a short silent prayer that the new message is from Monica and not Brian. This time her prayers are answered.

Jane,

I spoke to Stacey and Melissa. They can both meet tonight at 7:00 p.m. Stacey said we can all meet at her house. Let me know if you are okay with the time and place when you have a chance.

Monica

She was not expecting their meeting to be at Stacey's house. She is not sure how she feels about that. Meeting up with Monica, Samantha, and their yapping chihuahua in the pet park was one thing. Meeting up with all three of her high school bullies for the first time since high school in one of their houses is a whole other thing. Most likely Steve and their two boys will be there too. What if Melissa brings her lawyer boyfriend with her? Jane is starting to second-guess her decision to do the right thing. The only good part of meeting at Stacey's house would be that no one else could overhear their conversation. She does not want to keep Monica waiting for her response.

Monica,

I am okay with the time and the place if it will only be the five of us there. Stacey, Melissa, Samantha, you, and me. Please confirm that to be the case and send me Stacey's address.

Jane

This has been the most stressful staycation Jane has ever taken. So much for just relaxing and taking it easy with Blue for a week. Speaking of Blue, he needs to get over his temper tantrum. Enough is enough. Blue is the only positive thing in her life right now. There is only so much one person can take. Jane finds him still napping in his bed. She goes over to his bed, gets down on the floor near it, and gently rubs Blue's head. His quiet snores turn into low purring. He slowly lifts his head just enough so she can rub him in just the right spot: right between his eyes. His purring gets louder, and she knows all is forgiven. She picks Blue up out of his bed and holds him gently against her chest.

The sound of her text message notification breaks up her lovefest with Blue. He has been trying to break free from her hug for about a minute, but she was not ready for it to end. True love is hard to find these days. She loosens her hold on Blue, and he jumps out of her arms. As Jane goes for her cell phone, Blue goes to his litterbox. When she checks her text message app, she is again relieved to see the new text message is from Monica.

Jane,

It will definitely be just the five of us. The less people that know about this, the better, at least for now.
Stacey's address is 7103 Fisher Island Drive, Miami Beach.
See you there at 7:00 p.m.

Monica

That is a huge relief. Jane could not agree more about the less people that know, the better, especially considering she is the one that could end up in jail if more people find out about her involvement. This will be the first time she has come face-to-face with Melissa since graduation day, except for her close encounter in Marshalls. Fingers crossed; Stacey will not bring up their strange interaction in Whole Foods when Jane denied being herself. The night is going to be awkward enough as it is. In the meantime, she is going to take Blue on a little outing.

With the drowsiness of the Tylenol PM finally wearing off, Jane leashes up Blue and they head out the door. It has been quite a while since she took Blue to his favorite place. It can be a bit stressful sometimes, but she is still in her makeup mode after forgetting to scoop out Blue's litterbox for him once again. Is it really any wonder why Blue is as spoiled rotten as he is? She was going to drive, but it is a beautiful day out. Considering this walk is a bit farther than the pet park or the waterfront, Jane makes sure she walks on the inside while Blue walks closer to the curb. There are a lot less things for him to stop and smell this way. They make it to their destination in sixteen minutes. Although Blue is tired from the long walk, he is too excited to complain.

As she opens the door to Petco, Blue is as far ahead of her as his leash will allow. The cashier behind the register recognizes them and offers Blue a treat, which he devours. Jane shortens the reach of Blue's leash a bit so he cannot jump up on anything and start knocking things over. That only happened the very first time she dared to bring him here. We live and hopefully we learn. They head over to the aisle full of toys for dogs and cats. This is how they ended up with the catnip-filled mouse. Jane lets Blue pick out his own toy. The process can be a bit time-consuming. Blue will just toss the ones he is not interested in aside for Jane to pick up and put back. When he finds just the right one, he will keep it in his mouth until they get to the register. Every so often, Blue will pick out one with a little bell in it, which ends up driving Jane crazy. Those typically end up lost rather quickly. After only tossing three aside, Blue finds the one he wants. Jane is not surprised when she sees it is the same exact catnip-stuffed mouse he picked out last time.

When Jane and Blue make it back home, Blue goes right for his water bowl. He is not a young kitten anymore. He is beat from the walk. Jane had planned on playing a round of cat and mouse with his new toy, but Blue has a different plan. Within minutes, Blue is on the bed, snoring away on his pillow.

Chapter 39

Jane pulls up outside Stacey's house at 6:59 p.m. with her stomach in knots. Can she really pull this off? She is about to be surrounded by four very beautiful women, three of which bullied her every day of her high school years. Though Jane is not as heavy as she was back then, she is still not fit like they are. She is still the ugly, out-of-shape duckling. She has got to be out of her mind. Although she has driven by Stacey's house a few times over the years, she never knew it was Stacey's house. Occasionally, Jane would take Blue for a ride on one of her days off. They would usually end up heading to Miami Beach, which would take them right by Stacey's house, one of the many beautiful houses Jane would see along the way.

*****

"Jane, you better hurry up or you are going to be late." Being late was exactly what Jane was trying to be. Today was the day of their school outing. No matter how much she begged her mom to let her stay home from school, her mom would not have it. Her mom kept telling her repeatedly that she needed to make some friends. Spending time with kids her age outside of school was the best way to do that. Jane was sure to come home with at least one new friend. Moms mean

well, but they also see their children with blinders on. Jane's mom had already packed the new backpack she bought specially for the school outing. Jane put on her one-piece bathing suit, followed by a loose-fitting T-shirt and a pair of shorts. Her flip-flops were already packed in her backpack, along with a huge beach towel, extra sunscreen, and a couple of juice boxes, so Jane put her old ratty sneakers on for the trip. Before heading out the door, Jane tried pleading with her mom one last time to let her stay home. Her mom's response was "Try to have some fun for once."

When Jane got to school, most of the buses the school was using for the outing were already filling up with excited, screaming students. As she got closer to the buses, she tried to find the one with the least number of students on it. The first two were almost completely full. The last one was only about a third of the way full, so she boarded that one. Most of the students that were already on the bus were all the way to the back. She was happy to see that the front seat right near the driver was empty. Jane slid all the way over on the seat. She put her new overstuffed backpack right next to her so no one else could sit there. Not that anyone would if they absolutely did not have to. Only a few more students got on her bus before the driver shut the door. Stacey, Melissa, and Monica were nowhere in sight. Oleta River State Park, here we come.

Every student had to pay fifty dollars to go on the outing. The fifty dollars covered the cost for the buses, entrance to the park, rental of either a kayak or a canoe, and their lunch. Jane had no intention of getting into a kayak or a canoe. She was pretty sure it would sink or tip over as soon as she stepped into it. After a twenty-minute ride, they pulled into the parking lot. Jane pretended to be looking for something in her backpack as all the other students rushed off the bus. She exchanged glances with the bus driver. He looked like a sweet old man. Most likely retired from his previous job and only driving buses out of boredom. He looked at Jane with sadness in his eyes. It was like he could read her mind. "Sorry, kiddo, you have to get off now. I have another trip to make before coming back to pick you up." Just as Jane was closing her backpack, one of the teachers stuck her head into the bus to make sure no students were left behind. No such luck.

One of the park employees was standing in front of the huge group of students, trying to talk over them. He was holding up a map and explaining where everything was in the park. When Jane heard the words secluded beach, she knew where she was headed. He ended his speech by announcing lunch would be served at noon in the picnic area.

The lines for the kayaks and canoes were long. Stacey, Melissa, and Monica were at the front of the line in very skimpy bikinis. Jane took one of the park maps and headed to the secluded beach. She walked quite a distance down the shoreline before finding a tall palm tree. With the location the sun was in at this time of day, the palm tree made a nice, shaded spot for Jane to lay her towel. She took her beach towel out of her backpack and spread it out on the shaded sand. She sat down on the towel and took off her sneakers. Even though she had walked a bit to get to her spot, she still was not comfortable enough to take her T-shirt and shorts off. There was no way she would ever let any of her classmates see her in her bathing suit. She had only put it on to make her mom happy. Jane applied a heavy coat of suntan lotion on every visible inch of skin. If anyone did see her, they might confuse her with a large-size Casper the ghost.

As she sat there on the secluded beach all by herself, she realized this was the first time she has actually enjoyed being at the beach. Hearing the waves of the water relaxed her. She even got to see a few dolphins pop up and down in the water. Maybe this was not such a bad idea after all. She will not be going home telling her mom all about her new friend from school, but it was not as bad as she thought it would be.

Jane heard the announcement that lunch would be served in ten minutes. She had hoped her mom would have packed something to eat in her backpack with the juice boxes. Unfortunately, there was not enough room once she put the oversized beach towel in. She put her sneakers, sunscreen, and towel back into her backpack and slid her flip-flops on. She made her way back along the shoreline to the picnic area. She spotted Stacey, Melissa, and Monica right away. Jane mixed *into the crowd of students waiting to get a cheeseburger or a hotdog. When she finally made it to the front of the line, she could not decide what she wanted, so she asked for one of each. She then grabbed a handful of chips and a can of soda. She headed to the bench closest to the one the teachers were sitting at and sat down.*

Just as she was about to take her first bite of her hotdog, she heard the unmistakable sound of Melissa's voice. "Oink, oink." The teachers were so invested in their own conversation they did not even hear Melissa, but the students at the next table certainly did. They all turned to see what was going on. Luckily, Melissa had kept on walking, so the other students were not sure what they had missed. Jane watched Melissa as she walked back to the table where Stacey and Monica were sitting. It was obvious from the way all three of them were looking in her direction now that Melissa was filling them in on Jane's lunch choices. She could hear them laughing over all the other noise in the picnic area. Jane got up from the picnic table and dropped her plate in the trash can. Her appetite was gone.

＊＊＊＊＊

As Jane opens her car door, she sees a car pull up behind her and is happy to see Samantha getting out of the passenger's door. She was hoping she was not the last one to arrive. Just the thought of ringing Stacey's doorbell and standing there alone when Stacey opened the door was making her want to turn around and head back home to Blue. She waits on the sidewalk for Monica and Samantha. Although she does not really know her at all, Jane feels much better with Samantha there. The three of them walk up to Stacey's house together. Monica rings the doorbell, and Jane starts to sweat.

One of Stacey and Steve's sons opens the door. He looks about six years old. Though she hates to admit it, he is absolutely adorable. His younger brother comes running up behind him. He looks about four years old. Good looks definitely run in the family. They both have dark brown hair like Steven and bright blue eyes. The two boys hold the door open as Monica, Samantha, and Jane make their way inside. The inside of the house is beautiful. The decor is very tasteful and elegant. Whoever they used as an interior decorator earned every dollar they must have paid him or her.

Once they are all in the foyer, the two boys run past them and disappear. Jane can hear Stacey calling out for them to come on in from somewhere in the house. As they reach the end of the foyer, Jane sees Melissa sitting at Stacey's dining room table with a glass of wine in her hand. This is really happening. Stacey comes walking into the dining room with what looks like a platter with cheese and crackers on it. Is this a meeting to discuss the man that raped Stacey and Melissa or a party? Jane has never felt so uncomfortable in her entire life.

It had not occurred to Jane that this is the first time Samantha is meeting Stacey and Melissa until Monica makes the introductions. Jane notices that Melissa has not even made eye contact with her. Melissa is probably upset with her for not responding to her Facebook message regarding an apology. Stacey, on the other hand, comes right over to Jane and shakes her hand. She even thanks Jane for agreeing to come over. As they sit down at the table, Stacey offers her new guests a glass of wine. They all accept the offer, including Jane. She is going to need something to make it through this meeting. Stacey tells them that Steve and the boys are watching a movie in their downstairs playroom, so they will not be disturbed.

Once they all have their glass of wine and Stacey has joined them at the table, an awkward silence fills the room. Jane looks over at Monica, hoping she will take the lead, but it is Melissa that beaks the silence. Melissa looks over at Jane for the first time since she walked into the room and asks her straight out if it is true that she has proof of who raped her. Jane looks back at Melissa and tells her that she believes she does. Then Stacey speaks up and asks if it is definitely the same man that raped her too. To which, Jane says she believes it is.

Jane then takes them step-by-step through everything she knows about Brian exactly like she did with Monica and Samantha in the pet park. She even repeats her lie about leaving her cell phone at Brian's place and going back to get it. Melissa does not seem very convinced. Then Melissa asks Jane a question that neither Monica nor Samantha had asked her, and for a second, she thinks she is caught in her lie. Melissa asks, "If you were only there to get your cell phone, why were you looking in his closet?" Before Jane knows it, all four women are looking at her, waiting for her answer. She can feel the sweat dripping down her back, and her heart starts racing.

What can one more lie hurt at this point? She tells them that when she was at Brian's house, visiting him, she had gone to look out his sliding glass door while Brian was in the bathroom. When Brian came out of the bathroom, he started acting strangely when he saw that Jane was not sitting where he left her. Even though Brian saw her standing in front of the sliding glass doors, he walked right over to his closet and made sure the doors were closed tight. Jane found that to be odd. When she went back to get her cell phone, she opened the closet doors and that was when she smelled the foul odor which turned out to be old semen in used condoms. Not completely a lie, more like a stretch of the truth.

Monica asks Jane to show Stacey and Melissa the photos on her cell phone. Jane takes her cell phone out of her pocket and opens her photo app. She clicks on the first photo in the series. It is the one that shows all seven used condoms hanging on the wall. Jane hands her cell phone to Stacey, who is sitting right on the side of Melissa. They move in closer to one another so they can both see the photos at the same time. The looks on their faces tell Jane all she needs to know. They are just as disgusted as the rest of them were.

Jane knows there are eight photos in all. The first one shows all the condoms together on the wall. The other seven photos are close-ups of the seven individual condoms going from oldest to newest. Jane can tell by the movements Stacey is making with her fingers on the cell phone screen when she is zooming in and when she is sliding to the next photo. If she is correct, the next photo is of the condom with Stacey's name written on it. When Stacey throws Jane's cell phone down on the table, Jane knows she was counting correctly. Stacey gets out of her chair as quickly as she can and runs down the hall. Jane is assuming that is where the closest bathroom must be.

Melissa looks at Jane's cell phone sitting on the table, and Jane can tell the reality of what she told them has set in. Melissa knows without even sliding to the next photo what she will be looking at. Just like Monica, Melissa has had enough. She does not want to see the last photo. Jane grabs her cell phone and puts it back in her pocket. Melissa looks a little green in the face, but she remains in her seat. Nobody says a word until Stacey comes back to the table. The first thing Stacey does is down the rest of her wine and refills her glass. Then she apologizes for running from the table so abruptly. Samantha and Jane both tell her that they had the same reaction when they looked at the last photo.

Even though Melissa already knows the answer, she asks the question anyway. "Am I right in assuming the last photo has my name instead of Stacey's written on the condom?" Jane just nods her head, but then Samantha adds that the semen had not had enough time to dry out yet. Melissa follows Stacey's example and downs the rest of her wine. As Stacey refills Melissa's wine glass, she says in a very determined voice, "We cannot let him get away with this."

Chapter 40

Blue is waiting for Jane when she walks through the door. She is just as happy to see him as he is to see her. After the meeting at Stacey's house, all Jane wants is another glass of wine and some alone time with Blue. She heads to the kitchen and pours herself a big glass of white wine. Although she is willing to bet the wine she drank at Stacey's house cost about ten times more than what she paid for hers, she would pick hers over Stacey's any day. A wine connoisseur she is not. She heads over to the sofa with her very full glass of wine. Blue jumps up on the sofa with his new catnip-stuffed mouse in his mouth. He has been waiting for Jane to get home so they can play with his new toy. She had forgotten all about it after the night she has had.

After fifteen minutes of playing cat and mouse, Blue has had enough fun for the night. He jumps up on the sofa and settles down for a nice nap in his special spot. Jane tries to relax the best she can with the help of the buzz she feels coming on. Maybe she should slow down with the wine. She has a lot on her mind that she needs to work through. Did she really agree to go along with everything Stacey, Melissa, and Monica suggested? Were they serious, or were they just testing Jane to see what she would say? She feels like she is in way over her head. Talk about being out of your comfort zone.

In order for everything to work the way they all agreed during their meeting, Jane needs to make the first move. She knows once she does this, there is no turning back. Is she really willing to put her freedom in the hands of Stacey, Melissa, and Monica? If everything goes to shit, it is Jane that will end up behind bars. How much time would she get for breaking and entering? Out of curiosity, she walks over to her desk and turns on her laptop. When it is ready, she opens Google. She does a search for the punishment for breaking and entering in Miami, Florida. She is surprised to see it is only six months in jail and a two-hundred dollar fine. Six months is not that long, but who would watch Blue for six months? Jane looks over at Blue on the sofa making that cute little snoring sound. Then she opens her cell phone and clicks on her texting app.

Brian,

Did you hear Melissa was raped last weekend? How long before it is Monica's turn?

Jane

She sits there staring at her cell phone screen. She knows once she hits the Send button, it is game on. Brian is going to know that she knows he is the Miami Beach rapist or at least the copycat. Hopefully, Brian does not know that she was in his closet and saw his disgusting display of trophies. She looks over at Blue again and then back at her cell phone. Jane suddenly realizes that even though she is having conflicting thoughts, that stupid little devil is being really quiet. She takes that to mean that she is doing the right thing. She hits Send.

Approximately two seconds after she hit Send, she wishes she could unsend the text message. If there is one thing that Jane is sure of, it is that Brian is a dangerous man. What if Brian's reaction is not what the five of them are assuming it will be? What if instead of going after Monica he comes after her to shut her up? Damn that devil. Where is he when you need him to make you question your actions before you actually do them like usual? She hurries over to her sliding glass door to make sure the mop handle is still in the bottom track. She then checks and double-checks that the lock is locked. She walks over to her front door and makes sure it is also locked. For added protection, Jane grabs the chair at her desk and slides it under the doorknob. Paranoid, a little. Freaked out, a lot. Scared, shitless!

Once she is as secure as she can be, she goes back to the sofa. Blue peeks up at her for a hot second before retightening the ball he is curled in. Jane grabs her cell phone again and sends her next text like she agreed to.

Monica,

I sent the text. Do you think he will come after me instead of you once he reads it?

Jane

After she sends the text to Monica, she closes her texting app and shuts down her cell phone. She grabs her wine glass and finishes it off. It is getting late, and the wine is really kicking in. She makes her way to the kitchen sink to rinse out the wine glass and then heads to the bathroom to do her nightly routine. While she is brushing her teeth, she can hear Blue kicking around some of his kitty litter. Always the showman. They head to the bedroom at the same time. Blue jumps up on the bed and does his circling trick before, once again, landing in the same exact spot on his pillow. Jane gets in on her side of the bed and shuts off the light. For the first time in a long time, she finds herself with her hands pressed together, saying a prayer. It has been so long since she said any real prayers; she is not even sure she knows all the words. "Our Father, who art in heaven..."

*****

In the morning Jane is instantly reminded why she should never drink more than one glass of wine. How do you spell *lightweight*: J-A-N-E. Her head is pounding and the beam of light shining in through the slats of the blind in her window is so bright. If it was not for Blue staring at her as he patiently waits for her to get up and feed him, she would pull the covers as far over her head as possible and hibernate for the rest of the day. She squints her eyes until they are almost closed and slowly, very slowly, gets out of bed. She gets dizzy as the room spins around her, and her feet feel like lead. Blue's patience is wearing thin. He jumps off the bed and rushes past Jane. He walks to the end of the hall before stopping to turn around. He wants to make sure she did not turn around and get back into bed. Once she makes it halfway down the hall, Blue walks to his placemat and sits down.

With Blue disapprovingly eating his dry cat-food breakfast, Jane makes it to the bathroom and grabs the Tylenol bottle from the medicine cabinet. She pops three pills in hopes of getting the pounding in her head to stop or at least dull. She looks in the mirror and is horrified by her reflection. Her red frizzy hair looks like she stuck her finger in an electric socket. The bags under her eyes look like she is packed for a very long trip. She turns on the cold water and splashes her face with it a few times. Then she wets her hands and does her best to do something with her hair. It is a wonder Blue did not run and hide when he saw her this morning. He must have been starving.

Her stomach is too upset to eat anything for breakfast. She is not sure if it is all from her lingering hangover or partly from being under so much stress. Just the thought of food is making her gag. She starts up a pot of Cuban coffee. While she waits for the coffee to brew, she grabs a bottled water from the refrigerator. She has an awful case of dry mouth. Why in the world did she let herself drink a second glass of wine?

When the coffee finishes brewing, she puts two teaspoons of sugar and a splash of milk into the biggest coffee cup she owns. Then she fills the coffee cup the rest of the way with the Cuban coffee. She carries the cup of coffee in one hand and the bottled water in the other hand over to the table by the sofa. Before she sits down, she goes over to Blue's litterbox and does some quick scooping to prevent having to clean out the ficus tree pot again later. By the time she returns to the sofa, she has company by the name of Blue.

Jane sits down on her side of the sofa and takes a drink of her coffee, followed by a chug of her water. Her mouth is so dry it feels like sandy cotton balls. As she puts her bottled water back down on the table, she notices her cell phone is stuck between the cushion she is sitting on and the arm of the sofa. It must have slid down there last night. She slides her hand into the tight space and grabs her cell phone. She opens her cell phone and taps on the text message app. Her alert is letting her know she has two new text messages. One is from Monica and the other is from Brian. They both came in shortly after she went to bed last night. Jane does a quick "Eeny, meeny, miny, moe", before clicking on Brian's message first.

Jane,

I had not heard about Melissa. Why are you asking me how long before it is Monica's turn? I hope Blue is feeling better.

Brian

That was not at all what she was expecting as his response to the text message she sent him last night. Then again, Jane is pretty sure Brian is a psychopath. As if he cares if Blue is feeling better. She closes out of Brian's text message and then clicks on Monica's.

Jane,

I had not thought about Brian going after you instead of me, but now that you brought it up, it could be a possibility. We need to be ready for whatever he does. I will talk it over with Samantha in the morning and see what she thinks.

Monica

If that was supposed to make her feel better, it fell flat. She is even more worried now after reading Monica's text message than she was last night. It was bad enough when she was the only one that thought Brian might go after her now. Knowing that Monica agrees with her makes her entire body cringe. She closes out of her text message app without responding to either of her new messages. She cannot figure out what Brian is playing at besides trying to make her think he is innocent in all this. She is assuming Brian does not know that she broke into his place and found the used condoms. If he did know before Jane sent him her text message last night, his response would not have been so nice or he most likely would have paid her an unwelcomed visit last night.

The added stress from reading her new text messages is not helping her already-pounding head. She takes another sip of coffee, followed by another gulp of water. She gets up from the sofa and crosses the room to the sliding glass doors. Maybe some fresh air will help relax her a bit. She bends down and removes the mop handle from the bottom track. Blue comes running over from the sofa. She grabs the wand and pulls the blind open. Blue turns around and runs as fast as he can into the bedroom. Jane freezes right where she is with the wand still in her hand. Through the double-paned glass door, she can hear Brian say, "Wakey-wakey."

Chapter 41

As Jane stands there, unable to move, Brian slides the door open. It seems he had been able to pick the lock, but thanks to the mop handle, he could not get in. Did he spend the entire night out on her balcony? Blue comes running into the living room when he hears the door opening, but then he races back to the bedroom once he sees Brian is now inside. Jane starts sweating profusely. As Brian enters the living room, Jane slowly backs away from him. He is not saying anything, but the look on his face tells Jane all she needs to know. Brian knows that she knows his dirty little secret. *Hail Mary full of Grace...*

Of all days to have a hangover. Jane was already not feeling steady on her feet before finding Brian on her balcony. Now she is tripping over her own feet trying to back away from him. Although her condo is about triple the size of Brian's studio apartment, she has limited places she can go to get away from him before he pounces. She knows Blue is in the bedroom, most likely under the bed, so she does not want to lead Brian in that direction. The chair is still under the doorknob of the front door. There is no way she would be able to move the chair and get out the door before Brian van grab on to her. Besides, she would not want to leave Blue alone with Brian. That only leaves the kitchen or the bathroom. If she makes it to the bathroom, she can lock herself in, but what about Blue? If she heads to the kitchen, she can try to keep the island in between them and hopefully be able to get one of her kitchen knives as protection.

She clumsily backs into the kitchen. Brian could have certainly got a hold of her by now if he really wanted to. He seems to be having way too much fun watching her sweat and tremble just by his presence. She is feeling like the catnip-filled mouse being hunted by Blue. "You have been a bad girl. Jane" Brian says in a very sadistic voice. For the first time, she notices that Brian is wearing latex gloves, just like he did when he raped all seven women. There is no way she will be losing her virginity to a rapist. Nuh-uh, not today.

As she goes one way, Brian goes the other way. It is like they are doing some kind of dance around the kitchen island. From where she is now, she can see down the hall into the bedroom. She can see Blue's eyes under the bed. Blue is as afraid of Brian as she is. Jane quickly remembers how Blue reacted the very first time he met Brian. It was not caused by jealousy; it was caused by Blue picking up on Brian's true being. It seems Blue's intuition is spot-on where Brian is concerned. If she keeps going in the same direction, she will be on the outside of the island, which will put Brian in the kitchen near the knives and in view of Blue. She does not want that to happen, so she changes direction.

She keeps moving until she is standing right in front of the drawer with the knives in it, then she stops. As she grabs the handle on the drawer, the text message notification on her cell phone goes off. It must be a new text message from Monica. She and Samantha must have had their talk and Monica is texting Jane to let her know how it went. Brian hears it too and he looks around, trying to find where her cell phone is. No matter what, Brian cannot see that new text message. He starts moving away from the island and back into the living room. Jane slides the drawer open as slowly and quietly as she can. Blue starts creeping out from under the bed.

As Brian gets closer to the sofa, Jane takes the sharpest knife she owns out of the kitchen drawer. As she quietly slides the drawer closed, Blue emerges from the hallway. Jane can see Blue approaching and wants to warn him off, but she does not want to alert Brian to Blue's location. As Brian moves in closer to Jane's cell phone, both Jane and Blue start moving closer to Brian. Jane tries to silently deter Blue, but he is not having it. He is on a mission. As Brian bends down to grab Jane's cell phone, Blue jumps up and lands right in the center of Brian's back. He digs his claws in as deep as they will go. Good thing Jane never had him declawed.

Brian starts screaming in pain. He stands back up, but Blue's claws are in Brian's back so good he does not budge. Brian is now standing straight up, jumping around and trying to get Blue off his back. He cannot get his arms back far enough to reach Blue. Blue starts hissing very loudly. Payback time for locking him out on the balcony. Brian is flailing all over the place. Jane cannot even get close to him. He has not stopped screaming for even a second. Then Blue releases his two top paws for a nanosecond before jamming his claws into Brian's back again. Brian is so caught off guard by the new wave of pain that he starts losing his balance. Then he steps on Blue's brand-new catnip-stuffed mouse. It throws him so off-balance that he falls over and whacks his head on the chair under the doorknob.

When Brian falls unconsciously to the floor, Blue comes running out from under him, just like he did with the Christmas tree. Jane does not know what to do. She has no idea if Brian is knocked out, dead or faking. She inches closer and closer to him. She is on her guard every step she takes. Jane is still holding the kitchen knife in her hand. Once she is within arm's reach, she bends down and grabs Brian's wrist so she can feel for a pulse. She is surprisingly relieved when she feels one. Considering Brian did not grab on to her when she was right there next to him, she is guessing he is not faking. He is out cold.

Blue is nowhere to be seen. Jane would bet her life he is hiding under the bed again. He probably thinks he is in trouble, just like he was with the Christmas tree. Blue does not realize he is the hero of the day. Jane needs to act quick. She has no idea how long Brian will be out for. She grabs on to both of his ankles and drags him across the floor to where the heavy sofa is. Then she goes to the bedroom and gets as many belts as she can find in her closet. She uses two of the belts to tie Brian's wrists and ankles together. Then she uses another belt to tie the belt around his wrists to one of the legs of the sofa. She uses the last belt to tie the belt around his ankles to the leg on the opposite end of the sofa. Luckily, Brian is just tall enough to make it possible.

With Brian unconscious, tied, and bound, Jane gets her cell phone from the end table. In the state she is in right now, texting will not be an option. She clicks on her contact list and finds Monica's name. She clicks on the Call Now icon. After only two rings, Monica answers her call. Jane is so freaked out she can barely speak. She does the best she can to tell Monica that she needs to get the others together and get over to her place as quickly as possible. She does not even take the time to explain why she needs them. Jane blurts out her address and tells Monica they need to hurry, then she hangs up. Hopefully Monica takes her seriously and they will all show up before Brian comes around.

Within a few minutes, Monica calls back and lets Jane know that all four of them are on their way to her place now. Jane was not planning on visitors today. Not that her condo is a mess, except for Brian on the floor unconscious and tied to her sofa. Jane is not sure where Melissa or Monica lives, but she knows it is not too far away. They should all be at her condo shortly. Jane has two objectives before they arrive. She hurries to the bathroom and grabs one of her hair elastics and puts her crazy-looking hair into a bun. The bags under her eyes now only look like those for a day trip. No overnight stay at a hotel needed.

When she is done in the bathroom, she walks over to Brian. It looks like he is still out cold though Jane could swear she just saw one of his fingers move. She gently kicks one of his feet and gets no reaction. Satisfied he is still out of it; she bends down next to him. She cannot believe what she is about to do, but does she really have a choice? She sticks her hand gently into the right front pocket of Brian's jeans. Finding nothing, she moves on to the left front pocket. She finds his car keys but nothing else.

She then slowly turns Brian's body just enough to be able to get his wallet out of his back pocket. She thinks she sees one of his eyes twitch as she lets him roll back onto his back. She unfolds Brian's wallet and finds her piece of paper with her revenge list written on it. She takes the piece of paper out of his wallet, then refolds the wallet.

Again, she slowly turns Brian just enough to put his wallet back into his back pocket before rolling him gently onto his back again. She takes the piece of paper and tears it up into tiny pieces before walking to the bathroom and flushing it down the toilet.

Chapter 42

Jane hears a knock at her door. She takes the chair out from under the doorknob and moves it back to her desk, then she opens the door. Samantha and Monica are the first two she sees. Right behind them coming up the stairs are Stacey and Melissa. All three of Jane's high school bullies plus one lesbian lover are now standing in her doorway. Blue sticks his head around the corner, trying to see what all the ruckus is about. Jane never has company, well, at least not invited company. Today, she has an unconscious man tied to the legs of her sofa and four beautiful women. Blue heads back to his hiding spot.

As the four women walk into Jane's condo, they all instantly spot Brian on the floor. Jane assures them that he is not dead but that he has been unconscious for almost thirty minutes, so he may come to any second. They all stand there looking down at Brian. Samantha is the one that finally asks Jane what happened to him. Jane tells them everything that happened from the second she opened the blind on her sliding glass doors until the second she tied the last belt at his ankles. They all stand there with their mouths hung open, not saying a word.

Stacey walks over to Brian. As she starts to bend down, his eyes begin to flutter. Stacey is so startled she jolts back up. Brian is definitely starting to come out of it. They need to decide quickly what they are going to do. Melissa walks over and stands next to Stacey. They look at one another and then they both look down at Brian. The look on their faces makes it very easy to tell what they are both feeling: anger and hatred. The man that raped them both in their own houses, in their own beds is unconscious and tied up at their feet. Jane can only imagine what is going through their minds.

Monica walks over to where Jane is standing and asks her the question on all their minds, "Now what?" Jane looks over at Melissa and Stacey for an answer. Samantha stands off to the side. She seems to be very uncomfortable with the situation. Maybe Monica should have left her at home. Truth be told, none of them knew what they were walking into. No one is saying a word, which is making it even more awkward than it already is with Jane's only high school friend knocked out on her living room floor and tied to her sofa.

Out of the corner of her eye, Jane can see Blue creeping into the room. He does not know what to make of all these people in his space. Blue walks right up to Samantha and stretches up her leg. She bends down and picks Blue up. Jane is not at all surprised Blue picked Samantha out of all her visitors to go to. Blue starts purring so loudly they all turn to look at him. He loves the attention. They are all brought right back to the seriousness of the situation when they hear Brian say, "Well, well, look who we have here." Stacey and Melissa start backing away from Brian even though he is still tied to the sofa and cannot move.

As soon as Blue hears Brian's voice, he pushes his way out of Samantha's arms and makes a mad dash for the bedroom. None of the women say a word. It is Brian that does the talking, "Jane, you didn't tell me this was going to be a party with your bullies." Samantha's facial expression when she hears what Brian said makes it clear to Jane that Monica has not told her about their high school years. Sometimes the past is best left in the past.

The next thing Jane knows Melissa walks right up to Brian and stomps her foot into his crotch as hard as she can. Brian screams out in pain even louder than he did when Blue attacked him. As Melissa pulls her foot off Brian's crotch he yells out, "You fucking bitch!" In response to Brian's outburst, Melissa pulls her leg back and kicks him right in his balls. Brian lets out a scream that could most certainly be heard by Jane's neighbors. Samantha walks toward the sliding glass doors and blocks her ears. She definitely does not want any part of what is happening right in front of her.

When Melissa walks away from Brian, Stacey switches places with her. Stacey gets really close to Brian and asks him, "How do you like being tied up against your will, you freak?" Jane can tell by the dark shade of red that has taken over Brian's face that he is either in a lot of pain or he is extremely pissed off. Stacey bends down and unbuttons the button on Brian's jeans, then pulls the zipper down. Brian puts an evil grin on his face and says, "I knew you liked it." Stacey lifts her head to look at Brian and spits right in his face. As Stacey tries to work Brian's jeans down his legs, it takes all the power I have to make Jane stop her.

Jane walks over to Stacey as she fights to get Brian's jeans past his hips. Stacey looks up at her in confusion. Jane lowers herself so she is face-to-face with Stacey, and in a very calm voice, she says, "You do not want to do this Stacey. You are not like him." What Stacey does next surprises everyone in the room; she starts crying uncontrollably. Jane reaches over and wraps her arms around Stacey and holds her as tight as she can. This is probably the first time Stacey has allowed herself to cry since the night Brian raped her.

Once Stacey has pulled herself together. the five women unanimously agree on what they are going to do. Jane walks over to the junk drawer and gets the roll of packing tape she has had since she moved in. She rips off a couple of pieces of tape and gives them to Monica. Monica walks over to Brian, bends down, and puts the pieces of tape over his mouth to keep him quiet. None of them want to ever hear another word out of his mouth. Monica then grabs on to the beltline of Brian's jeans and pulls them back up. She pulls his zipper back up and buttons the button. Brian has no idea what is happening.

Next, Jane gets her cell phone from the end table and dials 911. She tells the 911 operator that a man broke into her condo and tried to attack her. The operator tells Jane the cops are on their way. The operator then asks Jane if she needs an ambulance to which Jane tells her that is not necessary. Jane hangs up and closes her cell phone. The five women gather around the kitchen island in silence. Out of nowhere, Samantha asks, "What did he mean by Jane's bullies?" Stacey, Melissa, and Monica all look at Jane. None of them have said one word about what they put Jane through for four years. An apology would be nice, but let's take this one step at a time, shall we? Jane looks over at Samantha and says, "Ancient history" and leaves it at that.

When they hear the police sirens approaching, Melissa asks Jane if she is sure she wants to do this. It is very possible that Jane could end up going to jail for breaking into Brian's place. Jane assures them she wants to do the right thing no matter what happens. Sorry, devil, not this time. Samantha has already agreed that she will watch Blue if Jane does end up getting arrested, which makes Jane feel much better about what she is about to do.

When the cops arrive, Jane lets them into her already crammed condo. There is one female officer and one male officer. The male officer starts asking what happened. He wants as many details as the women can give him. Jane tells the officers everything she knows about Brian being the Miami Beach rapist that they have been looking for all these years. She even admits to breaking into Brian's place. It is better they hear it from her now rather than learning about it at Brian's trial. When Jane tells the officers about finding the used condoms in Brian's closet with the victims' names written on them, they are both in disbelief.

Once the officers have heard all there is to hear, they free Brian from Jane's sofa. They leave the packing tape over his mouth. They obviously do not want to hear anything he has to say just yet. The male officer pulls Brian to his feet and starts walking him toward the door. When the female officer is face to-face with Brian, she looks him straight in the eyes and says, "You are one twisted fuck." She then turns to the five women and tells them she will be in touch soon, and then they are gone.

The snowball that was once the size of Frosty's head and then his stomach is now the size of one single snowflake. Snow in Miami? Not on my watch.

Epilogue

Three weeks later, when the five women are having brunch at Monica and Samantha's place, the paperboy shows up with the Sunday edition of the *Miami Herald*. Monica takes their copy from the paperboy and thanks him. She drops the newspaper on the table in the hall before rejoining the rest of them at the dining room table. Blue and the yapping chihuahua are having the times of their lives in every room of the house. It was Samantha's idea for Jane to bring Blue along with her.

Although this is not the first time all five women have gotten together since that horrible day in Jane's condo, it is a special time. A lot has happened in the last three weeks that they all want to celebrate together. Melissa is now engaged to her rich lawyer from Brickell. Jane has met him a couple of times. He seems like a great guy. Stacey found out that she is pregnant again, and this time, it is a girl. She could not be any happier. Jane got the promotion at work that she has been hoping for. She is now the lead manager of the hotel. As for Monica and Samantha, they are getting married in two short hours! It will be a small ceremony, but as long as all five women are there for it, they are happy. Blue and the yapping chihuahua are the special guests. They even bought matching pet tuxedos for them. Good luck to whoever is going to try to get that on Blue.

When Jane is done eating, she excuses herself to go to the bathroom so she can wash her hands. On her way back from the bathroom, Jane walks past the table in the hall. She sees the newspaper sitting there where Samantha dropped it. Jane is not close enough to read anything on the front page, but from this distance, it looks like the headline consists of the word *rapist*. Jane stops in mid-step and changes her direction. She walks over to the table in the hall and picks up the newspaper. She unfolds it so she can read the whole headline. She cannot believe what she is seeing.

In big bold letters she reads MIAMI BEACH RAPIST KILLED IN HIS OWN CELL. There is even a photo of Brian's mugshot right under the headline. Jane brings the newspaper with her into the dining room. She walks up behind Stacey and shows her the newspaper. The other women are looking at them for some explanation. Jane meets their glances and simply says, "Justice was served."

Dear Reader,

How did you do?

Were you able to figure out which character in the story you played the part of?

If not, or if you are not sure, I will tell you now that there are about six clues throughout the book that should help you. I will help you find three of them.

To prevent making this too easy, I will tell you the chapter numbers instead of the page numbers where you can find the clues if you missed them the first time.

Turn back to chapter eleven. Really get into character and read it as if you are telling Jane's story to someone you would normally spill the tea to. I assure you, if you find the clue, you will know exactly who you are.

If you are still not sure there are at least two more clues in chapter forty-two. Trust me they are there.

Good luck!

Sincerely,
Alan Sakell

ABOUT THE AUTHOR

Alan Sakell was born and raised in Fall River, Massachusetts, which is best known as the city where Lizzie Borden took an ax. He works in accounting for a nonprofit organization in the city of Boston. His first novel, *The Boy*, was released in the Spring of 2021.